Hers

Hers

BRILLIANT NEW FICTION BY LESBIAN WRITERS

edited by Terry Wolverton with Robert Drake

Faber & Faber   **Boston · London**

Introduction, Collection, and Notes copyright © 1995 by Terry Wolverton and Robert Drake

The acknowledgments on p. 195 constitute an extension of this copyright notice.

Library of Congress Cataloging-in-Publication Data

Hers: brilliant new fiction by lesbian writers / edited by Terry Wolverton with Robert Drake.
    p. cm.
  ISBN 0-571-19867-8
    1. Lesbians—United States—Social life and customs—Fiction.
  2. American fiction—20th century.   3. Lesbians' writings, American.
  I. Wolverton, Terry. II. Drake, Robert.
  PS648.L47H47 1995
  813'.5080353—dc20   94-48938
                                      CIP

Cover design by Susan Silton
Cover photograph by Connie Imboden
Printed in the United States of America

Contents

Introduction
TERRY WOLVERTON   vii

Bizarro
CHRISTINA SUNLEY   1

from The Dogs
REBECCA BROWN   16

Free Your Mind and Your Ass Will Follow
MICHELLE T. CLINTON   23

Mrs. Yakamoto Comes to Stay
HILDIE V. KRAUS   31

Welcome to Gaza
SARAH JACOBUS   39

Campers
ELOISE KLEIN HEALY   50

The Great Baptism
JANE THURMOND   61

Black Orchid
KLEYA FORTÉ-ESCAMILLA   74

Joshuas in the City with a Future
JACQUELINE DE ANGELIS   78

Against All Enemies
CODY YEAGER   85

Portraits of Desire
LISA ASAGI   91

Los Angeles, City of My Dreams
LISA JONES   97

Bitey Boy
MARTHA TORMEY   106

Self-Deliverance
ELISE D'HAENE   111

Bunco of Los Angeles
ALEIDA RODRÍGUEZ   128

Defiance
CAROLE MASO   133

E=mc²
WENDI FRISCH   148

from Clit Notes
HOLLY HUGHES   153

Joshua
ROBIN PODOLSKY   160

Rat Bohemia
SARAH SCHULMAN   169

Chinese Medicine
SANDRA GOLVIN   176

Notes on the Contributors   185

Acknowledgments   195

Introduction

Content or sensibility? That is the question.

Ever since the emergence in the 1970s of the notion of "lesbian culture" (that is, an above-ground, self-identified, visible collection of artistic products reflecting the lives and/or concerns of women who call themselves lesbians), a debate has raged over the guidelines for inclusion. Should the products of lesbian culture be considered those books, music, artworks, and performances that are *about* lesbians or those that are *by* lesbians? Is depiction of our lives the paramount concern, or is it the promotion of the talents of those within our ranks? Strict separatists may take the position that both conditions must be fulfilled for a work to be considered part of lesbian culture; others who are given to the long view certainly know that each is in its own way necessary and desirable. Still, publishers, bookstores, and other institutions charged with delivering these products have tended to gravitate toward one position or the other.

Events within gay and lesbian publishing over the last few years have served to reignite the controversy. The publication of some recent anthologies of lesbian writing has sparked debate because of their editors' decision to include stories containing lesbian characters written by (famous, to be sure) writers who identify themselves as heterosexual. The position taken by the organizers of the Lambda Book Awards—to disqualify some books by gay- and lesbian-identified authors for having insufficient queer content, and to nominate books with gay content by heterosexually-identified authors—has also ruffled more than a few feathers. For these editors, publishers, and booksellers, content is clearly the determining factor in deeming a literary work "gay" or "lesbian."

But that leads to a problematic question: Just what constitutes lesbian content? Must it involve a sexual act between two or more women? If so, is a kiss enough, or is genital contact required? If not specific behaviors, are there certain traits a character must possess in order to be certified as a lesbian character, and if so, what are they?

Can we conceive of lesbian content that is not about a preoccupation with relationships (having one, ending one, or seeking one) or about the pressures of coming out? And if lesbian content is limited to these subjects (or variations on them), doesn't that lead to a narrowing of self-definition, and thus of possibilities, for lesbians?

Rather than attempt to funnel creativity into some narrow definition of what we all can understand or agree is "lesbian," I'd rather see lesbian culture include whatever lesbians create, on any subject, with any content. To me, lesbian writing is writing *by* lesbians, and the more diversity of subject, point of view, and scope, the better I like it.

The stories assembled in *Hers* reflect this bias. The lesbians who have written these stories do not occupy some enclosed, marginalized ghetto of experience and perception; they are citizens of the world. Their characters have jobs and worry about politics. They get sick. Get married. Serve in the military. They have roots in their cultural communities. Some are women with male friends, some are women who sleep with men, and some *are* men. Some are children trying to make sense of a world that is inexplicably brutal.

Some stories do concern themselves with lesbian relationships, but minus both the soap-opera dramatics and the propaganda that would hold that women are different, better. In "Black Orchid," Kleya Forté-Escamilla's teenage heroine takes the risk of contacting an older lesbian, a pariah in their closed Latino community, for assistance in coming out. Lisa Asagi's "Portraits of Desire" is a spare and abstract study of the opposing pulls of nature and culture on the shape of longing. In an excerpt from "The Dogs," Rebecca Brown turns the whole issue of romantic dependency on its head by projecting it onto a canine relationship. Christina Sunley's gender-conflicted heroine in "Bizarro" finds a possibility of true love in a sex club after nearly being gay-bashed. "E=mc²" by Wendi Frisch is a bedroom farce for the nineties, and Jacqueline De Angelis contrasts the dangers without to the dangers within in "Joshuas in the City with a Future."

Then there are stories in which relationships are used to illuminate larger issues. The lovers in Elise D'Haene's "Self-Deliverance" are desperate women, bonded in their commitment to care for their friend Teddy, who is dying of AIDS; while the couple in Eloise Klein Healy's "Campers" fight to maintain their equilibrium as one of them battles breast cancer. "Mrs. Yakamoto Comes to Stay" by Hildie V. Kraus describes the plight of a lesbian in a green-card marriage to a gay man; the heroine in "Welcome to Gaza" by Sarah Jacobus finds relief in a sexual encounter while under curfew in the Occupied Territories.

Several writers revisit the terrain of childhood and find a landscape both hostile and bewildering. In Jane Thurmond's "The Great Baptism," a young girl cannot keep from betraying her best friend when confronted with forces larger than herself: the powers of natural disaster and adult evil. Another pair of friends, teenaged this time, attempt to help one another make sense of a world beyond the borders of their neighborhood in Michelle T. Clinton's "Free Your Mind and Your Ass Will Follow." Carole Maso's harrowing "Defiance" uses a fractured narrative as a woman tries to come to grips with a childhood tragedy, the twin losses of her brother and her innocence.

The aftermath of childhood is also a theme in Martha Tormey's brash, fresh "Bitey Boy," one of two stories in the collection with male protagonists. The other, Robin Podolsky's "Joshua," brings the perspectives of psychology, politics, and celebrity to her retelling of the story of Jesus of Nazareth.

Like "Joshua," the remaining stories all have social issues on their minds. "Los Angeles, City of My Dreams" by Lisa Jones immerses us in the cutthroat world of car sales, where "the survival of the meanest" is the dominant ethos. Holly Hughes utilizes acerbic wit and a flair for the outrageous to conflate the profession of waitressing, the politics of radical feminism, and a tendency toward performance art in her excerpt from *Clit Notes*. Cody Yeager's "Against All Enemies" describes firsthand the alienation

of a lesbian in the army reserves. Pride leads to vulnerability in
Aleida Rodríguez's "Bunco of Los Angeles," which explores a
crime in a community of Cuban immigrants. In Sandra Golvin's
"Chinese Medicine" the narrator examines the traditions of culture, her own and another's, and finds herself longing to forge
such a tradition for queer men and women. Finally, Sarah
Schulman takes on the breakdown of social order in the witty and
devastating "Rat Bohemia."

There is one further strand in the debate about lesbian culture. Should the work be only or primarily *for* lesbians? The stories in this collection say no. They have things to say to any
reader of intelligence and heart, any reader who seeks to view the
world through another lens. It is my hope that this collection will
find its way to that reader, lesbian or heterosexual, gay or
straight, or of any orientation in between. The more voices we include, the more people we are heard by, the more vital our culture will be.

TERRY WOLVERTON, 1995

Hers

CHRISTINA SUNLEY

"Free," says Jimmy as we step out the door of Cafe Pearl onto Market Street. It's a rare warm night in July, almost hot, past 9:00 P.M. and the sky still clinging to its blue.

"Fancy-free," I say. *Fancy-free*, according to my mother, means free to fall in love, unattached. Truth is we're exhausted, seven hours slinging caffe lattes, but we're ignoring all signs of mortality—we both turned thirty last week.

We start walking, heading south of Market, and I can feel my heart pick up speed, my blood stir. It's the sexiest part of San Francisco: old brick warehouses, earthquake-cracked pavement, not a darling Victorian in sight. We turn onto Harrison Street and stroll past a line of gay men waiting to get in at the Stud. Two bare-chested guys squeeze past us on the sidewalk and one brushes against me, his chest hairs tickling my upper arm.

"Sorry," he says, stopping. I stop too. Now it's my move. He's got perfect shoulders, arms to die for. Dark eyes perusing my body—until they flicker with doubt. So long, luscious shoulders. I grin quick and flee, catching up to Jimmy, who's used to this. Half a block later a woman in a red suede jacket, black lace bra, lime green tutu, and a tiara perched on the fuzz of her blonde head blows me a kiss from across the street. She's adorable and I want to follow her but of course as usual I don't.

"Aren't you the object of desire," Jimmy says.

"From a distance."

I'm a perpetual victim of mistaken identity: slight for a man, tall and big boned for a woman. I get a lot of attention but most of it never comes to anything. I attract, I confuse, I disappoint. Still, Jimmy gets jealous sometimes. Jimmy's fat, and a lot of gay men don't like fat. It blinds them to Jimmy's glory—the dreadlocks fanning out from the top of his head, his make-you-melt brown eyes, the cheekiness of his cheeks, the magnificence of his belly. Jimmy's less bitter now that he's found Martin, except he's always worrying it won't last.

"Martin's not the commitment *type,*" I hear him say. "I don't think he's ever been serious about anyone in his life."

Jimmy's staring at the ground as he walks, hands behind his back, serious beyond hope.

"Look, if you don't want him, I'll take him," I offer. "I saw him first." I used to use up film just to catch a glimpse of Martin behind the counter of QuickStop Photo, tall and lean and gleaming skin one shade short of midnight.

Jimmy glares at me sideways, like he wouldn't put it past me. "Where are we, anyway?"

He stops walking and looks around. I want to say I know exactly where we are, but I don't have any idea. We've been following an old set of train tracks, cobblestones still wedged between the rails, and they've led us out of clubland and into deserted warehouse territory. Plus it got dark when we weren't looking.

"We're drifting, Jimmy, we're fancy-free."

"I'm too old for this. Let's go back to the Stud."

"Go ahead," I say, knowing he won't. But there's a big silence between us as we walk, the kind that makes it hard to breathe, as if a pair of hands came up from behind and gagged our mouths shut. Things feel creepy. I keep thinking I hear footsteps, like an echo of ours, slightly out of sync, and I want to ask Jimmy if he hears them too but I can't because now it's fear that's gagging me. I glance back once, to make sure: red cap, American flag T-shirt. Baseball bat.

"Jimmy?" I whisper, so quiet I'm not sure any sound has come out. I see him nod out of the corner of my eye. We walk faster. The streetlights are so bright I can see for blocks ahead: just us, just *him.*

"*Asslickers.*"

The words clamp down on the back of my neck.

"*Fucking faggots.*"

I take Jimmy's hand. It feels plump. Soft.

"*Stop AIDS, kill a fag.*"

Sweaty.

"*A fat nigger fag.*"

Jimmy spins around. "That's right," he says, breathy. "I'm a big fat nigger fag."

Jimmy's huge, 220 pounds, not an ounce of it muscle but this guy doesn't know that. Besides, Jimmy's been training. He steps forward. The guy slaps the bat against his open palm, a warning, a hint of hard wood meeting soft flesh. Jimmy flinches, shoves his hands in his pockets like he's nervous. The guy snickers and slaps the bat again.

My turn.

I edge off to one side, as if I'm going to run. The guy turns on me, his mouth stuck open in anger.

"Faggot," he says, like it's my name.

And then he's raising the bat; he's so close I can see the stubble on his chin, I can see words carved into the bat, and then Jimmy whips his hand out of his pocket and I hear the sweet hiss of mace and screaming and screaming. The guy tries turning away but Jimmy stays on him, aiming for the eyes and it's working, the guy's dropping the bat, falling to the ground. For a crazy instant I get confused and lean down to help him, but Jimmy grabs me and we're running.

At the end of the block I stop and look back. Jimmy tugs my arm but I shake free. I can see the guy kneeling on the pavement, rubbing his face. Red baseball cap on the ground by his feet. I know I should keep running but I can't. I cup my hands like a megaphone. I want him to hear me.

"ME NO AM FAGGOT!" I scream. "ME AM GIRL!"

By the time the cops arrive the guy's vanished. The cop in charge, the older one, spends a long time scrutinizing Jimmy's mace license, like he's looking to charge him with something, anything. Maybe because he's black, maybe because he's queer. Of course being queer isn't illegal, not here anyway, but I can't forget how it was back in Indiana when I was growing up. Cops raiding gay bars, names in the newspaper.

While the older cop radios a description, the younger one comes over to where Jimmy and I are leaning against a car. "I need a full report."

Jimmy looks away.

"We already told you," I say.

"You want to meet up with this guy again?" He looks at me, then at Jimmy. "Or you want to get him off the street?"

OK, OK. I go over the story again, and the cop asks a lot of questions about our assailant. He's not exactly nice but he's not a jerk either. He's got steely blue eyes and blue-black hair, handsome, kind of like Superman in the old comic books. When I tell him about the words "FAG SMASHER" carved into the baseball bat, I think I see his eyes narrow, like it makes him angry, but I'm not sure.

"Are you going to report this as a hate crime?" I ask him right before he gets back in the squad car. I know he hears me but he doesn't answer, just opens the driver's side door and slides in next to his partner.

"To be a hate crime, something's gotta *happen* to you." He flicks off the emergency lights and starts up the engine.

His partner laughs. "That's right. All that *happened* here is your friend sprayed some guy with mace."

Jimmy's glass trembles when he raises it to his lips, and I can see a dark circle of sweat under his arm. We're sitting on stools at the bar, Martin on one side of him, me on the other, downing margaritas with salt and smoking Camels. As soon as the cops left, Jimmy phoned Martin, who woke up, dressed, and met us here at the Stud in less than fifteen minutes. Sounds like commitment to me. The Stud is jam packed, men crowding behind us, waving for the bartender's attention, reaching for drinks, and it makes me feel safe again, like I'm surrounded by bodyguards, except I can't convince my heart to return to its normal beat. Martin's massaging Jimmy's neck with his long, bony fingers, facing me but not meeting my eye. He hasn't said one word to me. I think he thinks I'm a bad influence on Jimmy.

"It could have happened anywhere," I say. "Someone even got bashed outside the Stud last month. Everybody watched, nobody helped."

"That's right," says Jimmy. "Lucky for us, we were ready." He starts telling the story again, for the third time. The Stud has a black light that makes everything white glow, and Jimmy's teeth flash like neon pearls while he talks. "The best part," he's saying to Martin, "is when Lindy screams, 'Me no am faggot—me am *girl*!'"

I know it's funny but I can't laugh with them. It scared me, the way I screamed. I can't figure out why I cared.

Jimmy and Martin went off to dance, so I'm sitting here by myself, watching them in the mirror behind the bar and licking salt off the rim of my glass. It's so crowded people are practically dancing on top of each other, but Jimmy's managed to clear a space around himself. He needs the room, not because he's fat but because he's a gorgeous dancer. People respect that. Martin's fast and jerky, all jabbing elbows and jackknifing knees, but Jimmy's got an even rhythm, a massive grace, a thing I can trust. I wish he'd come back from the planet Martin and talk everything back into sense for me, the way he used to.

A sweet-looking guy with ripped jeans and a flattop slides his arm around my shoulder and asks me to dance. Even though I'm lonely I shake my head no. I'm not in the mood for disguises. I just want to look as female as possible, so for once there's no confusion, but I can't remember how.

No one notices me, not Jimmy or Martin bumping hips on the dance floor, not the dykes playing pool in the front room whose tense elbows and jutting hips I thread past on my way out the door. It's cold now, a different night than the one we started out in. Goose bumps rise up on my arms. I slip into my leather jacket, my armor, and start walking back to the Mission. The streets are emptier, and I can't help wondering where *he* is. When I spot a cab I almost hop in, but I believe in getting back up on the horse; I believe in the hair of the dog.

At the corner of Valencia a group of men is hanging around outside a bar, harassing a couple of women crossing the street. I can't hear what they're saying but I can guess, so I lengthen my stride, expand my shoulders, think *male*, and it works—they ignore me when I pass. It comes easily to me, this switching. I grew up reading Superman comics, assuming I too would lead a double life someday, slipping in and out of my secret identity. But my super powers were slow in developing, so one day I went to Ernie's Trading Post and traded twenty-five comics for an old orange and blue football helmet. Ernie assured me it was the next best thing to being Superman. Ernie was a gentle guy with red hair and freckles, kind of like Superman's buddy Jimmy Olsen.

I tested my new invulnerability by tightening the strap of the helmet under my chin, lowering my head, and running full speed into a brick wall.

The light is on in Sam's bay window when I get home. He doesn't need the light—he doesn't even know when the bulb burns out; it's a signal to me that he's awake. I turn it off as soon as I walk in, tracing my way through the darkness, from the nubby back edge of the armchair, along the slick enamel surface of the mantel, across a gulf of empty space to the couch where Sam is sitting, grooming his dog, Carney. When he kisses me his hair falls across my cheek, soft and long like a girl's.

"Someone tried to bash me and Jimmy." My voice sounds trembly. I reach down and stroke Carney along the ridge of her back. "We got away. Jimmy maced him."

"You OK?"

I can't speak so I nod, then remember he can't see me. He reaches over and wipes tears from my eyes with the calloused tips of his fingers.

Sam is a bass player, my downstairs neighbor, my buddy. We fuck occasionally but mainly we hang out. He doesn't ask me to define myself, only to read to him things he can't get in Braille: punk 'zines, the *National Enquirer.* He doesn't care what I look like, he doesn't even care what *he* looks like. I keep my eyes closed during sex so I can feel what he feels, and every touch is intensified, electric. We don't talk, we simply float; it's like fucking underwater.

Tonight we don't even undress. Sam wraps his arms around me and we sink into the soft springs of the couch. I wake once during the night, from the dream of a baseball bat clattering onto cobblestones, then the rapid slapping of feet.

Jimmy and I always go out after work Sundays, but tonight I tell him I'm tired. I'm not, but after last Sunday I need to go where people at least know what gender I am. Club Frenzy is one of the new lesbian sex clubs, housed in the remains of an old ironworks factory not far from where Jimmy and I were walking last week, right before we got lost.

Once I snuck into a gay boys' sex party, just to see if I could, but I've never been to one for women, and as I climb a long flight of metal stairs I almost chicken out. It's not like the Stud, where I can be invisible. I get looked at here, and I'm not sure I'm pre-pared for scrutiny. I slip into the middle of a crowd watching erotic dancers on a tiny stage. I like the one dancing alone, in front but off to the side. A studded leather harness crisscrosses her small breasts, making her look somehow innocent. Her whole body is compact, fiery muscle, her movement splintery as shatter-ing glass. When I catch her eye I realize she's the woman in the tutu I wanted to follow last Sunday night—she must have been on her way here. A shiver squiggles up my solar plexus. I blow her a kiss and disappear into the darkened back room.

It's not fancy like the male club I snuck into. Mattresses draped with old bedspreads, a couple of couches, and an easy chair line the walls of the room. Women lie talking, kissing; I can see bare skin but no one completely naked. I find a mattress in the corner and stretch out, eye level with a pair of squirming bodies one bed over. I can see their breasts pushed against each other. I love that sight. Lesbian sex always seems so wholesome to me, wholesome but dangerous. I can be fond of men, but women I can love, al-though lesbians have less patience for me than almost anybody else. They think I'm in cahoots with the patriarchy, a sexual slacker avoiding my fair share of oppression. "You could at least have the decency," my last girllove informed me, "to call yourself bisexual." I suppose, technically, I am bisexual, but I hate to be pinned down. Lately it seems easier to stick with Sam.

I shut my eyes, and beneath the bass beat of the music I can *hear* this club, the thump and swoosh of dancers, the click of heels, the thunk of boots, the soft, fierce moaning of the women in the bed next to me, and I flash on Sam in one of the rare mo-ments when I open my eyes and glimpse his mane of long hair, his face so open, unaware of being watched, and suddenly I get the feeling that *I'm* being watched, here, now, at Club Frenzy.

It's the dancer in the leather harness. She's sitting on the edge of my mattress, breathless from dancing. Her eyes don't veer from my face, even when I look into them: gray, keen. I can see trails of sweat running down her breasts, drops hanging from her nipples. I sit up.

"Sally," she says, offering me her hand. Her palm is slippery with sweat.

"Lindy." Women this cute make me say stupid things. "I knew a Sally once."

She nods; she doesn't care. I'm trying to think of something else to say when a song comes on, new and jumpy, and the couple in the bed next to us suddenly rise and head for the dance floor, pulling on their clothes. Sally's shoulders start to sway and I get scared I'm going to lose her. "Sally and I started a club together," I say. "When we were ten. The Bizarro Club."

She gives me a look like she can't understand why I'm telling her this, but I'm too revved to stop. "We were hooked on old Superman comics, Sally and I, and our favorite ones were about Bizarro, which is a parallel world where everything is done crazy and backward and opposite from how we know it." I haven't thought about Bizarro in years, but suddenly the cartoon images are leaping in my head. "Everyone on Bizarro is a duplicate of an earthling. Except they have bright white skin and kooky grins, messed up hair, ripped up clothes. They're mostly Jimmy Olsens and Lois Lanes and Supermen. Lots of Supermen. And they speak a kind of idiot baby talk; they say everything in reverse." I take a breath. "Like, me think Sally ugliest girl at Club Frenzy."

"Hmmmm," she says, and lets her thigh rest against mine. I guess she's not going anywhere. I can see the down on her upper lip, still glistening with sweat. I brush my lips across the stiff blond fuzz on the top of her head.

"Go on," she says. I kiss her there again but she pulls away and turns around so she's facing me. "I mean go on with your story." She has a tough look, an almost smile, that I don't know how to read.

"So me and Sally founded the Bizarro Club with a couple of boys we knew. But Sally and I were in charge. On Bizarro, girls ruled."

"The boys agreed?"

"Oh, they were known sissies, that's why we invited them. We made them swear on an upside-down bible to do whatever we said. Sally and I stomped around in boots and long capes, and Frankie and Bill had to wear skirts and jewelry and shout, 'Save us! We scared!' On Saturdays we'd all go to this place called Ernie's Trading Post, and Sally and I would pick out girls' clothes for the boys to dress up in. But Ernie knew they weren't for us. One day he saw Frankie fingering some gauzy, beaded gown and told him he could try it on if he wanted. Of course Sally and I still did the trading at the counter, in case anyone we knew came in. Regular earthlings might misunderstand."

Sally's smiling now, I know exactly what she's thinking. Lesbians love these stories of kiddie gender rebellion, tomboy turns dyke. Things are simple for them. I look around the room, all the women in pairs, on the mattresses, on the dance floor, and I get struck with it again, the pureness, like they're full-blooded members of the tribe and I'm some distant cousin. Then I feel a hand stroking my shin and I decide not to care.

"Me hate to kiss you," Sally says.

She learns fast.

So here we are, just two nice girls locked in a wholesome embrace, and some idiot flicks on the lights. Women start laughing and shouting, *Turn them off! Turn them off!* but they stay on and then the music gets ripped off its track and there's nothing but light and silence and cops streaming in the doorway.

Sally flies off me and we start dressing, fast, but she has hardly any clothes so I give her my leather jacket and just as she's putting it on I notice flashes of white light popping around us—cops are snapping random pictures of the crowd. I've got my bra on but I can't find my shirt anywhere. Then I see him across the room. The cop from last week, the young one with the blue-black hair, the one who cared enough to take down our story. I head straight for him.

"What's going on?"

Instead of answering he looks me up and down—does he remember me?—and before I can duck, he lifts his camera and a flash goes off in my eyes. Where his face should be there's a white hole.

To be a hate crime, something's gotta happen to you.

Something's happening to me.

"You can't do this!" I shout. I'm crying, Sally's pulling me back toward her by my shoulders.

"Yes," he says, reloading the camera. "Yes, I can."

They don't arrest us, of course. No grounds. But they won't let anyone leave until the firemen finish their inspection. Finally they decide to cite the owner for not having illuminated exit signs. That means the rest of us can go. Sally and I are on our way out when I spot him again. He's standing by the door, arms folded across his chest.

"Why did you take our photographs?" My voice is shaky and I try to steady it. "We weren't breaking any law."

He won't answer, just stares at me, eyes like stones. Women are pushing past us on their way down the stairs, and I can feel Sally edging behind me, eager to escape. But I keep thinking about how his eyes narrowed when I told him about the bat; I keep wanting him to be on my side. "Could I at least have the negative?" I ask, trying to sound reasonable.

He shakes his head. "Not a chance. Official police evidence."

"Evidence? Evidence of what?" I know I'm hysterical but I can't stop myself. "Evidence that I wear a bra? Evidence that I have sex with women?"

"Come on." Sally grabs my hand and pulls me behind her. I look back at him, for a second. The bastard's smirking. Then we're running down the long, grimy steps and into the street. We don't stop until we're around the block, out of sight of cops and nosy bystanders. It's quiet here and I feel shy suddenly, alone with Sally, standing underneath a street lamp. My leather jacket is open on her chest and I can see her breasts, bare and vulnerable. I zip up the jacket and she pulls me into her.

"Come home with me."

"I can't." I slip out of her arms, lean against a parked car. Right now I just want what's easy. Home. Sam.

"OK." Her face gets that tough look again and I don't know if she's hurt or if she really doesn't care. She pushes her hands into the pockets of the jacket. "Can I have your number?"

She doesn't wait for an answer, just starts searching my jacket for a piece of paper. I'm scared she's going to find the condom I keep in the inner pocket, but before I can figure out how to stop her she comes up with a matchbook from Cafe Pearl. I write my number and hand it back to her.

"Don't let those cops get to you," she says. "Men are assholes."

She leans to kiss me good-night. I can see the gray of her eyes, the color of cement that hasn't hardened yet. It would be so easy to sink into them.

"I fuck men," I say.

I've already said good-bye and started walking away before she recovers.

"You want a medal?" I hear her laugh. "Or was that supposed to scare me off?"

It's not until I'm back home that I remember she still has my jacket on.

Sam's here, sitting in bed next to me, fingers skimming over a Braille edition of *The Unbearable Lightness of Being*. I've got my head on his thigh, my cheek nuzzling his soft hairs, when the phone rings. I don't move. Sam keeps reading, the words rising up through the little bumps into his fingertips.

The answering machine clicks on. "You make me so happy, Lindy, when you no call me back, because me never want to see you again anyway." *Click.*

Sam stops reading. "Why won't you speak to her?"

He doesn't sound jealous, just honestly bewildered. All week Sally's been leaving messages on my machine: *Lindy, me got your jacket. Lindy, call me back.* But I don't call. All I can think about is that photograph of me half-naked and some stupid pig jerking off to it. Sam says the film's probably sitting in a storage locker, but I think he's just trying to make me feel better.

"It's too hard to explain."

"It wouldn't be hard if you didn't make it hard."

I rest my head on his lap again and he lets me get away with not answering. I'm sick of explaining myself, I'm sick of my whole Bizarro existence. I'm too old for it. After work today while I was washing my hands in the bathroom a woman came out of one of the stalls, probably somebody's mother visiting from the Midwest, and when she saw me her jaw dropped. "This is the *ladies'* room!"

I could see her face in the mirror, eyes lidded with blue gunk, lips fuzzed brick red. I kept washing my hands, squeezing out more and more soap from the dispenser, building up a giant lather.

"Get out," she said. "Get out of here now!"

I turned around. I lifted up my shirt. I shook my tits in her face. Something's happening to me.

B79867. That's his badge number. The young cop. I memorized it right before Sally whisked me out the door. Minton is his name. K. Minton. Kenny? Keith?

I want my photo back.

One Saturday when I was eleven I got to Ernie's Trading Post early, before it opened. The door was unlocked. It was dark and I could barely make out the aisles of old clothes, battered pots and pans, army uniforms, books. I called Ernie's name but there was no answer. I was heading for his office at the back when I passed the dressing room and glimpsed a pair of legs behind the curtain. They were Ernie's. And someone was kneeling in front of him. Frankie. I recognized his red Pro Keds. I heard sounds. I stared at a large silver tack imbedded in the worn sole of Frankie's left sneaker. Then I ran out, on tiptoes.

I never went back to Ernie's. Maybe I would have, eventually, but I didn't have a chance, because a couple of weeks later they shut it down. Frankie showed us a clipping from the police report page of the daily newspaper. There'd been a bar raid, and Ernie's name was listed.

The Bizarro Club stopped meeting after that. We decided we were getting too old for it.

There are three K. Mintons in the phone book, but one is Kate and the second is so old his voice shook when he answered the phone. Jimmy and I are sitting in his van across the street from the house of the third one, 1245 Hayes. It's Saturday night and the lights are on, so I figure K. Minton is due to venture out soon in search of whatever off-duty cops do for fun in this town. And when he does, I'm ready. In the meantime, we wait.

I had trouble convincing Jimmy to come. He thinks I'm obsessed, that I should forget about the photo. Plus he's nervous the cop will recognize us.

"You he might recognize," I admit. "But he won't see you. Just me. And I'm a chameleon."

"Why do you look for trouble, Lindy?" He sounded like a parent.

"I'm not looking for trouble. I'm trying to figure out how to live on this planet, OK?" He's biting his lip, so I add, "I'm fine, Jimmy, I'm just fine."

He shakes his head. "Is this what you call *just fine*? Hanging out spying on some cop?"

I don't answer. I'm tired of Jimmy lately. I'm tired of everyone, even Sam.

We sit in silence for a while. It's cold and the windows are fogged up. I keep a small circle cleared with my finger, a peephole. Finally the lights go off and a man comes down the front steps. He's dressed in jeans and a polo shirt, but I can tell it's him from the way he holds his head, like he can't forget he's a cop, even on Saturday night. We pull out behind him and soon Jimmy forgets he's mad and starts getting into the cloak-and-dagger of it, keeping back far enough not to be spotted, close enough not to lose sight of K. Minton's dark green Triumph. We tail him all the way to Chestnut Street, a fancier neighborhood than I'd imagined for an off-duty cop. He parks in a lot and then disappears into the door of a crowded bar.

"Now what?" Jimmy asks.

"Now I go in."

"Lindy, wake up!" He grabs my hand. "You think he carries your goddamn photograph everywhere he goes?"

I jerk my hand away and climb into the back of the van where I stashed my bag. I crouch down on the floor and take off all my clothes.

"What are you doing?"

I'm putting on my stockings. I'm putting on my white lace bra. I'm putting on my tight black skirt. I'm putting on my yellow silk shirt. I'm putting on my high-heeled pumps. I'm putting on my long, blonde hair.

I climb into the front seat, switch on the light, twist the rearview mirror toward my face. Jimmy's not saying anything; he's just watching me while I flick mascara onto my lashes, draw my lips cherry red.

Me prettiest girl in San Francisco.

"Thanks for the ride," I say, meaning it. "Don't wait up."

K. Minton is leaning against the bar, sucking a Bud and watching the Oakland A's on TV. I'm standing by the wall across from him. It's a singles bar, an odd mix of regular guys, men in ties, and fancy women who ignore me as they glide past, immune to my charms. An investment banker named Jerry tries to buy me a drink. Everything is crazy and backward and opposite of how I know it. Anything can happen.

K. Minton is hungry. He asks me to dance. The floor is crowded, hot. I don't meet his eye, but I watch him. He moves like his body is a cage that's not quite big enough for him. I'm smiling, trying not to laugh. He sees me and smiles too. For a moment he gets a funny look in his eye, as if he were remembering something from a long time ago, but he pushes it away. Moves in closer. A slow song. His arm wraps around my waist, easy. I rest my head on his shoulder. He slides his hands down my back. We move casually, steadily, toward the back corner of the room.

It's dark here. I slide my hand over his, guide it past my hips, around my belly. Down down down to my big stiff—

"Hey!" he yells.

Him shocked. Him mad!

"Me no am girl," I explain. "Me am faggot!"

Me run, me kick off high heels, me faster than a speeding bullet. Me out the door, me in Jimmy's van, waving dildo out the window. Us drive off.

K. Minton sets his beer down on the bar, and for the first time since I walked in takes his eyes off the game, lets them rove around the room. They settle on me for an instant, small and blue and beady. I hold my breath, waiting for a flicker of recognition, but it doesn't come.

I cross the room and lean on the bar next to him, blocking his view of the game, heart pounding. I know I should turn around, walk out the door, let Jimmy drive me home if he's still out there, take a bus if he's not. But K. Minton took something from me, and I want something back.

"Ken?"

"Kevin." He squinches his brow, trying to place me. "Do I know you?"

"We've met here before." I figure it's better to plug him with a wrong memory than let him struggle to remember the real ones, and it seems to work. He smiles, nothing lecherous, and I get a flash of how he seemed that first night when I thought he was on our side.

"What's your name?"

"Lois." I lower my voice, not looking at him, just in case. I have things I want to ask him—did he catch the guy in the baseball cap, did he even try, where is my photograph—but I can't, so I ask him something I know the answer to, just to see what he'll say.

"So what do you do when you're not watching baseball in bars?"

"Work for the city," he says, like he has a job too boring to mention, and his face gets the same sealed-off look as when I confronted him in Club Frenzy, lips tightened into a line he won't let himself cross.

"What about you?"

"Work with addicts," I answer, thinking of all the steamy caffeine fixes I dispense each day. Then neither one of us speaks. I guess he can't think of any other questions, and I've got too many of the kind he won't answer. No matter how close I try to get I could never pry him open—I'm not the only one who knows how to switch. And even though he's no Clark Kent, I get fooled for a moment, watching him stare dully into his empty beer. There's something weary in his small blue eyes when he looks up at me again.

"Can I buy you a drink?"

I nod, and he makes his way to the other end of the bar. He blends in so perfectly he doesn't seem like a cop anymore, just one more lonely guy on the prowl. Every few seconds he glances back, without moving his head, to make sure I'm still here, and it gives me a surge of power, like right before we sprayed the mace. The only problem is, this time I don't have anything to fight back with.

I was half hoping to see Jimmy's van when I got onto the street but I guess he gave up on me, so I started walking down Chestnut, trying not to trip in my high heels, feeling idiotic and lonely and freezing cold, a true Bizarro. Soon all I could think about were the two things I wanted most—Sally and my leather jacket.

I called from a pay phone. I knew she never wanted to talk to me again, so I kept it simple: Me sorry, me want to see you, maybe us could meet? She wasn't happy to hear my voice but she said OK. I'm hoping that once I start explaining, the true Bizarro logic will come clear to both of us.

Now I'm on a bus, heading up Van Ness Avenue, and some jerk across the aisle is staring at me because my skirt keeps riding up my thighs. I can feel the cold plastic seat pressing into my legs and my wig itches, but if I look straight ahead, over the driver's shoulder and out the big front windshield, I can see Sally in my mind, sitting in the cafe where I asked her to meet me, looking up when I walk in. I don't know if she'll recognize me, even if I take my wig off at the door. I'm trying to concentrate on her eyes, but behind me, in the back of my mind, is another image: K. Minton waiting for me at the bar, holding his beer in one hand, my beer in the other, his empty, mine full, trying to remember where it is he knows me from. The farther the bus pulls me away from the bar the smaller the image gets, but it never disappears.

REBECCA BROWN

One night I found a dog in my apartment.

It was a big dog, tall and black and lean, with pointy ears and long taut slender legs. It had black eyes and auburn tips on its face and feet and it didn't move at all. I was afraid and held my breath and the dog did too. After a while its muzzle twitched and I could see its teeth. It growled very low in its throat and I was terrified. Then it stopped twitching and its mouth closed but it was like there was an X ray and I could see through the dog's skin to its teeth. I could see the tension in its mouth and how the dog was trying to keep from snapping.

I held my breath as long as I could. When I let it out the dog breathed too. The stomach of the dog was lined with tits.

Nice dog, I said as calmly as I could, Niiiice doggie.

The dog breathed out slowly, indignantly, like I had not shown right respect for my superior.

I wanted to get away from her but I was afraid I'd set her off. The closest place to get away was the bathroom. I slowly lifted my right foot—the dog watched every inch of me—and put it behind me. Then I moved my left foot back a baby step, but I was afraid to turn my back to the dog so I stepped sideways, very slowly, into the bathroom. When I got inside I shut the door behind me quickly, locked it, leaned against it, shivered.

I closed my eyes and pressed my palms to my temples as if I could squeeze something out.

I splashed water on my face and drank a huge glass of water. I looked in the mirror. I didn't look great but at least I didn't see a dog. I took off my clothes and got in the shower. I stood in the water a long time. I felt a little better when I finished. I dried off and grabbed my pj's from the hook on the bathroom door and put them on. The bathroom was steamy and the mirror was gray. I wiped a space in the mirror and I could see, streaked and dotted with tiny drops, my face, just me, no vision of a dog. Thank god.

My apartment is really tiny, just the main room with my bed and desk and chair, the bathroom and a little kitchenette. The overhead light is by the front door, so I shut it off and I stumbled to bed lit only by the pale orange blur from the street lamps coming in the window.

I got into bed the way I do every night. I rolled over on my side and pulled the blankets up to my face leaving only enough room to breathe. I pulled my knees toward my chest and my feet toward my butt. I tucked my head and pressed my fists into my eye sockets. It's the way I always have since I was young.

I was starting to fall asleep when I heard a click. Then there was another click. Then padding across the floor. One way, then still, then back the other way. And then toward the bed. I was scared. I could feel my body thinking, "no." There were the clicks and pads and then a few taut seconds of nothing, then the leap. I felt the weight as it fell on the bed. It moved toward the foot of the bed. There was the sink and then it moved around in a circle, then two, then three. Then it pawed at the blanket and mumbled something and lay down.

I pretended like I was asleep. After a while I thought I heard it breathing deep and evenly. I lay as still and quiet as I could. Then, when it had breathed like that a long time, when I'd convinced myself it was dead asleep, I pushed my covers down the tiniest bit and lifted my head the tiniest bit and I looked down over the lumps of me and at the foot of the bed, as if she belonged, as if the bed had always been hers, I saw the dog. Her butt was to the footboard and her paws were straight in front of her. Her head was up. And in the horrible light that came in from the street, I saw the outline of her body, I saw the wet shine of her open eyes:

The dog was watching me.

I woke up underneath the very heavy weight. My ribs were pressed and it was hard to breathe. I couldn't move, I could just barely

open my eyes and I saw it on me. It was lying all over me, pressing
me down. I wanted to get out but I didn't want to wake it if it was
still asleep. I wished I could shrink, or float above, outside us both.
But I was stuck inside my skin.

I tried to move my right arm. I pressed it down in the mattress
so I could move it over toward the edge of the bed. But it was
there too, on my side. I flexed my fingers. I could feel stiff fur, the
edge of a leg. I tried to move my arm again and I was slapped with
a paw. The paw was scratchy like the splintered end of a two-by-
four. Then I felt the tops of claws, like nails against my skin. They
were pressing down.

Let me out, I could only whisper, Please.

No response.

Please, I whispered again.

Nothing.

But then, and only in her own sweet time, and not because I'd
begged her, she shifted slightly and I could breathe. Then she
didn't move anymore.

I tried to not feel anything. Not the crush of my ribs beneath
her, not my arms and legs like sand. Not my neck pressed down so
every time I tried to swallow I was choked.

Please, I rasped again.

Then I felt her tongue and mouth go over mine and I couldn't
breathe at all. I thrashed and tried to suck the air but I couldn't. I
really thought I'd really die, I thought I was blacking out, and
then she moved and I gulped the air. Then she pulled away from
my body. I felt her butt and torso lift and I heard her straighten
and stretch. She smacked her lips and yawned like it was any, oh it
was a lovely, bright new morning. I sat up, when I could again, and
looked. Her teeth were white, her tongue was red, her eyes and
throat were black. She yawned a gravelly little growl that slipped
up the scale to a contented little yip. It sounded like a baby's
chirp. In another circumstance it might have sounded sweet.

Then she slipped out of bed. Her back feet jabbed me when
she jumped but I didn't make a sound, I was pretending I was
dead. I heard her walk into the kitchen and sniff around. Then
she came back by the bed. I lay as still as I could but I wasn't fool-
ing her. She stood with her head near the head of the bed and
barked. I tried not to flinch but I did. She barked again. She was
commanding me. I pushed down the sheets and sat up in bed and

dropped my legs to the floor. When I stood up my body felt like lead. I stood up straight, I was at her command, and she sniffed my feet and nosed my pj's and lifted the bottoms of my pj's with her muzzle: she was inspecting me. I stood at attention, eyes looking up and forward. I felt her wet nose through the flannel, then on my skin. After a while the dog stepped back, wiped her nose with a paw then wiped her paw on the floor. Then she sat on her haunches and waited.

I didn't know what I was supposed to do. The dog looked toward the kitchen so I went there. I didn't know what to do when I got there. She barked. She was looking at the tap. I got her a bowl and some water. I set the bowl on the floor. She examined the bowl very carefully to see it was clean enough. Then she dipped in her tongue, it was pink and wide, and drank.

She was suddenly smooth and graceful, she was beautiful.

And so the dog moved in with me. She lived inside my life.

And every day she woke with me, and every single night she filled my bed.

I got over my uneasiness, I put it somewhere else. I learned to accept the things she did, the things she made me do. I learned to fit myself around her ways, I learned to love her.

It became as if my house were hers, and I the grateful guest.

She met me when I stumbled home. I'd hear her whining all the way outside when I unlocked the street door, then hear her scratching, eager, as I hurried up the stairs. When I opened the apartment door she'd leap on me and press me with the pads of her feet and yowl. Her black stump tail and tongue would twitch, her open mouth would pant. I'd catch my breath and close my eyes and she'd back me to the wall and hold me there. I didn't tell her Down! or No! She'd get down in her own sweet time, and I was afraid to say anything that might really set her off. I was also afraid the dog might leave.

For, as much as she oppressed me, I required her.

And I was curious. I must confess I was a little flattered. Why had this monster chosen me? My home was humble, a dump in fact, too cramped for even me. If it had been a body it would be like mine—thin and spare and angular and empty.

The building doesn't have a yard. I'd picked the place with the

strictest lease: no roommates, no sublets, no pets. So I was afraid
to have her seen, afraid I'd get evicted.

But the dog did not complain about our secrecy. In fact she
thrived on how she was, and always only ever was, inside, alone,
with me.

One day when I walked home from work there was a butcher's
shop. I hadn't seen the place before, but I don't eat meat, and
maybe hadn't noticed it. I had not been in a place like that for
years. Not since I was a child and went with Mother out to get a
special cut of something when Father was coming home. But I was
led into the butcher's like something was pulling me. I walked up
to the counter and I looked down through the glass and said, like
someone else was speaking it, my arm was lifted up and pointing,
That one.

The butcher wrapped a single sheet of opaque paper around it
and wrapped it again in white. He wound the paper around in a
perfect swirl like a candy cane or a barber's pole. He taped it
smooth with clean white tape so it was long and round and like a
cast, like a dismembered thing. The butcher's hands were smooth
and white, his fingernails were very trim and tidy. He looked more
like a doctor than the thing he really was. He slipped the white
stump in the bag. He handed me the bag. It had a string handle.

I walked home quickly. The day was hot and I didn't want the
thing to spoil. I carried the bag by the handle. It knocked against
my leg like the bag of treats I carried when I was a kid on
Halloween.

Outside my apartment door, I shifted the bag to my other hand
while I reached in my jeans for my keys. I felt the swing of the
weight of the bone. I looked in the sack and it looked up at me
like a mummy's fist, like something from my childhood aiming up
at me.

I took a breath so deep I felt it in my blood. It felt like every
single cell of me filled up and emptied out at once.

I hid the bag behind by back.

I put the key in the lock. I opened the door. The bare bulb in
the hallway threw a line of light onto the apartment floor. As I
opened the door the line grew into a triangle. When I opened it
more I saw, inside the apex of the triangle, exactly where she knew
she would be centered in the light, the dog.

She sat as still and solemn as the Buddha. For a second I didn't see her breathe. Then the light seemed to pulse and I saw her stomach move. My eyes zoomed in on her belly like a scene from the movies. It actually felt a bit ridiculous. I stepped into the apartment, closed the door and switched on the overhead light and things looked normal, sort of. I began to move the bag in front of me.

And then the dog leapt. She sprang up against me. Her front paws knocked my collarbone. I lifted the bag above my head and she lunged toward it. She stretched her huge black neck, her huge white teeth and snapped. Then her back feet slipped across the floor and she fell. She whined like a baby and then like a boy.

I was convinced she would do anything to me to get the bag and I was terrified, but she didn't. When she got her balance back she jumped again, but didn't knock me down. I lowered the bag but she didn't grab. Instead she crouched and growled. She pressed her front paws flat to the floor and shook her butt and whined. The dog was *playing*.

Her growls sounded like she liked it, almost, but at least as much as she hated it. So I played with her too. I teased the dog to jump, then I raised the bag up high and shouted, No! She leapt and whined and cowered. I saw the tautness of her legs and thighs, the smoothness of her belly and the brilliance of her skin and she was beautiful.

I played with her, then after a while, in my own sweet time, I told her, I commanded, Sit.

She whined, then she was obedient and sat.

I looked her over several seconds then pronounced, like any proper schoolmarm with her pointing stick, Good girl.

The dog looked up at me and shivered, she was wild with need.

How much do you want this, I purred, How much does Baby Puppy want her bone?

She barked.

I snatched the bag up high. Polite! I ordered. We don't shout when we're polite.

Her muzzle twitched. I could see her teeth.

How much does Baby Puppy want her bone? I asked again, sing-song, through my teeth.

Her muzzle twitched again. Then she opened her mouth and yipped a perfect little yip like something begging.

Good girl, I said, Gooooood girl.

I held the bag a few more precious seconds. Her coat looked wet and shivering. Then I tossed the bag. She caught the thing midair. Then she didn't even try to act demure. She grabbed it with her teeth and shook it back and forth. She threw it to the floor and bit. She chomped and gulped. She was frantic to tear the paper off, frantic to get the meat. I saw white bits of paper fly, and strings of silver spit, then bits of red. I saw her stomach heaving and I heard her gnashing teeth.

When she'd torn the bag and paper off, she dragged the bone to the center of the room — onto the carpet, my carpet, of course — and gnawed. The thing was huge and wet and muscly and I could see where it had been hacked. The dog held it hard between her front paws and put her teeth in it.

Then suddenly, like a well-trained girl who realizes she's forgotten to thank her pretty auntie for the pretty, pretty doll, she stopped. She swallowed, licked her chops and caught her panting breath. Then, in a gesture I guessed meant Thank You, pressed her nose to my ankle and licked my shoe. I felt her tongue along the top of my sneaker. The spot was wet and very slightly pink.

You're welcome, I mumbled, as she grabbed the bone again.

But by then, of course, the dog was no longer listening.

Free
Your Mind
and
Your Ass
Will Follow

MICHELLE T. CLINTON

It was the time that made them get their hair all wild. Nappy is what Debra's momma called it. "Nappy, nasty, and downright nig- gerish, like some boo just crawled out of the bush," she fussed.

"But we proud, Mrs. Garnette," Sandra said. "God made us this way. We proud and happy to be nappy-headed."

"Them naps done soaked into your brains and kinked up your sense till you ain't got none left. How a nigger gone be proud of being a nigger?" Debra's momma kept fussing while Debra just snorted and grabbed Sandra by the forearm, and pulled her into the bathroom where all the hair care bottles, the afro grease and afro combs sat shining under the water-stained mirror.

"So what," Debra cursed, "fuck her," as she sprayed and picked out Sandra's hair. The tiny bathroom filled with the sour mist of the Afro Sheen. "We got something to do tonight, girl. Man and them want us to go riding. Plus they gonna pick up some juice, just like last time. You got to look pretty. You got any money?"

"Fifty cents."

"Okay. I got seventy-five. Let's only tell them we got a quarter apiece. I seen a picture in *Life* magazine of this white girl, must have been Jewish, 'cause her hair was rough just like a nigguh's 'cept she had braids on the side. Here. Hand me the comb." Debra plaited two braids right above Sandra's ears that framed her brown face. "Girl, you so cute," she said, and shoved the red, black and green comb in the back pocket of her jeans.

Their jeans were Levi's, shrunk bootie tight, cuffed at the bottom and topped by a solid color T-shirt. No bras: Their breasts bobbed when they left Debra's momma's house, nipples alert with all the juice and arrogance of adolescence. The beads around their necks were psychedelic rainbows, just the perfect touch, Debra figured, to telegraph to the wide and open world that they were ready.

Man and them were older and had a car. A nineteen-fifty-something Chevy that broke down once a week but could get to Venice Beach and back on one dollar worth of gas. Man and them meant some fast riding boys, but safe, 'cause Man was Debra's older brother, and Sandra was too young anyway and read too many books. Smart girls, Debra and Sandra, kind of cute, but way too smart-mouth for women, so didn't nobody mess with them. The Chevy got loaded down: Man, then Debra, then big Rufus, Man's ace boon coon, in the front seat, with Sandra and Stevie in the back.

"Debra," Man said, "you got Sandra looking like some kinda hippie white girl." All the boys busted up like it was a joke they'd been holding in. Sandra let out her breath and blinked.

"You so ignorant," Debra said, "you wouldn't know fine if it jumped up and slapped your ass in the face."

"We so ignorant," Rufus said, "we want to take you riding with us. You all got any money?"

"All we got is fifty cents between us. And we don't have to give you that. Better hope some fine white boy with a bunch of money don't see hippie-looking Sandra and snatch her ass up."

"What you got, Sandra, a quarter? I know you got more than that. Don't lie to me, girl. You want to have fun, you want to go to the beach, you got to pay," Rufus said.

"All I got is twenty-five cents. Here. Take it."

"Here's my quarter," Debra said. "You cheap-ass, broke-down nigguhs, always trying to take some woman's money." Man collected quarters from everybody and headed out to the Primo Discount Gas station, right next door to King's Liquor and Fine Beverages' blinking neon sign. Rufus, who had almost had a mustache, had to try and buy, but came back stomping to the car, pissed and frustrated that he couldn't pass for grown. Then four more liquor-store stops, four more ID requests that Rufus didn't have, until a half-buzzed, half-nodded wino offered to help.

"I could get that brew for you," he said, his eyes bloodshot.

"Don't want brew. We looking for that wine connection, Spanada, need three bottles."

The wino took the money and got four. He was already drinking, the bottles turned up inside the paper bag, when he walked out the store. He handed over three bottles.

"Aw man," Rufus said, "why you wanna do some kids like that?"

"You wanna play, you got to pay," the wino laughed.

"Fuck that drunk-ass, scabby motherfucker," Debra started up. "If you all was men, you'd take his money."

"Nigguh ain't got no money. Why you think he's drinking?" Man said. "Rufus, just get your ass in the car and let's ride. We got the juice, don't we? Let's just ride."

The clunky car made it up the ramp and whizzed into the lights of the Santa Monica Freeway. Man and Rufus and them always kept the window down in summer so the quick L.A. night air hit your face and made you feel like everything in speed. The white and red ribbonlike streaks of color could almost wrap you like wire and cut your happiness if you were too slow or thought too much. But Sandra couldn't help thinking, even riding the lucky ride to the beach with safe boys and her best friend: Nothing but fun was coming at her, she knew it and her mind kicked in anyway. The rhythm of the lights bouncing into her eyes made her wonder what was in everybody's head. I'll never know what's in anybody's head but mine, she figured, and that made her feel safe, that made her feel calm.

"I said free your mind," blasted out the radio, "and your ass will follow. The kingdom of heaven is within," said the music of the machine that carried them.

"Love me some funk," said Rufus, as he leaned over Debra and cranked up the radio. "Love me some hard-hitting, funkadelic music."

"Yeah, we ride," said Man, claiming the dark side of the night as his own. "Yeah, we drinking and we riding tonight."

The alleys of Venice are known to be sexy to men and dangerous to women, so teenagers are drawn like ants. Around the garbage cans and many arrogant cats, everybody thinks something is about to happen, something that you'll love, or something that will seriously mess with your mind. The wildest of the jealous gods is gonna go off on somebody with bad or excellent luck. Somebody, maybe you, maybe your running buddy, is about to pay or be paid, you could end up laughing so hard your stomach would cramp, or you might bust out crying, running back toward the car, or catch a brick in the lip and give up a front tooth: The alleys excited and warned them. But like most places everywhere, mostly nothing happens, mostly people wander and wait, mostly the alleys are still.

The front of Man's car bounced over the curb to the Clubhouse Court, an alley just three blocks off the beach, and began a steady creep up the alleys in prayer for the luck of an empty parking space. Man twisted the tops off the green wine bottles in the brown paper bag and handed one bottle to Debra. "This here is for you all," he said. "Best try and chug it. Drink it fast as you can without throwing up, gives you the best head rush." Debra turned the bottle up, gagged, wiped her mouth and passed the bag to Sandra. Sucking on the bottle like that, her neck all the way back, Sandra could feel a perfect loneliness, stronger than the lights on the freeways, thicker than the danger in the alleys, and even with the horrible liquor sourness in her nose, she was strong and got down three gulps. This is it, she thought. This is drinking now like a grown-up. This is what they do and I'm doing it now, she thought, because it was her first time and she didn't know shit and she always did what Debra told her anyway. She knew they was gonna get drunk and fucked up. Debra told her she did it last weekend and how she could be a wino. She could understand they trip. Because wine juice in the vein and head is a pure wish for fun and peace and no worry can make you mad. Which sounded pretty good to Sandra. So, with her head back, her nose fizzing with Spanada, she couldn't tell one reason not to gulp and drink. But how to tell if you were drunk and how much, were you really drunk? When does it get completely easy, she wondered when she hit the bottle a fourth and fifth time and then stopped counting.

"Yo, man, let's cruise," Man declared, and all four doors of the car opened at once; all five of them hit the pavement and turned in the direction of the waves. A big inhale of salt sucked in by open mouths made the whole gang light-headed and happy. That plus the booze.

The group split off into the boy bunch and the girl couple. The girl couple walked half a dozen paces behind the boys and in general made more noise, mostly laughing. They knew they wasn't nothing but fools; they liked to be loud fools, prowling for the trouble in fun, ready for the fun in trouble. Pretty scary for the fragile tourist white folks, but with laughing girls in back, that was the easiest way to make anybody willing to take a second glance comfortable.

But it wasn't hardly anybody on the boardwalk, no tourists at all, just a few of the local white folks, people of strange and mysterious culture. Beach people. Hippies. White people of peculiar color combinations: pink and orange, yellow and purple. Their hair dripped and hung shaggy. Their eyes all smokey and red, the hippie women obviously without bras, and everybody, even at night, barefooted. Just a few couples, a few small groups were out walking under the boardwalk lights, the rose color vibrated above them all. Like the same jealous god sent down a spotlight that seemed no relation to the beach at all, no relation to the reason all of them were there. The lack of shadow and electric buzz made them all look and feel cold, to themselves and to each other. But the light did not affect the girls at first. Debra eyeballed everybody. Sandra was busy with her Spanada grin, trying out her theory on telepathic communication with people of the same nature. She had on her tight jeans, true she wasn't barefooted, but she had braids in her natural and bells tied to her orange and purple beads.

"Can a nigguh be a hippie?" she asked.

"Hell yeah, look at you." Debra laughed.

"Debra, we dressed exactly the same way."

"Yeah, but I'm passing." Debra laughed more. "I'm visiting these white folks' planet. I would never act the same kinda fool as these fools act. 'Cept when I'm with you." She hit Sandra on the butt and took off running toward the water.

"Okay, so now I gotta run," Sandra thought, and walked to the nearest bench just past where the sand started and undid her shoelaces and carried her shoes. By then Debra was halfway to the ocean, and Man and Rufus was nowhere seemed like, the boardwalk totally empty. She wouldn't run in no cold sand, the cold bit into her toes and reminded her that the lights were hard, just like the lights that hit her eyes in the car, and maybe the whole night was poisoned and it wasn't even scary.

"Help. Help!" Sandra heard and she didn't even flinch.

"Help, please I desperately need your help," and it wasn't nobody but Debra, in a white lady voice, still wanting to be chased. "Please come to my rescue. I need help immediately." Sandra grinned and started an easy run toward the ocean. She could see Debra balanced on the rocks, waving her hands above her head, begging and yelling for attention.

"I have come," Sandra shouted, soon as she got close. "I am the lifeguard, the prince ready to do battle with the waves. Ready to protect you from the evil fish men!"

"Fish men!" Debra barked. "Fish men, girlfriend, I wish some fish men would try and come after me." She was busting up.

"Are you okay?" someone said behind her, and Sandra jerked around and faced him. A man, a white man hippie in thin beard and T-shirt said, "Is your friend cool? I came to see if anything was happening, anything weird."

"Nothing weird," Debra said. "Nothing weird happening here."

The white man exhaled. "She was yelling for help." Behind him Sandra saw other people, more than a dozen, coming toward them in a steady pace, their heads bent a little against the wind.

"We was just playing," Sandra said. "Wasn't nobody for real hurt."

The white man exhaled again and turned to the other people and yelled, "Everything is cool. Nothing weird is happening."

The people slowed down and stopped. They swayed a minute and looked at them.

"Then why the fuck did she cry for help?" a pissed-off somebody white said.

"Because they are kids," the man with the beard answered. "And they stink like they've been drinking."

"Hell, I was drinking too." The pissed-off one got closer and pushed his face toward Debra. "Listen, kid," he said. "It's not cool to stress out your community support, you dig?"

"We're not from here," Sandra said. "We was just playing. We didn't think nobody was listening." And by then most of the people had turned and begun to walk back to the lights of the boardwalk.

"Hell, I was drinking too," he said again, and turned away from them, and pushed his feet into the sand.

Then Sandra felt cold. She could see Debra sucking the corner of her bottom lip the way she did when she was tripping. Behind her the ocean was too big, too loud, and the air cut at her cheeks with soft slaps.

"I know where it's some swings," she told Debra. "And forget him anyway. What he know about nothing, white man who live at the beach." Their feet moved through the cold sand in one rhythm, Debra's shadow a few inches in front of Sandra, Sandra's eyes lowered like her friend's, their eyes stuck in the sand.

"I don't wanna go to no swings," Debra said.

"Tell me what he know, drunk sucker. He should have kept on drinking. Why he gotta come bother us?"

"They was good to come. They was good people." Debra's voice was depressed and scared Sandra.

"I don't like this wino mess," she told Debra. "Wine don't keep you from getting mad. And it tastes so nasty. Let's just find us them swings."

"The swings probably be broke anyway." Then Debra was silent. They were both quiet, and the wine and the cold and the human silence came down on them, and pushed them into the sand. "I feel so bad," Debra said. "I feel so bad."

Sandra loved the way Debra could loud talk and curse, the way her angry mother's fussing could never mess up her head. Teachers couldn't make her cry. Boys could not trip her out unless she liked them. When she was hurt she knew how to talk, she was quick and evil. All the bad-mouthing, all those pretty curse words were in public, outside the bathroom, in Man's car. But in front of mirrors, at beaches, times happened with Debra when sadness was a fist in your throat and you couldn't do nothing but feel it.

They were too big to ask for a push, so they got on the swings, in identical shadows, and they started to pump with their knees. Only way to get high fast. The sky looked blacker and blacker. There wasn't hardly no stars so nobody started dreaming: Debra hung her head back and kept her eyes open. Sandra closed her eyes when she was going backward.

"Free your mind," Debra whispered, her eyes wide, coming up and then down on the swing. "And your ass will follow. The kingdom of heaven is within," she whispered into the wicked lights of the beach. "Free your mind," she said louder and pushed her feet out over the edge of the black sky.

"And your ass will follow," said Sandra, lifting her head, her eyes greedy for the emptiness on the beach. "The kingdom of heaven is within."

"Free your mind," loud, together, they chanted, and sent out

the words with heat and arrogance, slamming them into the
spoiled night, like the threat of a whipping about to crack into
your body and make you bleed. Like some punishment that only
makes you meaner, like they found the secret of some sacred law
and it was a lie, like all lies, like everything.

"And your ass will follow." Sandra stood up on her swing. "The
kingdom of heaven is within." They swore it like an oath, like they
believed they could always hold back, hold in from the world and
the sneaky ways it hurts you. Underneath their voices the comfort
adolescents find in movement was faster and higher and cold.

"Yo, Sister Love," and it was big Man, his hands in his pockets,
his shoulders hunched, the color in his skin as regular as any
brother could be. "You all ready?"

"Check it out, man." Rufus showed his friendly teeth. "These
women is tore down. Look like that Spanada done done its work."

"Jump!" Man yelled. "Can you all jump?"

Sandra swooped straight out from her swing and came down
on her palms, her knees, with the palm trees and rose lights spinning with the dizzy sickness in her stomach.

"Bop on that," Debra said, and dug her heels down into the
sand. "You all help me stop this thing."

The five of them regrouped, again in formation, like the points
of a dark star, a whole unit, a perfect distance apart. They bent
their heads against the sharp nightwind and headed back to the
car, their faces and feelings finally ready for the foreignness to
close behind them. The bumper on Man's heavy car pushed
through the alleys of Venice and broke out into the wide city in-
tersections. With the streetlights and other cars, the city ex-
panded its indifference and they were small again, practically
sober. Their luck stayed halfway good and Man made all the
lights. Her head against the glass of the backseat window, Sandra
closed her eyes and gave her self to the car that slid back down
onto the Santa Monica Freeway, into the ribbon of white and red
lights that would take them back to their mother's home.

Mrs. Yakamoto Comes to Stay

HILDIE V. KRAUS

We'd been married two years and I had never met his mother. She sent presents sometimes: pastel sweaters, nightgowns, a glazed sake decanter and four small cups. I wear black all the time, sleep naked, and drink beer. But I was touched. I don't have a mother, she died a long time ago. My friends appreciated the clothes, and Nori used the sake thing for a vase. He has exquisite taste, according to him.

His mother left messages on the phone machine occasionally, and sent her regards, my name leaping out of the stream of Japanese like a fish from a brook—da de da de Bickie. She had a hard time with the *v*.

Nori sent her my regards too, presents he said were from both of us, infrequent photos of us dressed up, going out. Marital bliss, oh yeah. It wasn't much trouble to play along. One Saturday he comes into the kitchen all draggy and moaning about being up half the night, with Mark no doubt, and asks if I remembered to set aside Monday and Tuesday. Well, I hadn't, but luckily I wasn't busy. Tina had just left town to tour with her band, The Violent Contractions, and I was looking forward to solitude and hard work. I make ceramic tiles in a studio south of Market.

Then he tells me his mother is coming. And he wants me to go shopping with them, have a couple of meals, dress up like the wife. At first I was pissed, such short notice, why didn't he tell me she was coming? He might have thought I'd try to skip out. I had arranged to take a trip when his father arrived. But I wanted to meet his mother anyway. Mothers kind of fascinate me. Their comfortableness, that air of knowing everything—I mean, I know they're not all like that, but that's how I picture them: reassuring.

I would have practically spit-shined the apartment. Nori just straightened things up, put flowers in both our rooms, ran a rag over the kitchen surfaces. I shouldn't have been too surprised. It was like pulling teeth usually to get him to do his share of the housework. Sometimes I heard myself nagging and thought, "I don't need this. I don't need this spoiled man and his hair in the bathtub." But a deal is a deal; his friend Daniel married my friend Bharati. She and I compared notes sometimes, just like other women complaining about their husbands. Did they consider marriage a grim sentence too?

Monday afternoon I put on a sleeveless dress, then took it off and put a blouse on underneath so my armpit hair wouldn't hang out. I sat in the kitchen drinking coffee and thinking demure. Nori got the door when the bell went, and led Mrs. Yakamoto into the kitchen by the hand. She accepted my hug and kissed the air next to my cheek. She was as short as Nori, with small features huddled together under a graying Doris Day haircut.

Once he took off her coat, Nori was instantly fluttering around her, picking lint from her navy-blue pantsuit and making asides in English to me.

"She doesn't know how to dress, look at this scarf."

"Can you believe the shoes? You'd think she lived in a fishing village instead of Tokyo."

They were black orthopedic shoes, sensible for walking. I thought she looked fine. Who did he want, Elizabeth Taylor? It was as if he was apologizing for her, as if she reflected on his style. She probably thought he was complimenting her. I ignored Nori and offered Mrs. Yakamoto iced tea. She took the glass and said, "*Domo arigato.*"

"You're welcome," I said, bowing my head slightly. She asked Nori something and he shook his head. Mrs. Yakamoto raised her eyebrows.

"She wanted to know if you spoke any Japanese."

I flushed, feeling apologetic for no good reason.

She had brought us gifts from Japan, a red lacquered tea set, and a kimono for me, deep blue silk starred with chrysanthemums and cranes. Nori translated what she said as she handed it to me.

"Chrysanthemums are signs of good luck in Japan, and cranes signify health and long life."

I gave her a tile I had made, a red and white abstract design. She rubbed the smooth surface and cooed a couple of times. Then she wrapped it in the tissue paper from the tea set and stowed it in her suitcase. We started a new round of thank-yous. Thank God she and Nori went off for a walk and dinner. Already the tension of wifehood and bilingual goings-on had started a headache.

I took off all my clothes and put on the kimono. Its cool weight slid against my skin in deliciously reptilian silence. It hung on me, drapery rippling from my arms, folds pulling at my shoulders.

This one had a sash of the same fabric instead of the traditional obi, and as I tied it I imagined millions of Japanese women in the past, locking themselves into these silk prisons. It wasn't a garment made for striding or putting your foot down. You had to shuffle along, one baby step after another. I opened a Sapporo and lit a joint, propping my feet against the kitchen windowsill. The kimono poured open over my thighs. I sat there awhile, watching the dusk and the softening contrast between my woolly legs and the sheen of deep blue.

When Tina's mother had visited, she brought no presents. Tina was careful not to touch me during the lunch we all had, and I felt like some horrible reminder that Tina was not only queer, but actively practicing it. Her mother was polite and distant, meeting a schoolfriend of her daughter's, perhaps, or some stranger she had to be nice to. Tina's and my relationship was invisible. I had to fight the desire to lie and tell Mrs. Christenson that Tina and I planned to have several kids with the aid of a turkey baster. And your daughter's a great fuck.

Now the wedding ring was on the other finger. I worried that Mrs. Yakamoto would be offended that I didn't make a big meal, hadn't learned Japanese, took no interest in Nori's career. Some wife! Some reception for a mother-in-law, who should be honored in the wife's house... it was as if the kimono had subtly infected me with ancient traditions of duty and obedience.

God dammit, Nori should have told her about our marriage. And not only the marriage. Instead, here I was stuck in this travesty of a visit. The whole thing had been much easier at a five-

thousand-mile remove, when I didn't have to watch Mrs. Yakamoto's deadpan appraisal of the situation.

I hung up the kimono, resolving that I would not let Nori wear
it, and seized the occasion of an empty apartment to run up and
down the hallway naked, fast, twice. I ended up in my room,
breathless, staring at the framed picture of my mother on the bu-
reau. What would she have made of my life now? I was twelve
when she died in the fire. She escaped my adolescence, all the
things I might have lied to her about. It was easy to imagine that I
would always have told her the truth. I started to shiver from
being bare, and that old emptiness. I was no one's daughter. I
took a hot bath and put the good clothes back on for the return
of mother and son.

We had tea in the kitchen before bed. I made it in the new pot
and brought it to the table. Mrs. Yakamoto mostly watched Nori as
he translated for us. She darted glances at me when she thought I
wasn't looking. We talked about other stops on her trip, New
Mexico, Arizona. She was scared by the desert, Nori said, inviting
me to find this funny.

"Oh, absolutely," I said, bypassing him to nod at her directly.
She said something in Japanese and fluttered her plump hands to
indicate a lot of sky or light above her. He started to translate, but
I talked over him.

"And it's so quiet," tapping my ear and smoothing the air
with one hand. Mrs. Yakamoto nodded and pressed a hand near
her heart.

"She likes that part," Nori said.

"Me too." She and I smiled at each other.

Nori wanted her to sleep in his room—the "guest bedroom,"
practically a cubicle, with no light and a narrow monastic bed. I
insisted that she stay in "our" room, which had a double bed and
three big windows. Nori assured her that the living room couch
folded out into a bed for us. We waited until she was safely en-
sconced to go to our respective dreams. As I was trying to get to
sleep on the couch, it occurred to me that she might have been
happier in the small space.

The next day we went everywhere. Together. Nori and his mother
shopped while I fingered clothes dreamily, resisting their pleas to
get something. Mrs. Yakamoto stood patiently as Nori held severe

black-and-white dresses against her, allowing herself to be steered away from the floral prints.

"Come on," he said. "She'll be offended if you don't let her buy you an outfit."

Finally I gave in, stipulating that he had no say in the matter and should go to the men's department.

"I'm sure you'll find something to do there," I said sweetly. He laughed and pinched my arm in a way meant to be playful. He touched me more than usual that day—awkwardly, abrupt, like someone who doesn't know animals trying to pet a cat. I wanted to shrug him off, but I couldn't in front of his mother.

She and I turned silently to the racks of dresses. I chose a black-and-green number, plus black pumps with tiny vestigial tongues. Minimum fuss. She walked around me when I came out of the dressing room, adjusting the collar in an intent way that reminded me of Nori. But she wasn't bossy, just concentrating. She smoothed the dress over my shoulders. I could smell her perfume. I shut my eyes briefly and imagined I was ten years old, shopping with my mother for an Easter outfit. Then Mrs. Yakamoto stood off and clapped her hands. We tossed *arigato*s back and forth.

The rest of the day we rode around in the rented car and took pictures of places, and ourselves in them. I had a sudden fantasy that when the film was developed, my image would be gone, as if the camera knew what was true, and what was illusion. By the end of the day I was near collapse from all the family life. Back at home I called several friends to remind myself of who I was.

Only dinner remained, when to our little trio would be added Mrs. Yakamoto's sister, also on the bus tour, and Nori's "lawyer," Mark. Mrs. Mifune was taller and thinner than her sister. She taught English and had a teacher's crispness. Not as wild about Nori as his mother; I noticed a couple of cool glances toward the nephew. Mark arrived, immaculately suited and tied, and winked at my new outfit. Swallowing the last of my beer, I wished Tina was here to join us as my "sister." Then I thought, no, no more games, no more pseudo family members.

Off we went to a restaurant in the Castro nearby, a big round table by the window. Mrs. Mifune had her back to the window, and Mrs. Yakamoto faced it. The food was a small consolation. Every time two men or women walked by holding hands, Nori would nudge me and whisper, "Do you think she saw that?"

I was puzzled at first. Aren't there gay people in Tokyo? Then I realized he was titillated by the idea that his mother might see something while he sat all safe with wifey next to him. Once Mrs. Mifune overheard Nori and turned around, but the tall man in a dress had passed. Under cover of dishes arriving, I told him to shut up. I felt like pushing his face into the miso soup.

Mrs. Yakamoto's expression didn't change—she never appeared to register the occasional boy going by with nipple rings and leather chaps. Mostly she talked with her sister, or we all tried to have a conversation. Mark was content to eat and observe the scene. I could see his leg pressed against Nori's when I got up to go to the bathroom.

In the ladies' room I made a horrible face in the mirror and grimly pulled up my stockings. It was almost over. Tomorrow morning Mrs. Yakamoto would be on the bus to Seattle. She would leave San Francisco with the nagging sense that something wasn't quite right with her only son's marriage, but she would never really know why. I couldn't imagine Nori telling her any part of the truth, because then the rest of the deception might unravel. The unaccustomed constraint of a brassiere chafed my breasts, the hose clung to my legs like tight spiderwebs, and I felt like tearing the new dress off and emerging from the bathroom naked and real.

I forced myself back to the table, fuming inside. Nori and Mark were impatient to leave, ostensibly to sign some papers. On the sidewalk I grabbed Nori's elbow.

"You're coming back to the house, right?"

He gave me a warning look. "I'll be there in half an hour, don't worry."

Mrs. Yakamoto, Mrs. Mifune and I made our stately way down the street. The new pumps were killing my feet, so I had no trouble matching my gait to theirs. It almost felt as if we were out of school, playing hooky away from the men. At the door to the apartment, Mrs. Mifune shook my hand and was about to say good night when I stopped her.

"Please come in for a cup of tea." She pled tiredness, but I insisted gently.

While we were all blowing on the tea, I slipped off my shoes under the table and spared a moment to wish I had smoked a roach in the bathroom.

Then I said to Mrs. Mifune, "There's something I need to tell your sister. Will you translate?"

"Of course." She looked at Mrs. Yakamoto quickly and turned back to me.

I spoke in a rush, half-listening for the door.

"Nori and I don't have a real marriage. I mean, it's legal and all, but we're friends, and that's why I agreed to get married, so he could get a green card and become a citizen. Eventually. Do you understand?"

"Mmm-hmmm." She spoke to Mrs. Yakamoto, the words rapid and almost angry sounding. But Japanese always gave me that impression. Mrs. Yakamoto sighed and was silent a moment. Then she said, "*Domo arigato.*"

Looking at her, I continued. "I wanted to tell you because maybe... you wondered what kind of wife I am, not cooking for you or learning Japanese. I didn't want you to be offended, or think I was disrespectful. Nori should have told you from the beginning."

Mrs. Mifune nodded sardonically and translated. While she spoke, Mrs. Yakamoto watched me, some question in her black eyes. As soon as her sister finished, she answered, leaning toward me as if I understood what she was saying.

"She says she has appreciated your hospitality very much, and she would be honored to have you, ah, as a . . . 'real' daughter. So please don't worry about this. She wants to know if Nori has another girlfriend, maybe?"

Mrs. Yakamoto and I locked gazes. Mrs. Mifune stirred her tea, the spoon clinking in the sudden stillness. I shook my head. Not my job.

"I don't know. We don't talk about it." Mrs. Yakamoto's shoulders sank a fraction, and she pursed her lips. She asked something else.

"And doesn't this hurt your opportunity to find a husband?"

I smiled broadly, and it felt so good I realized my face had been tense for hours.

"I'm not too concerned."

Mrs. Mifune grinned as she passed that along, and Mrs. Yakamoto added her own kind smile. Never mind what we were all amused by. I was awash in relief.

After we finished our tea I excused myself, thinking the sisters might want to talk. I kissed Mrs. Yakamoto on the cheek. From the couch I heard Mrs. Mifune go out, and Nori came in shortly after that. The uneven rhythm of Japanese voices followed me to sleep. I woke up wondering what Mrs. Yakamoto had said to her son on the last night of her visit. Stumbling down the hall to the bathroom, I saw her fully dressed already, poised with a camera. I mustered a gummy smile as she clicked away. My hair stood up in tufts, and I was wearing an old T-shirt and sweatpants.

Nori had made some coffee, thank God. I checked him for signs of unwelcome news last night. There were none. Mrs. Yakamoto seemed the same too, bustling around getting her shopping loot packed away. Finally we were all on the front stoop waiting for the cab. She hugged me tightly, saying *arigato*, and we went into all that for the last time. I got a little catch in my throat. Nori and I waved good-bye and he put his arm around me. From the taxi window Mrs. Yakamoto wiggled her fingers, and I thought a glint of sarcasm flashed behind her glasses. But it could have been the sun.

As we turned to go in, I said, "What did you and she talk about so late last night?" Casual-like.

"Oh, nothing special. My job, the family. She thought you were nice, by the way. She said I was lucky."

"Yeah, you are. More than you know." I pushed him inside and started up the stairs.

I never saw Mrs. Yakamoto again. I moved out when Nori got his green card. But she sent me birthday presents for several years after that. No more pastel nightgowns. Instead, terrific black sweaters arrived, a very cool pair of sunglasses, the black leather bag I carry all the time. The kimono shimmers away in my closet, like a tropical fish in the depths of a pond.

Welcome
to
Gaza

SARAH JACOBUS

I stare at myself in the mirror as I drape the black wool scarf over my hair. "Better to cover your heads when you go out," Nada, one of the kindergarten teachers we are to spend the day with, has counseled. "They will see that you are foreigners, but still, it is better not to take chances."

I make a strange sight in my pullover sweater, flannel skirt, tights and Reeboks with my head covering, an awkward visitor from another world. Wearing the scarf seems an assent to an oppressive religious practice, which makes me uneasy. But the Islamic resistance movement wields a powerful influence here in Gaza. Accounts of bare-headed women pelted with eggs or stones in the street cause me to take Nada's admonition about attire seriously.

My nerves have been jangling since I arrived four days ago on my first trip to Gaza. Being in the Middle East at all is almost an accident, based on one of those chance moments that could easily have passed without special notice or action taken, but did not.

At the root of this journey is my friendship with Karima, a Palestinian woman I met my first year as a graduate student in public health at the University of Michigan. Karima was from the West Bank city of Nablus and had moved with her family to Detroit when she was ten.

"I've never been friends with a Jew before," she had told me, laughing but wary. Not that I knew all that much about Palestinians. I harbored some vaguely formed ideas about the injustice done to them and the legitimacy of their cause; I had never actu-

ally known any Palestinians. Yet it was the very fact that Karima
was Palestinian and I a Jew that had cemented the bond we shared
and created a rich, if at times thorny, texture of experiences and
discovery between us.

Her family welcomed me with warmth and curiosity. I often
spent weekends with Karima in Detroit, where I developed a taste
for both Arabic food and music. I learned enough Arabic to ex-
change pleasantries with her older relatives, who spoke no English. I was especially fond of her grandmother, an energetic old
woman with gray hair pulled into a knot at the back of her neck, a
weathered face and alert black eyes that sized me up in a single
glance. She'd slap my arm and toss her head back with laughter as
we sat close on the sofa, piecing together conversations through
smiles, body language and fragments of phrases.

It was Karima who first spotted the tan flyer on the bulletin
board outside the department office at school one afternoon in
early October. An international children's relief organization was
sponsoring a delegation of health care workers from around the
United States to visit the West Bank and Gaza and gather first-
hand information of services for Palestinian children.

"You should apply," Karima had announced in a somewhat
brusque tone she had that let me know she expected me to do it.

"Me? Why don't you? You're the Middle East expert."

"I've promised to spend the end of the year holidays with the
family. Besides, it's not easy for me to travel there. It'd be a good
experience for you, wake you up. Do it."

We spent the first week of the trip in the West Bank, long days of
visits to clinics, hospitals, nurseries and cooperatives. I could not
stop thinking of Karima. One moment, I longed to thank her for
encouraging me to make this revelatory journey. Then I was just
as suddenly furious with her for pushing me into an uncomfort-
able experience that was compelling me to confront so much suffering and raising so many questions that I could not answer.

There are eight of us in the delegation, including a few doctors
and nurse practitioners, a San Francisco chiropractor who has
practically disappeared behind his video camera, and a midwife
from Boston named Susan, the only other Jew in the group.

It is with Susan that I have come to Gaza, our group having split
into pairs so as to call less attention to ourselves. Or at least that's

the idea. Traveling with Susan, I wonder. She is a tall woman, a good four or five inches taller than I, with a disarming intelligence in her gray eyes and dark hair braided down her back. Everywhere we've been, children have wanted to play with her hair.

She has made many trips to the Middle East and came to work for two years in a clinic in the West Bank when the *Intifada*, the Palestinian uprising, first started at the end of 1987. She has an unassuming ease with people that seems to invite their trust and confidence, enhanced by her proficient Arabic. Her attitude toward me has been respectful, not at all condescending, which I appreciate. We have formed a congenial alliance around the work we are doing.

Susan and I travel to Gaza from Jerusalem in a Mercedes Benz *service*, a group taxi, with three Palestinian men, an old woman and her daughter. We speed past low-lying citrus groves, an occasional factory puffing steam from its metal stacks and boyish Israeli soldiers with Uzi machine guns slung over their shoulders, hitching rides by the side of the highway. The car radio blares Arabic music and news.

Suddenly, traffic slows, then comes to a stop. In the road ahead is a maze of large chunks of whitewashed concrete and corkscrews of barbed wire that force all the cars into one lane. The driver snaps off the radio and shifts in his seat. Conversations among the other passengers stop abruptly, as if on cue. We pull up to a tollbooth where an Israeli soldier leans over the *service*, scanning all of us through mirrored sunglasses. Beside him in the booth is a pile of burlap-covered sandbags supporting a machine gun propped on a small tripod. A border. We have reached Gaza.

The soldier at the checkpoint motions for the *service* to pull over to the side of the road. Every muscle in my body tightens. I look toward Susan. Without turning her head, she whispers to me, "Have your passport ready and if they ask us anything, stick to our story."

Another soldier issues some sort of order in Arabic to the driver, in response to which the men begin to get out of the *service*. I start to slide across the seat to get out as well, but Susan holds my arm and hisses, "No, just the men. They're checking their IDs." Perhaps seeking to share my anxiety in this encounter, I turn around to the two women sitting in the rear seat behind us.

Earlier in the trip, they amiably shared bread and *zatar*, the tangy wild thyme, with us. Now their eyes will not meet mine.

The men are lined up on the side of the road, each one extending his identity card to the soldier. When this procedure is completed, they get back into the taxi. I am seething at what appears to be ritual harassment, but the faces of the men are blank masks, registering no reaction whatsoever. To my relief, the soldier ignores Susan and me. The driver pulls away from the curb in silence, his jaw twitching slightly.

Just past the checkpoint, a thin white wooden sign arcs across the road. "Welcome to Gaza," it proclaims ironically in English, Arabic and Hebrew. Strewn around its base are the skeletal remains of dozens of cars, like dinosaur bones, gnarled with rust and half-buried in sand. I cannot imagine a less welcoming stretch of road.

A blanket of gray dust and sand glazes every surface. Decaying buildings droop wearily on their foundations. Our *service* lumbers through muddy potholes in the chaotic streets of Gaza City, narrowly avoiding collision with donkey carts, small white taxis bulging with passengers and cars that look as if they will soon end up with the others we saw decomposing in the sun on the way in.

Kaleidoscopic arrangements of cucumbers, tomatoes and citrus fruits press against the glass of vendors' carts. Clouds of pungent smoke from grilling meat at sidewalk stands fill the air, sent spiraling into the streets by electric fans that blow across the coals inside sawed-off oil drums. Clothing shops display long dresses for women, the essence of modesty, draped stolidly on mannequins or dangling from the awnings. And on every wall there is layer upon layer of political graffiti, the colors splashed into each other like Jackson Pollock paintings.

Suddenly, Susan elbows me in the ribs and jerks her head slightly toward the window. A drab green watchtower hovers over the corner where we are stopped. Israeli soldiers with binoculars perch there, surveying the crowded streets below.

The longer we stay in Gaza, the more familiar the military presence becomes. Army jeeps patrol ominously. Shopkeepers and passersby ignore them with studied indifference, yet their presence creates an almost palpable tension in the air. Thunderheads of violence gather, waiting to break in sudden storms anywhere, at any time. The *Intifada* is still in full swing here in Gaza. Almost every day there are reports of clashes between soldiers and people in the streets, mostly teenagers throwing rocks.

At night, the streets are black and silent. Curfew for Gaza residents begins at eight P.M. and lasts until dawn. One night, Susan and I ride back to the guest house where we are staying with a UN refugee affairs officer, who is allowed to drive about as he pleases in his official white Volkswagen station wagon. We pass through deserted streets, the pale blue UN flag whipping about from the rear of the car in a bitter wind. The full moon is brilliant in a cloudless sky. I wish that the women who have shown us such kindness in our time here might emerge from behind their locked doors to see it.

Today, we have come to the Breij refugee camp to visit a kindergarten. Children stare uncertainly at us from the doorways of crumbling cinder-block houses, dressed in flimsy polyester sweatshirts with incongruous logos in English on them, like "X-press yourself" or "Party Animal," and plastic flip-flops. The air is rank with the smell of sewage running in open ditches down the middle of the narrow dirt streets.

The rubble of houses demolished by the Israeli army is scattered throughout the camp. Sometimes only one wall is gone, like a missing tooth. There is a sense of almost embarrassing intimacy in glimpsing the exposed interior, often still furnished, of a stranger's house. In other places, a tangle of broken concrete, stones and wire is all that remains.

The kindergarten seems an island of normal life in the midst of this misery. Inside, the walls are painted bright blue and white, lined with children's crayon drawings and posters of the Arabic alphabet. A map of Palestine hangs beside a cartoon cutout of a grinning pink bear cub. Groups of noisy children finger-paint, have snacks of biscuits and milk, giggle and pinch each other. An atmosphere of relative safety prevails here in the kindergarten, which I cling to, even knowing that it is illusory.

Nada begins a new game, holding up frayed flash cards with pictures of animals on them for the children to identify. They shriek each answer in a gleeful and knowing chorus.

Susan's long frame is huddled onto a small wooden chair next to several little girls of four or five. She smiles and encourages them in Arabic when they answer correctly. They grin back at her in delight. Although I have spent the last four days in the constant

company of this woman, I barely know her at all. Our days have
been long and consuming, our attention fastened upon our hosts.
By the time we return to our room at night, we either fall into bed
exhausted or spend our remaining time awake reading or writing,
relieved of the need for further interaction.

Suddenly, the uneasy quiet in the street outside the kindergarten is broken by angry male shouts, followed by the crack of a
rifle shot. Startled, my heart pounding, I look out the window to see
a group of boys and men running down the street, an army jeep ca-
reening in pursuit. Nada's eyes dart nervously toward the door, but
she continues the game, not wanting to call the children's attention
to the turmoil in the street. Two other teachers, Aisheh and Fatima,
open the door slightly and lean out, but quickly pull back inside the
room, coughing and rubbing their eyes. As the door closes, the
sharp, sickening odor of tear gas begins to drift into the kindergarten.

Nada signals the other teachers, who gather the children into a
tight circle in the center of the room. Susan springs from her tiny
chair. She and Nada begin wetting handkerchiefs and handing
them to the children to cover their faces. The children don't
panic. This ritual is obviously familiar to them. A small girl in a
sweater knitted in the colors of the Palestinian flag offers me a
damp handkerchief, which I gratefully accept.

The noise in the street continues—the shouting, the roar of
an army truck grinding through the dust, a few more shots—but
it is impossible to tell what is happening. Moments later, another
jeep passes. A loudspeaker mounted on the back blares a warning
in Arabic. I recognize the word *manatajawal*—curfew.

"A total curfew is beginning," Susan barks at me. "Everyone has
ten minutes to go to their homes and stay there."

I look at her, stunned. We are miles away from Gaza City. It is
clearly impossible for us to get back to where we are staying. She
reads the question in my face. Our eyes lock for a long moment,
but we do not have a chance to ponder our dilemma further.
Nada is formulating plans. She grabs my hand and pulls me
toward the door, speaking rapidly in Arabic. Susan trots along
beside us.

"Nada says we'll go home with her," she reports. "But first, we
have to get the children home. There's no time to wait for their
mothers to come here."

Along with the other teachers, Susan and I form a circle around the children. Clutching as many small hands as we can, we move together out into the street. People are scurrying in all directions, herded like cattle by Israeli soldiers in jeeps shouting at them to go home and close their doors and windows. Above all of this, a nauseating cloud of dust and tear gas hovers in the air.

We all stumble along together, delivering the children to their homes, in some cases met by a frantic family member before we arrive. When we have parted with the last of the children, we shake hands and wave good-bye to Aisheh and Fatima and run along beside Nada toward her house. She suddenly disappears through a door in a gray cinder-block wall. We follow. Apparently, we are home.

We are greeted by an old woman in a long traditional Palestinian dress, densely embroidered in front, her head covered in a scarf of filmy white material. When she sees that there are strangers, she pulls her scarf across the bottom half of her face. Nada's introductions in Arabic reveal that the woman, whose name is Um Khaled, is her mother. Um Khaled shakes hands with Susan and me. As she does this, she lets the scarf fall. Her leathery face is lined with worry, but she smiles broadly at us and repeats the customary words of welcome, *ahlan wa-sahlan*, several times. She acts as if it were nothing at all out of the ordinary to open her door to two unknown foreigners in the middle of this violence and sudden curfew. She motions for us to follow her.

The room we have entered from the street is unfinished, with a dirt floor and a bare lightbulb dangling from the ceiling. We climb a flight of cement steps with no railing that twists treacherously upward in an open stairwell. Nada's mother directs us into another room arranged in Arabic parlor style, with low rectangular cushions lining all four walls and colorful mats woven from plastic threads on the concrete floor. The one small window, high in the wall, has been securely shuttered. The room is ablaze with fluorescent light. It is no longer possible to tell what time of day it is. A space heater glows uselessly in the corner.

The room is full of women, chattering nervously, several of whom hold young children. They fall silent at the sight of Susan and me, staring at us in fearful surprise. A child of around two begins to cry.

Nada quickly explains to them who we are. I hear the word

Israiliyyeh; she is assuring them that we are not Israeli. Susan
recovers her composure and begins to greet the women in Arabic,
moving around the room shaking hands. I am rooted to the spot,
jarred by the baby's wailing and the thought of the fear I have
caused these women. At a sharp look from Susan, I too begin, in
my clumsy Arabic, to try to put the women at ease.

At the insistence of Um Khaled, Susan and I settle ourselves on
the cushions. Nada's mother disappears from the room, along
with two of the other women. I loosen the scarf I had hurriedly re-
placed on my head as we left the kindergarten, and let it fall
around my shoulders. Nada and Susan are talking to several of
the women, who are apparently Nada's sister, sister-in-law and
cousin, about what has happened. Susan translates. I listen atten-
tively, steadied by her even voice and level gaze.

"They say that the soldiers chased a group of boys who were
throwing stones at them. They raided several houses where they
thought the boys had gone."

She listens for a few more minutes, then continues.

"The soldiers were firing at the boys as they ran. The women
think that one boy was shot, but they're not sure. The soldiers also
fired tear gas into the courtyard of one of the houses."

Susan stops to catch the rest of what the woman is saying. She
nods sympathetically, then turns to me.

"Some of the women are concerned," she says in the somewhat
clipped cadence of one who is translating a foreign language, "for
their brothers and husbands who are still at their jobs in Israel
and have to get home tonight. They're wondering what will happen to them, if the soldiers will let them come home."

I am about to ask how news of this incident can have traveled
so fast under curfew, when Nada's mother and the other women
return. They carry trays laden with tiny cups of Arabic coffee and
a huge platter of food—plates of hummus and eggplant, pickles,
olives, tomatoes, hard-boiled eggs and a bowl of *lebeni*, the rich,
sour cheese.

Nada's mother pushes warm pita bread into my hands. I tear
off a piece and smear it across the plate of hummus, suddenly ravenous. I sip the sweet coffee, struggling gamely to have a conversation in Arabic with the young woman next to me, who gazes at
me intently with piercing green eyes. I am reminded of all of the
meals, not unlike this one, that I have shared with Karima's fam-

ily, of her grandmother's admonishment, *"Kulli, kulli!"*—Eat!—
if I slowed for even a moment, of chatting around the table with
the women and kids after the men had adjourned into a haze of
cigarette smoke in the living room.

But this is no Sunday dinner in Detroit. There are soldiers with
guns patrolling the streets outside the door. We are all prisoners
inside this house and would risk being shot were we to go out. Yet
here I am, like Alice in Wonderland, a guest of honor at this
strange tea party. I am frightened. There is too much here to ab-
sorb. I need to have some sort of contact with Susan. We have
been so caught up in conversations with our hosts that we have
barely spoken to each other at all since we arrived.

I finally excuse myself and step out of the room. The hallway
opens to the outside on a large covered balcony. The woman with
the green eyes follows me. I assure her that I am all right and will
not go near the edge of the balcony. She retreats back into the parlor. I breathe deeply. The afternoon has faded into a pale purple
twilight. The air is cold, with only a faint lingering scent of tear gas.

As if reading my thoughts, Susan slips up quietly behind me. I
turn and look at her, my throat knotted, embarrassed at the sudden tears that have begun to spill down my cheeks. I can hear
Karima's voice chiding me for this reaction, telling me that I know
nothing of real danger, that I am spoiled and soft.

Susan reaches out and takes my hand. "It's a difficult place to
be, isn't it?" she says gently.

"I feel like such a wimp," I tell her, sniffing and brushing awkwardly at my tears. "These women face this all the time. *They* seem
to manage."

"Yes, but that doesn't make it any easier, never knowing what
will happen, if maybe the next time it'll be your house that's
raided, one of your own kids who gets shot. Don't be hard on
yourself."

"What about you?" I ask. "What do you do with your feelings
about all this?"

"Well, for one thing, I draw inspiration from the Palestinian
women's example, their strength and courage. And, I try in whatever way I can to do something of use." Susan pauses for a moment
to consider, then smiles. "Do you think that's a Jewish thing?"

Impulsively, I touch her cheek, leaving damp traces from the
tears on my hand. She leans over and lightly kisses me.

The evening wears on, through cup after cup of coffee and countless games of peekaboo with the children. Word comes that all the men are being held for the night near the checkpoint. They will not be coming home. My Arabic vocabulary is exhausted, and I am exhausted too. I am enjoying the company of these women, especially Nada, who has remained unwavering in her hospitality. But I am restless and claustrophobic.

Curiously, a tendril of attraction has begun winding its way between Susan and me. Our eyes linger upon each other, full of meaning that I do not completely understand but have no inclination to analyze. We brush against each other as we play with the children or shift our positions on the cushions.

This is ridiculous, I scold myself. Can't you leave the intrigue out of it? But at the same time, I sense that it is precisely this unspoken intrigue that is sustaining me on this night.

Finally, Nada asks if Susan and I would like to sleep. She ushers us into a side room and begins to pull the floor cushions together to form a bed. I feel both relieved and guilty that we are offered this room to ourselves, that everyone else will sleep in the parlor.

"We can sleep with the others," I tell Nada. My voice seems to lack conviction, so I add, "Please don't make anyone move for us."

"It's okay," she answers, her tone discouraging further protest. She brings covers in some fuzzy, synthetic material from neatly folded piles in the corner. Susan and I help her spread them out over the cushions, all the while not looking at each other.

After Nada has left the room, Susan and I undress to our long underwear, shivering in the cold room, still not speaking. She slides under the covers. I flick the light switch on the wall and feel my way back to the bed in the blackness. I lie for a few minutes under the scratchy covers, feeling the warmth of Susan's body beside me. She sighs deeply. I try to relax, but between the tension outside and the tension between Susan and me, this is impossible.

"May I hold you?" I ask her, surprised by my own boldness. The question hangs disembodied in the chill air for a few moments, like a balloon of words in a comic strip conversation, before she turns and curls into my arms, nestling against my side. We lie like this for a while, still tense, listening. The voices in the other room subside. Outside, there is only silence.

We relax into each other. How good she feels, how comfortably our bodies seem to fit together. Our hands begin to explore each other, tentatively at first, reaching and caressing. The rhythm quickens. Our mouths search skin until we find each other's lips, breasts, bellies.

I am now naked and feel a stab of defenselessness in this unsettling environment, a need to be more on guard. But I cannot stop what is happening, cannot stop the movement and heat between Susan and me. Our warm nest is a place of life, a heartbeat, in the dangerous night. This coming together has become a necessity, a means of defying the nightmare that is all about me, the violence that my people are bringing upon another people. Susan and I make love greedily, as if we could stop the madness by the sheer force of our passion.

Hours later, I am awakened in darkness by the eerie sound of the call to prayer from a nearby mosque. The undulating voice through the loudspeaker is scratchy as an old record. I want to believe that there is a man in the minaret from whose throat soars this haunting cry. But perhaps it is only a recording, automatic and impersonal, that pierces the predawn desolation.

It must be evening in Detroit now. Perhaps Karima is studying for the final exams that await us upon our return to school. Or she has taken a break to read to her grandmother or go to a movie with her sisters. I am comforted to think of her engaged in these simple rituals, safe and far away from here.

Daylight seeping through the cracks around the shuttered windows grows brighter, illuminating the room in narrow stripes full of floating dust motes. Susan sits up, yawns and stretches. I start to touch her, but hesitate. She seems almost a stranger again. Something has shifted with the passing of the night, the tension released, passion dissipated.

Finally, Susan speaks. "Well, that was a surprise," she says with a slow smile. "A nice surprise." She gives me a kiss on the forehead, crisp and final.

"*L'chaim,*" I answer, raising an imaginary glass in her direction. "To life."

We rise, dress, restore the cushions and covers to their proper places and join the other women to wait out the curfew.

Campers

ELOISE KLEIN HEALY

The skinny older boy brought his little brother over to our camp-fire. "Can Chris sit with you?" he asked, motioning to the lawn chair next to me. "It would be for just a while." With that he left and Chris pulled the chair a little closer to the fire, half-climbing, half-heaving himself into it.

His stiff blue parka engulfed his body, except for his legs, which stuck out straight ahead—pajama legs covered with car-toon designs. His very round head also stuck out, as well as his hands, in which he gripped a giant family-size package of M&M peanut candies. He said nothing.

Janet and I had been talking about cancer. She has it. Or, had it. She's been having chemotherapy, although we both know it's been having us. Suddenly it became hard to continue the discussion. The child was there. Not like an empty chair or fixture, but a per-son we didn't know and at an age we aren't ever in contact with.

We're the kind of lesbians who never had children, technically always "aunts" to kids, not "moms." And we never taught elemen-tary school or babysat much, so having a child in our midst feels like having a foreigner in our home who doesn't speak English.

The skinny tall kid should have taken his brother to the new motor home next to us. Inside it were two mainstream adults. One was a blonde middle-aged woman, a WOA, as Janet and I would say—a "Woman Our Age." By that we mean a straight woman who wears what we know we're supposed to wear and doesn't have a haircut that you can slick back or make stand straight up, depending on the social occasion. Most WOAs don't have goddess-consciousness or know which actresses are really dykes.

The woman in the motor home had sons, told us all about them at various times during our stay in the campground. Her husband hadn't said much, except to offer us a box of wood, two-by-fours he'd taken home from a construction site, cut and packed in a cardboard box. I knew he couldn't quite figure out who we were.

When he offered the wood, Janet took the axe I'd borrowed from my dad and started to sliver some kindling and stack it in the fire pit. She's a good traveler and knows the tasks that need to be done. Even with her energy shot to hell from the chemo, she'd picked a job she could handle and went to work. I think the husband wanted to help and I think the woman wanted us to have some drinks with them, but I could tell we weren't going to have much more to talk about than what we'd already covered—that Janet is a college counselor, that the woman is a school aide, that the husband's in construction, and that their youngest had just graduated from high school.

So that's why Chris should have been sitting on their doorstep, learning about what little boys are supposed to do instead of being here at the fire with the two of us. What do we know about little boys except that we both wanted to be one until our bodies hit that proverbial dividing line and marked us forever "female." There went two dreams out the window—second base for me and shortstop for her. I think of what great double plays we could have turned and I hear in my head that voice I heard when I was a kid, a scratchy radio announcer voice over the roar of the crowd calling out our names in the play-by-play of the game that sends our team into the World Series.

I didn't catch the name of the Woman Our Age next door in the motor home. Just after dinner, she and her husband had lowered the blinds in all the windows and stretched a curtain across the inside of the front windshield. I could hear a TV playing, and occasionally somebody running water. The vehicle was still new enough so the aluminum trim hadn't gotten that moth-wing dusty surface to it yet. The couple had a boat, too, in a matching color scheme they said, but it wasn't along on this trip. Their sons liked

boating better than camping, but the woman said they were out-
growing both. "All these blessings," she'd said, "and now they're
wanting to live on their own."

Without looking at me, Chris poked the torn top of the M&M
package in my direction. "I think Chris is offering you some
candy," Janet said. I reached into the bag and came up with a
brown one. "Can I give this one to Janet? She loves the brown
ones." He shook his head and offered the bag again.

"Do you like camping, Chris?" He nodded but kept looking
straight ahead into the flames. "Did your mom stay at home?" I
asked.

"No mom. We don't have a mom." He looked up at me.
"Where are your kids?" Janet jumped in to say that we had none.

I didn't know what to say next and looked at Janet, trying to
read her sense of it. Her face said—don't pursue it, maybe it's bad.

"We lost our mom at the hospital," Chris added.

I looked at Janet again, confused by this information. Was the
mother dead? Was she in a sanitarium? How do you ask a kid
those things if he thinks his mother got lost at the hospital? What
kind of world does he live in—lose your mom and whoops! she's
just gone. You do without.

He held out the bag again and I took two M&Ms. "My brother
caught ten fish today and my dad took us to a restaurant." I had
seen the fish—ten to my one—and had thought there must be
some compact between kids and fish. One time in Minnesota,
when I probably wasn't any older than Chris, I caught twelve little
sunfish on a homemade pole with a safety pin hook. I was pulling
them out of the water as fast as they could bite.

A flashlight beam weaved and bobbed into the circle of night
around us. It was Chris's brother coming for him. He thanked us
for watching Chris, though I still didn't know why he had brought
him in the first place. Chris slowly climbed down out of the chair
and rolled the paper bag shut. He'd eaten about two thirds of the
M&Ms, enough for a great sugar rush. Stiffly, he held out his
arms, bumped into my leg, reached over the chair arm, and then
embraced me.

When the boys had gone, Janet held out another length of two-
by-four. "More fire?"

I pulled the hood of my sweatshirt up over my head and hun-
kered down into my parka. "Strange visit, huh?"

The smoke spiraled straight up. Above us in a small cone of night at the treetops, moonlight was just beginning to wipe out the stars. All around me I felt the deep life of the trees. I felt like I've always felt in the big trees, that our home is really there among them. Even though they know neither father nor mother, they live long and well.

Janet put three more boards on the fire and we began to talk again, rambling, not directed at work or the chemo or how we fit into the world—none of the usual knife blades we balance on. It was dreamlike talk, barely audible, belonging to a context surrounded by the night.

There were twelve messages on my answering machine when we got home. "I only have three," Janet said. "Be a volunteer more often," I offered. "Oh, I'd be the great volunteer, wouldn't I? Checking my cell count to see if I could stay through the whole meeting!"

Cell counts, yes, a new addition to our vocabulary. Janet's white cell count had dipped dangerously low several weeks before our camping trip, so low they wouldn't give her the scheduled treatment. The cure would have killed her.

We went crazy, of course. Everything had been planned around her "up" and "down" times, a three-week wave that rose and fell as she alternately plunged and recovered from her shot. When the treatment was put off for a week, it skewed all our plans for taking some time off. Our cleverly constructed calendar crashed—how could we go camping when she wasn't up to strength? But we took the chance, cooled her participation in day hikes, and celebrated being able to get into the open air of the Sierras.

I unloaded the car while she sorted the mail. There was the usual assortment of flyers, announcements, and lots of coupon books addressed to "New Neighbor," that being me. There was also a bundle of stuff forwarded from my old address. "How long does the post office forward your mail?" Janet asked.

"No idea. Maybe after a while they just route it to some landfill." I leafed through the junk mail following me around and counted the weeks I'd lived with Janet before she'd found the lump—eleven. I felt the whole swirl of it wash over me again. Too much to handle, one part of me said. You get what you can manage, another part answered.

Here's what it feels like now. We were strangers to each other. Lovers, yes, but strange to each other. Not worn into each other's habits, patterns. Not alert to the minuscule changes in the muscles of the jaw that signal an entire shift of mood. I look at the photograph one of Janet's friends took of her a few days after her first treatment and I remember saying, "Hey, this is a good picture, Janet. She really captured you." What did I know? When I look at that picture now, it chills me to see the depth of pain in her face, her eyes dulled from medication, her smile tentative and questioning. She doesn't look happy, she looks stunned.

I was pretty off myself in the first weeks after her diagnosis. There were two speeds in our lives—faster and no speed at all. Stasis, stone-still terror right in the center of a furious spin of activity. Right away I'd called a friend who's a medical reporter and she did a database search for us. Then another friend in Minneapolis had a number for us of a Chatsworth chemist who was keeping people's hair from falling out. We'd plugged into the ad hoc national lesbian cancer info network, and, in turn, as the weeks went by, people started calling us. In one of my journal entries from those days, I'd written, "No one has been saying the *E* word, but it's really true—EPIDEMIC. Breast cancer is at epidemic proportions. And I'm going crazy over the silence and lack of reality about this disease in the media."

Under the pretext of normalcy we tried to do things like taking in a Dodger game with four other lesbians who are rabid fans. Janet did fine walking from the parking lot up to the cheap seats, but she did look a little green when it came time to decide what to eat. Big choice to begin with—Dodger dog on regular bun or spicy Dodger dog on onion bun. "I think I'm living dangerously enough," she said. "Get me the plain model—no frills, no onions, and definitely no mayonnaise."

The guy sitting next to us sloshed some beer on my leg when I stood up. "Whoops, hey, where you goin'?" He had on a Cardinals cap and a red-and-white baseball shirt with the name Mike in script on his chest. I figured, "Be friendly—he probably isn't the jerk you think he could be."

"Well, Mike, I'm off to get the Dodger dogs."

"So, why don't you sit and talk?"

"I said, I'm off to get the hot dogs, can't chat right now." He turned around in his seat to face me, then turned and pulled on the cap of the guy in front of him. "Hey, she won't talk to me. She probably doesn't talk to anybody but those Dodger dogs." Well, he cracked himself up over that one, and as I started to squeeze by him, Janet gave me that look which said, "Don't get mad enough to kill him; we have to sit here the rest of the night."

"Maybe your friends want to talk about the game with me." He gestured broadly to take in Janet and the two other couples who were sitting in our group. "Maybe they had a better night last night than you did." His friend joined in, "Got home too late, did ya, feeling grumpy 'bout now?"

I decided the best course would be to ignore what was building, fueled by beer and the assumption that all women really want to do is talk to half-drunk balding guys they don't know.

"C'mon," I said, "let me get by," and with that I tried to pass in front of him, stepping on his toes in the process.

"Watch out where you're going, you fucking dyke," he said.

"Pretty good," I replied. "Looks like you're one guy who can tell the players without a program." And with that I kept going past him and out the row, though I wanted to add a quick knee to his face.

When I got back to our aisle with the food, he and his friends were gone and in their places were two teenaged couples.

Janet said, "The Cardinal fans didn't really have tickets for this section, so when the kids showed up, the ushers busted the bozos pretty good. Mike pushed a female usher a little, and she called a security guard down. But the excitement was good for me."

She did look perked up by it all. She loves to see swift retribution, but she's always afraid I'm going to get in fights with guys when I feel challenged.

"You don't need to protect me from men." I know that's what she'd say, and ordinarily I wouldn't. Trained killers, we laughingly call ourselves. Really ready for situations that get out of hand. But what I couldn't protect her from was the attack directing itself at her body and the counterattack by the chemicals that was really knocking her out. What I couldn't protect myself from was my anger and fear of death. They orbited inside me like twin stars spinning around a darkly hollow core.

I needed to be mad at the Cardinal fan and the regular stupidities of the world instead of the really serious stupidity of the medical practitioners who couldn't even tell us what she ought to be eating to help combat the onslaught of the injections. "Choose a balanced diet from the four major food groups" is what the pamphlet from the American Cancer Society advised.

"The last time I heard anyone say that was on the 'Sheriff John Show,'" Janet said when she read it. "I was eleven and knew we'd never have Ovaltine at our house."

"I'll put it on our list, if you like. You're never too old for Ovaltine."

"If it has too much iron in it, I can't have it. Just get me Hershey's chocolate syrup."

"If you add pickles to our list, we're in trouble," I said.

"I can't talk about food anymore, OK?" she asked. "Just get whatever you think. Everything either makes me sick or reminds me of throwing up. Let's go back to eating what we always ate. I can't look at another bowl of chicken soup."

And so it went for a long time, and last week when we were down in the desert to celebrate Janet being out of treatment for a year, I saw somebody on a Sunday morning science show discussing breast cancer and I started sobbing. Janet had just come out of the shower and there I was, almost in a collapse.

"I still can't stand it," I cried. "It's still going on out there, the cancer, and it's still going on in me, the being afraid. I can't stand that I can't make it go away."

She wrapped me in her towel. "It's gone away from me. I'm OK, I know it."

"But we know nobody's telling how bad it is. Think of Susan and then Melanie and her ex-lover. Just think of the lesbians you know, let alone the straight women we don't hear about and the poor women who can't begin to afford mammograms. I can't stand that there's so much terror and nobody makes a public stand about it."

There were many kinds of terror for me from the beginning. We were just beginning to live together. Living together was a big step. Not just that I left my house to move to her house in the Valley—but that I left living by myself. I left my private view of the Griffith Park Observatory and the lazy mauve sunsets. I moved back to the flat, arid floor of the San Fernando Valley, closer to my work, yes, but back in time to where I'd gone to high school, played softball, been a model student, where I'd tried the normal routine of being a married woman. But now suburban streets felt too straight. And what that meant to me was regimentation, regulations, regular expectations. It made my head start to pulse. What if I couldn't stand the strictures? What if I really fell back into "normal" existence, only this time as a lesbian?

"Normal existence"—what a misnomer. Here I was in the middle of my life—someone once told me I'd never understand the concept of middle age—still wondering how other people lived. I hadn't given up wearing Levi 501s, a hankering for black tennis shoes, or buying plain colored one-pocket cotton T-shirts from Penney's. I was as far in my concerns from a Woman Our Age as I was in my dress. Instead of wondering how my offspring were going to get through high school, I was wondering how I could get to the island near Borneo where the tribal elders instructed you in having a dream, then tattooed symbols representing your vision in dark blue ink on your shoulder with a nail.

Janet was a lot like me except she had lived with a woman before, had travelled to more obscure, out-of-the-way places, and knew no amount of living in the San Fernando Valley would make her normal. Living, living, living, living—you have to wonder why humans complicate the issue to the degree we do. Is it the easiest strategy to keep from facing death? When Janet was diagnosed with breast cancer, the initial terror and the continuing terror was that she was not going to get free of it. I remembered my grandmother. She was my favorite person ever, the first person close to me who had died. (Of course, in those days we never could tell her she had cancer.) The long, unhealed hurt of that silence howled through my heart again. In not telling her, we never really told ourselves either. And I never trusted talk of illness again, no way.

I had seen how we covered up death that time, covered it up again when grandfather died shortly after her. There was no way to avoid the tragic ending to my other grandparents' lives. The TV news had aired the twisted frame of their silver station wagon prime-time.

Lots of times lately I have flashbacks about dead people. Whenever I come to a certain Y in the road on Pass Avenue, I think of a girl named Michelle I ate lunch with my second day in high school. I thought she was really nice to sit with me and talk.

She was a sophomore and a class officer, kind of a bouncy blonde cheerleader type. A day after I met her she was dead—somebody ran the stop sign at that Y and broadsided her car.

I think of that little boy we saw who said he had no mother and I wonder if she really had died or if she just wasn't along on the camping trip. I imagine him growing up in some fifties tract house in Northridge, and I have this fear that he'll resent learning to take care of himself and doing laundry and vacuuming and cooking. He could turn out like the kid who lives next door to my sister, the one she complains about all the time. The dad never really recovered from his wife's death. The house got ratty, the dogs run all over the neighborhood, and the boy has been alone too much. He has one of those heavy-metal hairdos now and looks like a male anorexic. My sister used to be afraid of him because he stared at her a lot. But he's made some friends and he barely says hello to her anymore. The guys who hang out at his house drink beer and get pretty loud. They have mock fights and tumble around on the lawn, which scares my sister, but I tell her it's better they do that to each other than to their girlfriends. There's a lot of that now, guys hitting their dates.

Maybe the little blond kid we met camping will keep his sweet and loving nature. Maybe he'll get a new mom who really likes him and he'll be able to bury the dead. Maybe he won't turn out to be like the Cardinal fan or my sister's neighbor or the slimeball I share an office with. Maybe he'll even like women.

This last summer, Janet and I took a trip again, camping all the way up to Canada and back. We had some disagreements about which tent to take, which stove to take, how to pack the car. Janet accused me of needing my big stove along to feel like we'd have well-cooked meals. I thought the little one-burner propane promised us a regimen of thin soups and unappetizing vegetarian chile. We ended up packing both.

We were sniping at each other over missed turnoffs and freeway alternates, and choosing a campsite at the end of each long day of driving made us tense and confrontational. We were settling on KOAs instead of exploring the side routes and the Forest Service sites.

By the time we got to Vancouver, I had even suggested in a huff that she let me off at the next airport so I could fly home.

That way she could drive my car exactly the way she wanted, she could choose campsites after dark had fallen, and she could live on carrot sticks and plain yogurt if she felt like it.

Then we arrived in Vancouver a day ahead of our reservations (two Virgos can get too careful), and the town was booked to the hilt with Gay Games participants. Luckily, a noisy group from San Francisco arrived two people short and we got their extra room for the night.

Once we had dragged all our gear up to the room, I forced a showdown. "As far as I'm concerned, this trip is terrible. We aren't acting right. I don't know what's the matter, all the power struggles, I just don't get it."

"You want to control me," Janet answered. "You can't get over the fact that I'm well now. You just want to be the one who decides everything. I know you had to be that way last summer when I was sick, but now I don't need it. I need to make my own decisions."

"You're practicing on me, that's how it feels, Janet," I replied. I knew I was really getting mad because I wanted to pitch my binoculars through the window. "You're practicing having power again and I'm not the one to practice on. Big power I ever had when you were sick. Big power," I cried, "helping you out of bed, telling you you needed to rest, cooking food you couldn't eat or threw up. Oh, yes, that suited all my fantasies about controlling a lover."

By that point we were both crying because we were both right. I was always scared for her and thinking to protect her, and I was the one she initially had to test her strength against.

"You remember the first time I went with you into the room to get your chemo shot?" I reminded her. "You claimed you wanted me to see how cute the nurse was. But you wanted me to have that shot with you. It was a test. And it was terrible watching her wrap that rubber tube around your arm and draw the fucking poison out of three vials. When your blood raced into the syringe and bloomed there for a moment, I thought I was going to crash to the floor. There's never any way to forget it. It was like the day the vet stuck the needle into my old dog's arm. I knew that what was coming was more terrible than I could ever have imagined."

"Let's not make this harder," Janet said. "Don't you keep bringing those pictures up. I'm OK, I just need to remember I don't have to prove it all the time.

So we kissed and made up and went out to the opening ceremony of the Gay Games. We sat next to a guy from Texas and his brother from the Bay Area. We even ate a hot dog and some nachos, much to our distress. There were dancers of all kinds, some elegant queens, and athletes in all stages of "shape." We promised ourselves we'd find an event we could compete in the next time, and we took ourselves back to the hotel, a couple of true campers roughing it in the urban wilds.

The
Great
Baptism

JANE THURMOND

There is a time in my memory when my age is not measured in years. "Before the flood" or "after the flood" suffices. Days convert to watermarks, distances calculated from the lapping surface of the lake to the roofs of houses. The flood must have come when I was nine. I've determined this by the watery memory of my possessions washing out my upstairs window—my birthday tea set bobbed by and Tiny Tears reached for me as I was dragged by my father toward the chimney. And then, of course, there are the people I knew before the flood who I would never see again.

For months Mother called the flood the Great Baptism because, at first, it put us on the path to a better life. My own baptism happened in the church before the flood, but I was never better for it.

Eternal Life Baptist Church was saved from total destruction by the slope of the earth, but after the flood, when most of the survivors moved away and businesses shut down, the church followed. Last summer I made the trip back to see what was left. Eternal Life Baptist still stood. When I pried open its rotted walnut doors I could still hear the echoing microphone, the gallant choir and the gentle sloshing of water. Not water from the flood, but baptismal water. Yet when I think of how baptism feels, it's something like a flood. Or like falling off a dock with a dress on, the skirt billowing up around you as you sink. There comes an instant when you must choose whether you will punch against the preacher or simply lean back and trust the weight of his hand, strapped across your gaping mouth, blocking the water.

When my mother was twelve, she was baptized in a river. On the bank she stood in starched white lace, orange mud oozing around her ankles, until she was led into the water by the preacher in his soggy suit. She promised herself an indoor ceremony for me.

Perhaps she chose Eternal Life simply because of its baptistry, which loomed like a large fish tank implanted in the wall high above where the choir stood. Facing the choir, we sat in stiff pine pews, our necks hinged back, lulled by our aquarium view. In a blue sea of organ chords we drifted with the waves on the other side of the glass and watched the preacher push the heads under, watched the elegant legs float up. Behind ripples and splashes swayed swirling aqua tile. Above the waterline, the tile burst into a bright mosaic sky where two enormous hands, God's hands, reached down as if they could scoop us all right up to heaven.

When I was eight my mother's wish was realized—me and the preacher chest-deep in water, lit up from underneath so we were glowing.

Baptism is supposed to save you. That's the good part. The bad part is that it doesn't change you; it doesn't suddenly make you do right.

Our town was perched on a limestone rise overlooking a narrow lake as smooth and green as a chalkboard. We lived in one of the split-levels built along the bank by the oil company and provided as part of Dad's pay. That's when my parents were still in love, before he started traveling. Each night sweets followed pungent plates of food set on crocheted trivets. Dad would hunch over his dinner, his hair falling across his forehead, one arm encircling his plate, and consume helping after helping of my mother's dishes. Mom would round the counter, drying her hands on her rick-racked apron and she'd reach for Dad's cheeks, bobbing his head back and forth. "Judy Ann," she cooed, "who's the *best* father in the world?" I sang back, "My dad." Sometimes we'd wrestle on the living room carpet or they'd spin around the pink stone patio pretending it was a ballroom.

One summer night Mom was out playing the organ for church choir practice while Dad worked late. I rocked alone on the patio glider, listening to neighbors' lives open up through lit windows that fell in yellow rectangles on the water. Across the inlet, the church steeple shot up with its stained-glass window the size of the moon. Through the colored glass, music melted over the tops of trees. Lights flickered like blue flames across the lake. Someone over there was splitting wood. Coyotes moaned and dogs barked back. Fireflies darted through darkness. The seniors had just graduated and the engines of their cars droned up and down Lake Avenue. Whooping boys and squealing girls kept time with the even squeak of my glider. I climbed down to the street and walked while the music calmed the whole town. Cars slowed, drivers straining out windows. People stopped on sidewalks to sit under trees and gaze out over the lake and listen. Sometimes there would be a long prelude of organ chords, and I'd call across the water, "That's my mom."

When I wandered past the corner park I heard someone humming and turned toward the monkey bars where I found a girl hanging upside down. She stopped singing when she saw me. "Is it always this hot here?" she said, her arms dangling in the dark.

I leaned in close and squinted. "Who's there? Do I know you?"

"You know me only if you met me in the last few days," she said, swinging from her knees. "I just moved into a house down River Road. Our furniture filled up three pickup trucks. They're *still* unloading."

I climbed a few rungs to get a closer look. Her yellow hair fell like an undone bolt of silk. Her cheeks were dark, reddened with blood settled in her head.

"My name is Judy Ann Wiggins," I said.

"Laura Leigh," she announced, sticking out a hand for me to shake. "Porter's my last name now. Before that, in Idaho, it was Villanueva, and before that it was McDougal, in Montana."

"Why does it keep changing?" I asked.

"Mom keeps changing husbands and houses. After each wedding she sits my brothers and me around the kitchen table, passes out paper and pencils, and we practice our new names. P-O-R-T-E-R," she recited. "This one's easier than the others."

Leaves high in the elm trees shuddered. The chorus swelled. I pointed to the steeple. "Listen for the organ. The person playing it is my mom." The music had captured me again and I climbed down. "See you around, Laura Leigh." I waved and walked backward, watching the tangle of arms and legs and bars fade into the shadows.

"Hey, kid," she called. "What grade will you be in come September?"

"Fourth, and my name's Judy Ann."

"I'm older than you are, Judy Ann," she sang, then hummed along again with my mother's music.

Before I knew it I was down at the church in the blackness of the balcony, sitting with my feet up on the seat like I'd never do in a Sunday dress. No one even saw me. No one knew. Chandeliers brightened the rows below. The choir roared above the steady tap of the director's stick against his metal music stand. My mother bowed toward her sheet music, her fingers crawling over the keys, her feet dancing on the foot pedals. I leaned my head back and listened until their hymnbooks thumped shut, the organ lid snapped and everyone shuffled outside toward the cafe. The chandeliers finally faded and the door slammed, leaving me alone with the rafters swelling and creaking in the dark. And then, more than ever, the baptistry was a blue square of light, beckoning me like the doorway to heaven.

Heat engulfed me and sweat wet my back. My bangs dampened against my forehead. Is it always this hot? Laura Leigh had asked me this and I had never answered. Now all I could think of was yes, yes. I wilted as I gazed at the baptistry until it occurred to me that I could be up there swimming.

I pulled myself from the bench, tiptoed down the balcony stairs and slowly walked the center aisle, scanning every seat. Chandeliers barely swayed, creaking from the arched ceiling. The smell of newly-laid carpet rose around my feet. At the preacher's podium I turned and faced the empty pews to be certain I was alone, then slipped through the door to the tunnel that climbed to the choir loft and above to the baptistry. On all fours I felt my way up the stairs until I stumbled onto Reverend Culpepper's thick-soled shoes stashed on a shelf and his baptismal gown hanging from a hook.

When I realized where I had ended up, I crouched close to the cement floor, recalling the last time I was there, for my own baptism. I had been ordered to change out of my Sunday clothes near this very spot, in the dressing room next to the reverend's. Behind the drawn curtain I folded my sailor dress, stuffed my socks into my patent leather shoes and slipped the gown that he had tossed me over my head. I smoothed out the creases and stood motionless in the center of the dressing room, listening for the others to emerge in their gowns. Instead, from the stall next to me, I heard the reverend's pants unzip, saw them drop and bunch around his feet. I imagined him in his shorts. His chalky knees. The little hairs curling against his chest. He cleared his throat and scratched.

Stretching the gown toward my ankles I had struggled to hide myself entirely with cotton so thin my nipples showed through. Finally, I filed out with the others, folding my arms across my chest, and waited in line for my sins to be cleansed away.

I rolled on my back and opened my eyes wide to remind myself I was alone. My face felt cool against the cement. I stood and slipped out of my shirt and shorts. In my underwear, I crept to the edge, then slid into the tile-lined tub of water.

Pretending to perform for a large audience, I staged my own water ballet. I rocketed up, slicing the surface with a twist, my toes pointed, my hands pressed against my thighs. I jackknifed under water, every muscle straining for balance and grace. My stiffened arms spiraled up. The waves sloshed and broke against the tile. Underwater flips, handstands, floating on my back.

No one came in. No one saw. I pressed my face against the glass and stared out into the church to check. Nothing. Only rows and rows of pews. Dark aisles. Just me in my private pool. A seal slipping under water.

So this became my secret. Nightly, I continued to swim.

Don't let me mislead you into thinking I led a lonely life. Before the flood I had friends on every corner. On warm summer nights as I walked home from the church, children dodged in and out of shadows, racing under streetlights clicking with June bugs, calling to me from games of kick-the-can. I recognized their Hula-Hoops spinning from dark yards, the shush of their Slinkies, and I'd wave their way, tossing my damp hair.

Weeks later, in a game of hide-and-seek, I met Laura Leigh again, hidden behind a house in a maze of hedges. Soon we were spending entire days together. She was from a large family, farther down River Road where the earth swelled with the bare roots of trees. Although she had passed her eleventh birthday, she was smaller than me. Her two brothers, three stepbrothers and Mr. Porter were rarely home. She could never guess the day of the week because for her, summer days all seemed the same. No one left her house for work on weekdays, and Sunday was a day no more special than the rest. At their kitchen table her mother sat like a statue, examining a deck of cards stacked and restacked in a never-ending game of solitaire. Through a cloud of smoke, she gazed up at us from her scorepad and took another sip of scotch. "Bring Mama somethin' sweet," she slurred as we passed, tapping her cigarette into an ashtray that overflowed onto the linoleum.

Some nights Laura Leigh slept over. We'd lie in my wide bed and count the stars Dad had painted on the ceiling with phosphorescent paint. Big Dipper, Seven Sisters, an oversized North Star. From piles of stuffed animals we contemplated the universe. I imagined heaven on the other side of the ceiling. Who ended up there and who didn't was as clear to me then as the differences in the sun and the moon. You were either saved or you weren't—as easy as an instant under water. In Sunday-School-teacher fashion, I recalled the topics of my Sunday lessons, explaining to Laura Leigh the features of heaven and hell. But soon I would learn that, baptized or not, I would do unforgivable things that even a flood's undoing could not wash away. A flood I saw coming because of the bats.

One evening, just before sunset, Laura Leigh spotted my father's binoculars sitting on a shelf. Soon we were perched on the patio, staring at the bridge at the far end of the lake. Tiny cars crossed silently through the lenses. Beneath the bridge the water glowed like stained glass. "There they are!" she finally cried, thrusting the binoculars to my face. I peered through the lenses until I spotted a colony of thousands of bats spiraling upward from under the bridge. They swirled up like a pillar of smoke, then dispersed to specks in the purple sky.

"The bats feed every night," Laura Leigh explained. "They'll return to the bridge when the sun comes up." She slipped the binoculars back inside their case. "I've got another secret that I'll trade for one of yours." I nodded. We hadn't yet told each other everything. She leaned close to my ear. "Those bats were only the beginning of mine. Follow me."

We took the road along the lake past her house, under a moon so bright we cast long-legged shadows that slipped in and out of trees. Gravel crunched under our boat shoes. She led me to a metal shed nearly covered over with vines and pushed the door open, yanked me inside, then sealed the door behind us. I stood in the dark, trying to identify the musty smell. Laura Leigh's hands fumbled until an old Christmas candle in the melting shape of an angel lit up the room. She pointed up to the corner of the shed, and I squinted in the dim light until I spotted a bat hanging upside down from a dowel. Its face had the look of a tiny newborn calf, with a mouth as pink as my mother's lipstick, its nostrils like pinpricks, its eyes two black beads, its head crowned with oversized ears. Its wings fell like portions of a split parasol.

Laura Leigh stepped on a stool and stretched her arm up. The bat squeaked and bared its tiny teeth. "Her name is Barb. She can't see us so she's afraid. After she smells me and realizes who I am, she won't bite." Laura Leigh slowly turned with the bat hanging from her finger. Barb was as small as the palm of her hand. "Judy Ann, open that jar of bugs," she ordered. "Grab hold of a moth. Now, put it close to her nose." Barb grabbed the beating moth with one clawlike thumb, covered half her own body with a cloaked wing and ate. I ducked as Barb flew above her bowl of water, lapping with her tiny tongue, wings a brown blur.

"Did you get her from the bridge?" I asked.

"My brother caught a bunch in a net. Barb's the last one. The others died or got away, but Barb's stayed on for weeks." Laura Leigh blew out the candle and we stood silently in the dark. She added in a whisper, "I've thought about letting her go, but she depends on me."

Once outside Laura Leigh poked me with her index finger. "Now it's your turn. Tell me a secret."

I trotted ahead. "Follow me," I said over my shoulder.

The breeze coming off the lake had stopped completely, and after our run to the church, even the outside air felt stuffed up and soupy. When we pushed open the sculpted doors, Laura Leigh glowed in the blue shaft of light from the baptistry, her blond hair tinged green. I slipped my arm around her shoulders and coaxed her up the aisle, past the podium, until she stumbled through the secret door. "You're going to love this," I promised as we climbed through the tunnel, up the stairs and emerged, finally, at the edge of the water.

"Well, this is it. Welcome to my private pool," I said, unbuttoning my shirt.

She twisted her hair around her hand. "You're kidding, aren't you? What if we get caught?"

I draped my clothes across the back of a chair. "Don't worry," I said. "No one's here. I've been doing this for weeks."

Peering over her shoulder into the darkness, she undressed while I floated on my back. I pushed the air from my lungs and lay on the bottom of the pool. When I came up for breath she had perched at the edge, filling her chest until her ribs resembled the fine bones in Barb's fanlike wings. As Laura Leigh stepped into the water, her cheeks grew pinker and her lips drew into a perfect O. When she ducked her head under, a halo remained on the surface of the water until she popped back through it, slick and smiling.

"I'll show you what it's like to be baptized," I said, my left hand pressed between the wings of her bony back, my right palm raised and facing the glass. "I baptize you in the name of the Father and of the Son and of the Holy Spirit, Amen." Then, just like Reverend Culpepper, I pressed my hand over her mouth and nose, and pushed her head under. Her legs floated up. She didn't fight. Laura Leigh came up laughing, like people sometimes do with a real preacher, happy that they're safe now, saved.

I performed my newest water ballet. My triple floppy. My five-way splash. She turned three somersaults underwater without coming up for air. We sank and rose up pressed together and then, without thinking, we clutched each other and kissed. Like we'd seen on TV. Like my mom and dad. The water slapped and churned. I pulled her toward me and we kissed again. "Let's try it this way," she said, arching my back over her arm, dipping her shoulders to meet mine. My legs slipped up and I started to laugh, until I heard a bump from the pews in the dark. We lurched forward and peered out into the church.

"Don't stop," came a choked voice muffled through the glass and sloshing water. "Kiss again." I sank back and looked at Laura Leigh. The color had drained from her face. Again, the voice ordered, "Judy Ann, do it. If you don't, everyone will know about your little swims."

Our limbs stiffened, but I obeyed. When we kissed for him our mouths were hard. Our bony chests bumped under water and our eyes blinked back the beginnings of tears.

When I heard the faraway click of the door to the tunnel, I let go of Laura Leigh. "He's coming," I whispered. "Let's get out of here." But she couldn't move, so I grabbed her arm and pulled.

But she slipped away under the shadow of the man reaching for her. I can't fault myself for trying to escape. She lost her nerve. She wouldn't run.

I clamored down the stairs in the dark, bumping against the banister, then sprinted up the aisle. When I looked back, the baptismal tank was empty except for water churning against the glass.

Outside, I crouched with no clothes behind the azaleas. My pulse pounded in my neck. Even in the still heat, goose bumps spread across my arms. In the distance, children laughed, but the church was quiet. The cold stone wall supported my spine.

I slowly counted backward from one hundred, sang songs to myself and studied leaves on all the branches before me until the door finally opened, and Laura Leigh stepped out, fully dressed, her blouse blotched with water. She stood on the top step examining her arms and legs as if she were checking to see if they were still attached. When I whistled, she jerked her head my way. "It's me," I whispered. She came over carrying my clothes and threw them across the hedge.

"Why didn't you stick by me?" she cried. Her eyebrows were drawn together, setting a deep crease in her forehead.

I was silent for a while before I answered. "I didn't have my clothes." Slowly, I pulled on my shirt. "Besides, no one can find out about the swimming. We would have gotten caught."

"*He* would have gotten caught," Laura Leigh whispered between her teeth. Muscles in her cheeks tightened and squared her face.

I stopped dressing and studied her. "What did he do?"

She shrugged her shoulders. "You know," she said, letting her arms go limp at her sides. "You should have helped."

My breath choked in my throat. "Did he hurt you?"

"What do you think?" she said, pressing her palms against her eyes.

"Who was it? Have you seen him before?"

"I don't know anybody in this lousy town." She backed away. "Not even you."

As I wrestled with the buttons on my shirt, she turned and ran. A group of boys under the streetlight drop-kicked a football back and forth. The ball arched high until it slapped onto the sidewalk. Laura Leigh kept running as if she didn't notice. Her clumped hair thumped her back. My hair dampened the collar of my shirt. Zipping my shorts, I stepped into the churchyard and the boys

paused and waved, but I looked straight ahead and forced my legs
to walk.

When I reached my house, I stood in the yard. My father's silhouette slipped back and forth across the window. It was Saturday,
his evening to putter around the house wearing a tool belt, fixing
leaky faucets and tightening loose screws. Through a crack between curtains, I could see my mother on the couch reading her
Sunday School lesson. I entered through the back door, a smile
plastered across my face, as if this were any other summer evening.
"Good night," I said, kissing their tender cheeks, and ran up to my
bed.

I pulled the soft sheets around my neck and faced heaven. The
four walls fell away. The painted stars began to move until I
couldn't tell if I was looking at the ceiling or the sky. I grappled
with what I could or should have done. I sifted through whispered
stories I had heard while sitting on dark curbs or gathered with my
friends on the school ground. My face grimaced again in disbelief,
recalling girls giggling through sordid stories. They illustrated with
their hands, stroking their own bodies, or drew impossible pictures
in soft sand.

I sorted through this gibberish again and again, trying to make
sense of the deep crease in Laura Leigh's forehead that had sliced
through the darkness. The stories followed me into my dreams. I
slept twisted and trapped in sheets.

In church the next morning, as the sun streamed in on the rows
of people filling every pew, I memorized the faces of the men as
they bowed their heads in prayer, trying to figure which one. I listened to their voices in the lobby. I examined hands as the ushers
passed offering plates brimming with dollar bills. From the balcony I studied Reverend Culpepper through binoculars, following him back and forth across the pulpit, focusing and refocusing
my eyes.

After lunch I walked down River Road where Laura Leigh's
mother sat in the open doorway. "I ain't seen her all day," she said
without looking up. Every day that week I wandered past her
house, peeking between leaves. I checked their dock and found
one brother dangling his feet above the water and baiting a bamboo pole. "Not here," he said, shrugging his shoulders and shoving a hook into the brittle belly of a cricket. I walked to the shed

where I found Barb alone, silently hanging in her corner. Beneath her on the shelf, the angel candle was reduced to a small puddle of wax and a crisp wick that hardly held a flame.

A few days later at dusk, I stood on our patio thinking about Laura Leigh. My constantly churning stomach had lessened to flinches of nervousness. I tried to relax each night, pressing my eyes to Dad's binoculars, waiting until the gray spiral of bats emerged from under the bridge and circled and spread across the darkening sky. You might say I owe my life to the bats. Had I not watched for them, I would not have seen the wall of water burst through the bridge as the flapping wings emerged. I would not have shouted for my parents who ran outside in time to register the danger.

They dragged me by my shirtsleeves from the patio across the balcony, then boosted me to the roof. Water roiled around us. As we all teetered at the top, waves crashed against our house. My mother prayed aloud, her cheek pressed against the chimney. My father encircled us with his arms. We all shouted above the roaring waves. Beds and drawers and rooftops pummeled past. A car carried a howling cat. Tree trunks were tossed in the current like toothpicks. With each gasp for help that wrenched past, my father reached into the waves but came up empty-handed.

In a matter of hours our town shattered to pieces that scattered and finally settled in silt, like our next-door neighbor's chess set that floated through our kitchen window, popped open in the grand piano, and spilled and sank against the strings.

In the middle of the night, I woke up in the school gymnasium under dry blankets surrounded by rows of creaking cots. Wailing voices filtered through the bleachers from the doorway. My mother's dark hair spread across my bed where she rested, waiting for me to come alive from a fitful sleep.

A few hours later I awoke again. "No, I won't have it. We won't be separated. We're going with you," my mother said as she tightened a blanket around me. She carried me through the gymnasium behind my father to the company truck. We piled in and rumbled down a back road, washed over with water. My father hunched over the steering wheel, his clothes still caked with mud. My mother's breath frosted the side window. Her bruised and fragile fingers rested on my cheek. It was daybreak and the sun had drawn its first pink streaks across the horizon. The CB radio crackled with static. "Didn't Laura Leigh live somewhere out here?" my mother whispered. I sat up and tried to recognize what was left. We moved slowly, surveying the clogged path the flood had taken, crossing into pasture when the road swelled with water. "Survivors could be hanging on to anything," Dad said, his eyes darting from tree to tree. He pulled to a stop and examined every branch. I searched for waves of yellow hair.

"Hold on, would you look at that." Dad lifted me out of the car still bundled in a blanket and pointed across the water.

Bats were plummeting out of the sky toward the place where the bridge had been, nose-diving into nothing but splinters and air instead of the cool dark space below the bridge where they had left their children hanging upside down. "They'll have to find another home, like us," he said, rubbing his bristly cheek against my forehead.

I heard my mother sigh. "Poor little things. I always feel sorriest for the innocent animals. They don't know what a dam is. They can't understand a flood." She rolled down her window to get a better view. "There's a difference in being spared and being saved."

Back in town I watched the sun rise higher in the sky. The flood water looked dreamy, steaming in the heat. By the third day, no trace of high water remained, but the town was coated and clotted with mud. The summer sun dried this silt to dust, and the wind blew it into muted clouds that hung over the jumble of houses, branches and upturned cars. Each day in the gymnasium, a miracle survivor appeared. Men sat on the edges of cots in mud-streaked waders, wads of tobacco puffing their cheeks, and swapped stories of daring rescues. Trips were organized to view the great gash in the dam. I walked up and down the streets, studying the face of every child. I checked and rechecked lists of names, searching for Laura Leigh. Kids from the neighborhood wandered through the rubble and I asked each of them if they had seen or heard. My parents and the other survivors sadly sifted through their belongings. An air of reverence hung over the town as the death toll rose.

Reverend Culpepper conducted daily services in the high school auditorium, where we clamored to make sense of the disaster that had destroyed our town. From the back of the auditorium where I remained, the reverend shrank to the size of a moth. I sprawled on the cool linoleum and drew a picture of Noah's ark. Soggy animals bloomed from the butcher paper, paired on the deck of their fragile wooden ship. Hours passed. Under my stubby crayons, fog rolled in until all the animals' heads were draped in smudged gray clouds.

Within a week Dad had loaded a car with the little we had left. We coasted down Lake Avenue for one last look, then pulled out onto the main highway that paralleled River Road. Alone in the backseat I knelt on my knees, facing the rear window, and looked in awe for the last time at the tangled mass of uprooted trees with rowboats lodged in the branches. From the front seat my parents said their soft good-byes. "The world is recovering and so are we," Dad said, patting my mother's shoulder. Yet we left without learning the fate of my friend. Watching the town disappear, I tried to find comfort in recalling her baptism. How she went under water without flinching, and the look on her face as she came up laughing.

KLEYA FORTÉ-ESCAMILLA

She went down there again the next day after school. A side street
not many people passed by. The VFW was across the street but
could have been ten thousand miles away. The bar had no windows at all, a brick wall with a solid door in the middle. The small
sign over the door was faded, impossible to read.

Chula inched along the wall, looked both ways, saw no one. So
she leaned against the wall right at the edge of the alley, ready to
run back. She was a young woman, with a soft, innocent, well-
formed face, saddle shoes, a narrow blue skirt and gray sweater,
dark, intense eyes. She held her schoolbooks locked against her
chest. It was mid-afternoon. She waited until the very last minute,
until she had to run home to keep from being late.

The next day she came again. It was not a good time for people
to be coming to a bar, but it was the only time she had and
maybe...but no one came.

Chula waited, nervous, practicing to herself what she would say.
Maybe she wouldn't have to say anything. Maybe all she had to do
was see her and the woman who dressed like a man would understand everything. But another day went by and she didn't come.

Then it was Saturday and Chula came downtown with her *tia* to
buy some *tela* for her home ec class, but Tia had forgotten her
purse. In a rush to get to Tia's house because the store was near
closing, they cut through the alley to avoid traffic and get more
quickly to the south side of town. Just as they reached the end of
the alley and were about to jaywalk across the street, an Impala

came around the corner and roared to a stop. The woman Chula
had been waiting for all those days got out right in front of them.

Chula saw all of her in one frozen instant: black eyes and
molded lips, wild hair brushing her tan cheek, breasts taut beneath a blue western shirt, Levi's ironed and creased, a silver chain
hanging from the pocket. *Y esas movidas,* and that incredible energy. Chula just hung there and Tia tried to pull Chula one way
while she stumbled another. The woman who dressed like a man
steadied her and stood her on the curb again, saying, "Watch out,"
in a throaty, laughing voice. The air around them was drenched
with the hot smells of skin and cologne and Chula's feelings—paralyzed and burning. She stared into the woman's face with lips
trembling, and then her *tia* jerked her away and across the street
as though a rabid dog were at their heels.

Chula started to turn around, catching a glimpse of the woman
standing next to the Impala, watching her. But her *tia* hissed,
"*Ponte cara en frente!* Don't look over there!"

"Why not?" said Chula.

"*Te agarra una de esas, y ningun hombre te quiere de mujer.* If one of
those women touches you, no man will want you. Do you understand?" Who cares? thought Chula. But she made an effort to
keep her face straight and her *tia* didn't notice, still talking with
disgust and venom in her voice. "*Una muchacha como ti son las que
quieren. Te siguen y te agarran.* They run after young girls like you
and ruin you. Never go near that place." She kept her hand firmly
on Chula's arm, pulling her along.

The next Saturday Chula got permission to go to the library
with her cousins, Amalia and Tootsie, and then she told the girls
she had to go buy something in a flash. Already flirting with some
cute boys, they hardly noticed her leaving. Chula ran all the way
from the library to the back of the building and then up the alley.
It was almost time.

Panting, Chula peered around the corner, but there was no
Impala. The late afternoon sun was hot and blistery on the pavement. She had waited as long as she dared when she saw the black
car coming down the street. Before the woman who dressed like a
man could get out, Chula opened the passenger door and jumped
in. The woman, startled, stared at Chula.

"Will you take me someplace?" asked Chula. Disbelief, amuse-
ment, concern—all struggled in the woman's face. She reached

across Chula's breast, pushing her back gently against the seat, and made sure the door was closed. As she double-clutched at the corner, she said, "Where do you want to go?"

"I don't know," said Chula. Her throat got tighter and tighter. She swallowed. "I mean, I just want to be with you."

The woman didn't say anything but drove down a side street skirting the barrio and along the edge of the South Side. When they came to a piece of desert, she pulled away from the road and stopped the car. She left the engine running.

"You're the one who's been hanging around."

Chula, afraid of the anger in the woman's voice, said, "I've been waiting for you."

"How old are you?" The woman reached out as if to touch her, then pulled her hand back. "Do you know what they'd do if they found us together?" Chula heard her fear now. "They'd cut off my hands," the woman said.

"Take me someplace," Chula pleaded.

"Take you where? For what? You have to wait until you're eighteen."

"When I'm eighteen maybe I won't want this anymore."

The woman's voice was soft. "When you're eighteen maybe you won't want this anymore," she agreed.

"Please. I'll never bother you again...."

The woman dropped the car keys she had pulled out of the ignition, found them, and put them back. Her face was pale. "Come on, kid, you'll get me into trouble."

"There's no one I can talk to. There's nobody I can tell about this," Chula said.

The woman drove out on Saguaro Road. She drove all the way with both hands on the steering wheel. They got off the road at a ranchito. They passed the big house, vacant, windows broken. Farther back, behind a stand of tamarack trees, was a little casita with a pink door. On it, someone had painted a beautiful black orchid.

They both got out. The woman leaned against the car. Chula walked around looking at the mountains turning purple, at the dancing tamarack sweet with the voices of birds. It was quiet; she could hear the bees buzzing.

The woman watched her, silent, tense, knowing she'd come back.

She did. With a cry, Chula pressed herself against the woman's body. The woman didn't move, turned her head aside. Chula forced her face against the other's face, put her hands around the hot skin of her neck. The woman's breath quickened but still she didn't lift her arms, only her breast heaved up and down under Chula's breast.

Chula's need was like a pain filling her body but not telling her what to do, how to move. The sensations started in her legs where they pressed against the woman's legs. Small, sharp bursts of electricity—the sensations came and went, over and over again, and stronger. She trembled against the older woman's body. Until at last the woman's hands encircled her ass and pressed—that was all —pressed her tighter and held her that way, without moving. The burning turned liquid, flowing into Chula's thighs, bursting between her legs. The woman's own breath came out in a moan of pleasure and despair. But she never moved her body. They stayed like that until Chula stepped back—of her own will.

It was two years later, the day after Chula's eighteenth birthday— the day when Chula had said she'd look for the woman. It was a Saturday, and that evening Chula went down to the VFW. She stood in the shadow of the doorway and waited a long time before she saw the black Impala come rumbling to a stop. It had new skirts and whitewall tires. A pink streamer was flying from the antenna.

Chula ducked behind the door and saw the strangely beautiful woman: molded lips, shaggy black hair, strong, lean body in a blue denim shirt, sleeves rolled up, new Levi's with a long silver chain hanging from the watch pocket. Chula saw the woman reach for something behind the visor, lock the car door, and step into the bar.

Chula came out of her hiding place and went slowly back the way she'd come. She didn't see the woman come out and follow Chula with her eyes for several long, breath-held beats of the heart. Then the woman carefully placed the orchid in her hand on the fender of the Impala, turned, and went back inside.

Chula stopped and stared at the traffic for a while, then crossed the street. A few minutes later, legs shaking, she came back. Slowly approaching the Impala she saw the black orchid, and picked it up with trembling fingers. Chula opened the door of the bar.

Joshuas in the City with a Future

JACQUELINE DE ANGELIS

The Black Rock ranger leaned on the counter at the visitor's center to inform us that the San Bernardino county sheriff had lost the trail of some armed and dangerous bandits out by the water tank. "Bandits," I said and giggled. Marge shot me a look and crossed her arms. The camp host standing next to the ranger cleared his throat and spoke up, "They're both white, one male, one female. They have dirty, stringy blond hair and bad complexions. They fled the scene after officers ran them onto the shoulder of the road just outside Joshua Tree. They're somewhere out in the Monument with only one pair of shoes between the two of them." He gestured knowingly toward the topographic map under the glass counter between us. "You ladies are welcome to stay in site number two. It's right across from my Airstream. The wife and I will watch out for you." He gave me a grandfatherly smile.

I thought it was a pretty good deal, but Marge held on to her checkbook and had this look on her face that means she's not negotiating.

"Bandits have guns," Marge shouted as she marched on ahead of me back to the van. "Bandits take hostages, Charlene."

Bandits, according to Marge, were hard to catch. They were even harder to predict and were renowned for digging shallow graves. Marge went on and on about the nature of bandits. By the time she finished enumerating Los Angeles County statistics on crimes committed with automatic weapons, we were seven miles away from Black Rock back on the Twentynine Palms Highway heading east toward Amboy.

"Marge, bandits are small potatoes next to what's going on in the world right now."

"The war is in a different desert, Charlene, but the bandits are here, and I'm not taking any chances."

"Fine, don't take any chances," I said, "but I'm *not* driving back to the city, so we have to find someplace to stay out here."

Marge put her feet up on the dash and started to thumb through the campground guide. "OK, Charlene, there's a Big Sky RV park one mile west on Highway 62." Marge opened the California map too fast and I heard it rip.

At that moment I couldn't figure out why I ever thought it was a good idea to go on a last-minute desert trip with Marge, whose caseload was driving her crazy and to whom the ocean is paradise. I was in rotten shape myself. I had been completely frightened and obsessed by the war. For weeks it dominated my every gesture. I had maps taped up over my paintings in the living room and a list of military hardware on my refrigerator. Fuel Air explosives, Stealth bombers, and Wild Weasels were more familiar to me than the faces of my cats. There was no landscape, only information. I moved through radio waves, satellite broadcasts, cockpit videos. I had to know who said what on every front, in every briefing, in every paper. I kept running into the bathroom at work to listen to my transistor radio. I was lucky I still had the catering business after the burnt pizza fiasco earlier in the week. I wanted to get away from all the coverage and just be with Marge.

Once we got to Big Sky I realized it looked like the parking lot of a discount membership store, but I would stay there and compromise if it made Marge feel safe. But Marge was so stressed, even the Big Sky RV park, with its 160 sites on cement slabs overhung with mercury vapor lights, seemed suspicious to her. I thought I had made headway in convincing her that the senior citizens seemed harmless. But no, there was something about that RV park, even with its wide variety of hookup options, that smelled like the Bates Motel to Marge.

"Charlene, you think because they're old they're safe. What about that nice Ohio couple who ran out of farmland to bury their hired hands in so they started stacking them in their cellar? Real sweet old couple."

I turned back toward the main road and kept driving. Marge switched the radio stations in search of news of the armed and dangerous couple. There was nothing but CNN war coverage and occasional sports updates. Marge was frantically chewing her gum and flipping through the camp guide. We were running out of places to camp and I knew it.

The desert does strange things to people sometimes. It is all that space stretching out and beyond. And the light coming down directly without passing through the filter of smog or coastal moisture. And the sky so vast and prominent that it is unmistakable proof that we're on a planet. It sent Marge right to the edge. I'd never seen Marge frightened, even when she comes home at night and walks up the long series of steps past the Vietnam vet who randomly shoots a shotgun from his patio, and then through the unlit garden to her front door. It pissed me off that in the desert, where she could see something approaching her for miles, Marge was ready to turn around and drive back the two and a half hours to a city where drive-by shootings compete with car alarms for her attention.

We drove on silently; I turned off the radio reports of the ensuing ground offensive. I wasn't really sure what to do next so I kept the van in high gear. At the turnoff for Amboy I decided to continue on toward Rice, Earp, and Parker. It was early sunset and the desert light was rapidly altering the landscape. The little San Bernardinos and the buttes to the south were blue-gray. Backlit from the setting sun they looked like a pop-up card. The alluvial fans of the Pinto Mountains in front of us were splashed with pink and the Joshua trees seemed to lift themselves up from their concentration on the crops like Coachella field-workers.

"Look, Marge," I said, gently, "we better turn around. I've never been to Rice or Earp and I have the funny feeling that Parker really isn't much of a town, and besides, with all the sheriffs around, Black Rock is safer now than it's ever been."

"Safe." Marge's voice had an unmistakable edge to it.

"Well, let's face it, Marge, we have a van that locks, I mean how could they get in without our knowing it?"

"I hate those trees," Marge answered.

"What trees?" I said, going along with Marge's stalling tactic.

"Those trees," she said, waving her arm furiously out the window at an immense stretch of desert to my right.

"The palms?" I asked. We were entering Twentynine Palms; the sign said it was the City with a Future.

"No, not the palms, you know I like palms, those twisted things over there."

"The Joshua trees?" I said, as if she had just said she hated my guts.

"Yes, those trees, they're ugly."

"Ugly," I said, offended. "But they're from the lily family! Oh, fine, Marge, they're just nine hundred years old and only exist in our Mojave Desert. Have you ever seen one bloom?"

"Those things bloom?" Marge flicked her Zippo lighter. I saw the orange red light at the end of her cigarette out of the corner of my eye.

"Open the window if you're going to smoke," I said harshly.

Marge opened the window and the cool, dry air began to rush into the van. I realized that I had to calm down. I had done it again. Why hadn't I learned my lesson that time in Anza-Borrego when Rosy packed up and left because it was 103 degrees and she saw a sign saying Rattlesnake Danger. But no, I had to talk Caesar into coming so that he could see how cactus grew in the wild. He saw, all right. He stepped on a jumping cholla and the spine dug deep into his foot. He swore to his *orishas* that he would never step out of West Hollywood again, then raved at me half in English and half in Spanish all the way home about how he was from Honduras and it was a tropical country—he wasn't made to live in a booby-trapped wasteland that dried out his skin.

So there I was, making a U-turn on the Twentynine Palms Highway with poor frightened Marge, as if we were two lady passengers in dusty hoopskirts riding in a stagecoach rather than two women driving in a Westfalia through the City with a Future.

"Why isn't anyone on the streets in this city?" Marge jammed her cigarette into the ashtray. "This *really* reminds me of some 'Twilight Zone' episode. Look at that, all four corner gas stations are out of business." Marge lit another cigarette. "I don't know how people do it. Over a hundred degrees every day in the summer and nothing to do the rest of the year. You see, Charlene, this landscape compels people to pass through it. Boy, you can really

see how a war could get started in a place like this. Now the Pacific
Ocean, Charlene…"

I knew Marge's story of the ocean; it was a primal tale of west-
ward migration, the color green, and the balance of negative ions
and fluidity. I stopped listening to her. If I had to hear her oceanic
lecture one more time I thought *I'd* be the one digging a shallow
grave for her.

"Pull over at the McDonald's," Marge ordered suddenly.

"McDonald's," I said. I figured Marge had lost her mind.

"Yeah, I want a coffee and some french fries."

"They fry the potatoes in rancid oil, Marge," I said with superi-
ority. It didn't faze her. Marge moved to the back of the van to
drag her handbag out of the closet before I made a left turn into
the parking lot. Marge opened the side door and jumped out as
soon as the van came to a stop. I watched her walk toward the
doors of McDonald's before I went to the back of the van to consider my options. I wanted to leave her at the Twentynine Palms
McDonald's.

It was already dark but the McDonald's was as bright as high
noon. I watched Marge pick up her order and select a table. She
sipped on what looked like a milkshake for a long time. Finally,
she picked up a french fry. I opened up the refrigerator and rum-
maged through the nonfat, fiber-loaded contents and found an
apple. I stood up and washed it in the sink. Marge was reading
some newspaper and eating one french fry at a time. It looked as
if she was demonstrating proper food chewing techniques. I was
so furious that Marge really had more to fear from me than from
those poor stupid bandits wandering around in the desert with
one pair of shoes between them.

I opened the side door of the van and let in the cold night air,
then put new batteries in my transistor radio and started to eat
some blue corn chips. Oil fields were burning all over the Kuwaiti
desert, some reports said at least sixty fields, others said hundreds.
I turned off the radio and noticed that the Joshua tree in the center of the parking lot had the beginnings of a bloom. A creamy
white bullet-shaped cluster pushing out from the tip of one of its
twisted arms. The tree was so irregular, all at once lopsided and
tall, babies growing out at all angles. Its older, spinelike leaves
gave in to the pressures of heat and gravity and formed a fierce
guard around its trunk. It demanded respect even though it was

encircled by asphalt. It had to have been there before the wave of
cattle rustlers and after the great Keys fire. I saw Marge push open
the door and walk toward the van. I imagined the Joshua stretching its tangle of arms and lifting her up, up through the field of
stars into the safe light of the full moon. But I could tell by her
walk that there wasn't going to be an ascension.

"You know, Charlene, this *just* isn't working."

There it was. Marge was dumping me again. As she lit another
cigarette, I knew by the angry snap of her lighter that her well-
ordered mind was stacking the deck against me. Before we were
on the outskirts of Twentynine Palms she said what I've come to
resent more than any other pronouncement.

"You know, Charlene, at the heart of it all you really are a good
person."

"Don't do this, sweetie, not again, not tonight."

"I really just can't stand it anymore. You have to have control
no matter what we do, Charlene."

"Marge, I mean it, don't start this control shit."

"Look at your house."

"My house?"

"Oh, please, stop the innocent routine. Every inch of that place
of yours reeks of control."

"Okay, everything in my house is under my thumb. Shoot me,
I'm well-organized, I clean up right after I mess up."

"Let me just put it this way. I didn't want to come on this trip in
the first place. I wanted a simple two-day vacation in a motel room
near water—any kind of water. But no, General Charlene had to
orchestrate this brilliant maneuver."

"Christ, Marge, can this junk, will you?"

"Sure, so you can have your pleasant desert weekend."

"Pleasant? You call driving back and forth on the Twentynine
Palms Highway pleasant? It's dark; you know I can't stand to drive
in the dark."

"Did you bring the tent?"

"Why?"

"I'm going to sleep in the tent; it will be better that way."

"*What!* Where, where are you going to sleep in the tent, Marge?
You want to go back to the McDonald's parking lot? Or should I
stop right here and you can pitch it on the shoulder."

"Anywhere's preferable to being cooped up in here."

"You know you can't smoke your guts out in a tent, it will blow up on you."

Marge shut up. I drove. The full moon lit up the Mojave, making it a giant diorama, a flawless mirror of its own surface. We were two forgotten astronauts flunking our psychological compatibility test in the face of minor adversity. I laughed at this thought and Marge snapped off her seatbelt and went to the back of the van.

I kept driving until I saw the sign and pulled off onto the side road leading us back to the Black Rock campground. I decided that we were going to stay in the supercivilized National Park system where bandits hadn't a chance and where no doubt Marge would once again return the ring I gave her and tell me she expected me to return the St. Joan reverse painting on glass that she'd lent me. I could see us both drinking hot chocolate, sitting in our lawn chairs, facing in opposite directions but near enough to maximize the warmth of the campfire.

Against
All
Enemies

CODY YEAGER

Raise your right hand. Swear to defend the Constitution of the United States against all enemies, foreign and domestic. Swear this. Believe it. Spend the next nine years of your life fighting to believe this.

Tell your parents what you have done. Their silence on the telephone says it all. How could you?

Tell your best friend what you have done. His shout deafens you. Weren't you listening?

Tell the woman you love what you have done. Her tears stun you. Weren't you watching?

But you do it. You do it anyway. There is no turning back. Your family's silence increases, though they try to hide it. Your friend's protests grow fainter, though his voice grows louder. The tears of the woman you love suddenly go dry, but they are still there. Though you never see them again, you know they are still there.

Practice push-ups until you can do forty in two minutes. Start running with your dog every morning before breakfast. Start walking in step. Try thinking in step. You are not good at this. Keep trying.

The day before you leave, get a military physical. This will be the most humiliating experience of your life. You could not realize that in advance. Get lots of inoculations with air gun injections, no needles. Waddle like a duck naked in front of two men in lab coats. Do this so they can judge your coordination. Important for a soldier. Tell yourself this. Step on a scale. Almost two pounds light. Same men shout at you. Eat the candy bars they give you. Hate Nestlé. Eat three doughnuts. Eat a peanut butter sandwich. In a little while, get back on the scale. They take your measurements. When they step out of the room, throw up in a trash can. Do this quietly, glancing around you, nervous as a caged mink.

You are learning.

Fail the eye test miserably. More men shout at you, men with gold trim on their uniforms. Be impressed by this. Feel patriotic. Feel guilty. Fail the test again. Now they are really angry; they thought you'd be smart enough to memorize the answers from the first time. You didn't realize you had been expected to cheat. The third time, you pass.

When a nurse shouts at you to take your clothes off and get up on a steel table, you tell yourself you've had these physicals before. Tell yourself this, over and over. The major in the white coat has cold hands. He doesn't warm his instruments under hot water. He doesn't have to. When you jump, he snaps at you to lie still. But you can't lie still; you are suddenly in too much pain to lie still. He asks how you can possibly be a virgin at your age. You can't even wonder where he got that idea; you are too close to fainting from a stabbing pain. In a disgusted rage, the major shouts at the nurse. He hates it when they bleed; he can't see what he's doing.

Feel nauseated again as you realize he means you. Feel ashamed.

The major informs you that you'll probably never have a normal sex life because you're so tense. He has seen a lot of them like that. Feel sicker. When he finally tells you to *get up, move like you got a purpose in life,* you slide off the table through your own blood. *Don't forget your paperwork, Private.* You passed.

On the bus, you stop bleeding and begin to notice the people around you. You wonder how much you will learn from each other. Some of them don't speak English; some of them don't want to. One of them threatens to cut the fingers off your left hand if you look the wrong way. This doesn't scare you. It's the ones who don't talk who scare you. Pile off the bus. Men shout at you to get your duffel bags. All the bags look alike. You tied a bandanna to yours so you could find it quickly. This pleases the men. They designate you platoon leader.

Get uniforms. Look good in dress greens, Class As. They take them away. You won't see them again until graduation. Put on sweats. Everyone runs one mile. Everyone hates it. Except the one who was a track star from Mississippi. Jones. Everyone hates Jones. Learn to sing together while you run. This makes it better. *I wanna be an airborne ranger, live a life of sex and danger, I wanna go to Vietnam, I wanna kill some Viet Cong.* Don't realize that you couldn't be an airborne ranger even if you wanted to. Feel like part of something bigger than yourself. You are learning.

Get fitted for a gas mask. The men tell you this is really important. They tell you gravely that it will save your life; wear it like your boyfriend's kiss. While you are figuring that one out, get kicked into a hazy room full of shouting drill sergeants. Do some push-ups. Do thirty-five push-ups. Do some sit-ups. Suddenly, your mask is pulled off from behind. You start to choke. Recite the Pledge of Allegiance. Gasp for air. Your lungs are on fire. Before you get to *one nation under God,* they drag you outside. Everything is a blur. But you passed.

Polish boots in the evening after taps. Your buddy shows you how to heat up the can with a lighter so the polish goes on smooth. This is the time of day when stories are told, haircuts are given, stray threads are burned off uniforms, buttons sewn on. The stories fascinate you. Rodriguez who joined up to get out of Puerto Rico; Rossano who joined up to escape a coke habit. And there was Gallagher who joined up to get out of the house and Berger who joined up to get her brothers off her.

And there is you. You who didn't join up to get away from anything at all. You, who felt painfully removed from the blue-collar steelworker you once were, who could never get enough, feel enough from any one person or experience. You, the academic, strolling across campus one day when a recruiter with a slow Southern drawl and a fast line spotted you and said there was something you should do for your country. Basic training, then, just one weekend a month. Twenty years later, you'll get a pension. And you said yes, you would, yes.

Learn little tricks those first couple of months. Like: Sleep on top of your bunk so you don't have to waste time in the morning making it up. Get up at four A.M. Like it. Have exactly two minutes in the latrine; don't call it a bathroom. After a two-mile run, have exactly three minutes for a shower with forty buddies. Forget to be shy. Rush through morning chow; don't call it breakfast. Buddies who are too thin get plenty of hamburger gravy along with their eggs. They are watched. Buddies who are too fat get no gravy and only one egg. Nobody gets coffee. After chow, learn to march in endless straight lines. *Your left, your right, now pick up the step, your left, your right, your left. Get in step, Private, do you fuck like you walk?* Wonder what that means.

March to grenade ranges. Put on a flak jacket. Get in a cement foxhole with your buddy. You are both scared. Your turn first; hold the fragmentation grenade to your chest, pull both pins. Extend one arm in front of you, draw back the other one and throw. You have three to five seconds after pulling the pin to complete this task. Afterward, you shake. Your buddy draws back one arm, but forgets to extend one for balance. The grenade falls. You're not sure how many seconds go by as you throw it out of the foxhole and throw yourself on your buddy all in one movement. Both of you shake all over. Learn some more.

Take a rifle apart and put it back together in one minute. Don't wonder how that will help your civilian teaching career. Know it doesn't matter. All that matters is the moment you're living. March to rifle ranges. Stay in step. Discover that if you hit all forty targets you will get an afternoon pass. Make up your mind to hit all forty without a miss. A couple of the three-hundred-meter targets are tough, but the rest are easy. You have made up your mind. When the last Soviet silhouette has fallen, your buddies cheer. You use your afternoon pass to go to the post library, where you sleep the afternoon away, inhaling the comforting smell of the books no one ever checks out.

Feel that you are part of something beyond yourself, beyond the scope of all that you have known. This excites you. The Expert Marksman medal they give you pleases the drill sergeants. You are pleased too until you stop to think how real the faces on the Soviet targets were, how easily your bullets took them out. Put the medal in the bottom of your locker. It will be a long time before you look at it again.

Move on to attack drills. Lots of things to remember. Three kinds of attack: nuclear, biological and chemical. *NBC.* The men keep telling you that the most important thing after one of these attacks is *Charlie Mike*—Continue the Mission. When you see the blast caused by the Soviet threat, put your rifle between your knees and fall on it. This will protect it. After the fallout settles, jump up, regroup and *Charlie Mike.* You will have plenty of decontamination kits and plenty of packaged nuclear-proof chow. The chow comes in green and brown pouches with silver lining. Some of them have little bottles of Tabasco in them; some have Chiclets. Everybody fights over the brownies. The men say there is nothing too good for the American soldier. You have plenty of ammo too, so you can continue the mission. Don't stop to wonder what the mission could be after a nuclear, biological or chemical attack. Yours is not to question why.

Home again after basic training, despite your excellent, no-expenses-spared training, you do question why. Realize that this is dangerous to your military career. Tell yourself you are a career Reservist. Tell yourself this over and over. Swear this. Try to believe it.

You are grading essays in your study that October evening when the phone rings. *Report.* Grin to yourself, thinking, *Just another drill,* as you kiss someone you love and pat your dog on the head. Three weeks later you return. But it is not you; it is someone thinner and tanner who won't sleep in a dark room, who keeps reaching in her sleep to see if the next banana clip is loaded. Your no-expenses-spared military education has paid off; you have defended the Constitution of the United States. Bang, bang, ketchup color.

You don't know, will never know, if your Expert Marksman badge was deserved. But you will know what fear is; you saw it in the eyes of women who just wanted to feed their children, in the eyes of men you interrogated who just wanted work. And you saw it in yourself; you felt it when someone shouted, *Cover!* as you stepped off an airplane onto a beautiful island, British but not Britain.

When the recruiter stopped you that sunny day, he didn't tell you any of this. Maybe he didn't know. He didn't tell you that being part of something bigger than yourself might cost you part of yourself. Didn't say anything about being afraid of the dark, of not looking in the mirror because you don't recognize the person looking back at you. Didn't warn you that no one would understand. No one.

Nine years later, stand in the middle of a university classroom wondering if you have anything to teach anyone. Your students teach you so much. But still, no one experience is enough. Realize it will never be. When reenlistment time comes around again, raise your right hand. Higher this time. You are learning.

LISA ASAGI

1. CHAOS.

Tonight they lost track of the Mars satellite. It completely disappeared from the screen and no one knows what it's doing. Something just happened. A slight malfunction and now it's on its own, closely slow dancing with the red planet. Gazing intently, unaware of its newly freed status.

Scientists are disturbed. Its body will reenter the atmosphere at some point; they calculate and obsess about this loss of logic. A randomness possesses them and promotes sleeplessness. They dream of its body, hum slow, wordless songs, and draw maps of islands in the margins of textbooks.

Go live and everything comes to find you. Like a small car in a dream.

Once, there was this woman. Once, she was the world and I slept with my face in her nape. Sometimes she'd reach over, rest her hand near the hollow of my neck and count for the room how often my heart moved. Maybe one day this will all find her in the middle of a story, sheets of words around her. A way to keep her warm, having stood so long in my memory.

Perhaps a well-thought-out tale about love, passion, the human condition, etc. But this isn't possible at the moment. I can't stop thinking about her. Can't stop interfering with the nature of motion, have it grow out of me enough to encircle, gradually expand into one big picture. Paintings, photographs—although not excused from the concept of time—sometimes get away from gravity. Unlike a story.

The earliest remembering that she ever shared with me was to tell of her first airplane ride. When she was seven. To Maui. Said that she has never been able to fly in her dreams since, but instead can pilot airplanes in them. So far, of sixteen, only three have crashed. No one ever dies. One, three years ago, actually stopped in midair. "What did you do?" I asked. She stood up and walked to the back, climbed out and realized the plane was floating in water. Then she woke up.

In August I walked through a Paul Klee exhibit and hated everything until I reached one notebook paper–sized sketch. It was pencil, watercolor, barren, insectlike except for one thing. Looked like the moon, it was a musical note called a fermata—an extended pause.

This is not about how I keep seeing things about her. Even if it were, no one would know. My body uses my mind and believes it is still falling and so it stutters. Says nothing at all and then says too much. At this moment, I am working for a documentary filmmaker. For lunch we talk about rendering. *Rendering* is not an honest word. It feels responsible for considering all seemingly unrelated ideas so much so that sometimes it prolongs, searches for connections in contradictions in order to create a place for a feeling that it believes exists.

Look. Looking is standing at a bus stop or the desire to fall in a wide open space for an indeterminate length of time. But *once* implies a decision of a singular beginning.

2. THE SPIRAL.

I first saw *Vertigo* two years ago, during a weeklong Hitchcock festival on cable. Every so often it is natural to come across a passage in a book or a scene in a film that firmly grasps an evasive part of your mind. Maybe it is near to the part that controls the body's blinking reflex. The part that understands the emotion of psychological thrillers. How memory will replay it over again for the mind. Sometimes you watch.

I watch and when the sound fades away, images start melting and everybody forgets their lines. When this happens, I rewind and play and rewind and play, try to remember what the words were from the look in the eyes and shape of mouth. When I do this, it keeps changing and I can never keep up until I forget. Until nothing makes sense anymore, except that I am making them repeat everything they did. Like bubbles climbing the walls of a shaken bottle. Like an animal trying to understand that the world is actually outside of the cage.

> I am trapped in jimmy stewart, on the twelfth day of filming, dropping the glass for the second time and trying not to scream when kim novak looks at me.

> I am trapped in the twelfth day of filming, trying not to fall for kim for the second time. Jimmy stewart drops the glass and stares at me.

> Kim dropped the twelfth day of filming. Jimmy stewart stares at me. I am trying not to fall for the glass.

> For the second time, I am trapped in jimmy stewart on the twelfth day of filming, dropping the glass and trying not to fall when kim stares at me.

3. GRASPING.

Maybe I fell. Maybe I stumbled on the way she placed her hand upon the last inch left in the circumference of a perfectly round table.

They say the cure for fear is desire. That the only way to conquer fear is to master it, replace it with something just as strong. Just as accurate and ambiguous, in potency. Immediate, like an angle of a sound tearing through a large city, untranslated.

> Garnet is said to be the protector of all born in the month of january. She is the dark sister to the fire of ruby, and she is the wine of diamonds. Once, garnets were used as sling darts. Because of this dark shade of red, upon entering the human body, they were indistinguishable from flesh or blood. Rescue was based on a pinching search for hardness.

When I was nine, I got sent to a speech therapist because of a certain lisp. We sat in a quiet room, my therapist and I, deep in the school library. She gave me cherry LifeSavers. The object of the exercise was to speak about she who sells seashells by the seashore, while my tongue held a LifeSaver up against the roof of my mouth.

They say that the Mars satellite is so far that the planet on which I lie will not see her body again in the next hundred years, so I walk for as long as I can every night before going home and sometimes imagine that I am being watched.

4. THE UNDOING.

In order to deconstruct, there needs to be an underlying longing for another structure. So I am walking home and studying the hues. The grass is not just green, those leaves are also not just green. This is not my apartment because when I open the door, the walls look at me suspiciously. Nothing is the same. It is not three-thirty. This is a glass of water, but when it falls in me it becomes different. I lie and face the ceiling. This is not only my body anymore.

An excerpt from the essay "Poetry, Madness, and the Inner Ear"*:

> We are now inside the cochlea, an exquisite miniature spiral curled in upon itself, no bigger than the tip of the little

*By Douglas Thorpe, *Parabola*, vol. XVII:2, Labyrinth.

finger. Here pressure from the stirrup creates a wavelike ripple in the thin basilar membrane. Alongside of this membrane, still within the spiraling cochlea, lies the organ of Corti. Thousands of tiny hair cells convert these hydraulic pressure waves to electromagnetic impulses, which are conducted to the brain by the 30,000 or so auditory nerve fibers. But these impulses are no longer sounds: they are, as one source says, "symbols of sounds."

Some nights, she'd ask me to read to her. Open a book and read to me, she said. I read, and after each paragraph, would glance quietly at her face. Until she was asleep. Until her mouth had that softness and her head lilted so definitely that I could never reach the lamp.

Some nights, some days, I'd do nothing but watch. Maybe I said a hundred things, but I don't remember. All I know is what she said, the angles of her face, textures, glistenings, the manner of her breath.

5. ENCHANTMENT.

The placement of sound is as direct as the focus of an image. What the eye sees is influenced by what light will allow. What the ear perceives is tone in vibration, sound starts as a disturbance of the air. The brain coordinates data from your eyes and ears, from muscles in your body and the sensory nerves in your skin to assess your exact position.

It is two o'clock and I am a hazard to her agreements. In turn, she is an enchanting. A condensation across the edge of a very steep cliff.

6. EMERSION.

The earth is almost seventy-five percent water. Like the human body, so much blood. And because there is so much gravity in liquid, the moon pulls, stretches biological bodies too far outside of themselves. They say that the moon orbits the earth and her volume influences the motion of the earth's element. But the moon was not placed there for the earth. The moon just happens to be much too close.

Once, there was a woman. Once, every day, I would leave a peach in her mailbox and one night we were at a party standing on a pier. Always somewhere now, she is breathing that way, leaning, tilting, an arm across a pillow.

LISA JONES

At the end of May I pointed my car west and went screaming over the Rockies, across the dry floor of an ancient Utah sea, through Las Vegas and the Mojave, to stand here in a gray wool gabardine business suit and sell cars under the bright Los Angeles sun.

I came to L.A. to continue an affair with a woman named Marta, the first woman I'd ever made love to. That was back in Denver— she was on a business trip, visiting from L.A. We met in a bar and spent the night in her hotel room. "You should move to L.A.," she'd said. I had just graduated from the University of Colorado and I had no goals, no plans. A couple of days and a thousand road miles later, I knocked on Marta's door and met her angry lesbian lover, Joy.

The three of us went to dinner together that night. Joy didn't know about the affair—but maybe she had an intuition.

"L.A.'s a hard place to live, Suzanne," Joy said. She swigged her beer and smirked. "This isn't a place for losers."

"I'm not a loser, if that's what you're saying."

I had no idea what I wanted to do with my life, but at that moment I knew that I wanted to do it in L.A.

The only thing I knew about this city was *cars*. There were lots of cars everywhere. I found work as a car salesperson—although my sales manager calls me a car sales*man*. I'm the only woman on the lot and, apparently, it would be too taxing for him to add a whole extra syllable to the job title just for my benefit.

Some people say that personal identity and choice of career

are inextricably linked. You are what you do. I stood among the legions of cars, looking at myself in the windows and windshields, my reflection distorted, amorphous—captioned portraits, "No Money Down," "Low Mileage," "Fully Loaded," "Bargain Price." The new me.

"Incoming Volvo. He's mine," I shouted, calling my first "up" of the day. An up is what we call a customer.

I tried to remember all the coaching that Squatty, my sales manager, had given me. Smiling, I extended my hand. Squatty insists: first thing, always shake hands with the customer. "Once you touch 'em, you own 'em," he says.

"Hi there. Welcome to Southland Auto Acres. My name's Suzanne."

He squeezed my hand limply as if I were too delicate to warrant an actual handshake. He flicked his mustache with the tip of his tongue. *Leering at me.* "I'm just shopping," he said.

As Squatty says, there's one thing to remember about customers: "They want to buy, even if they say they don't. It's your job to sell 'em."

"What can I show you?" I asked. "Cars? Vans? Trucks?"

"My wife and I are thinking about getting a FamleeVan."

"You've come to the right place...." Squatty Principle Three: Always refer to a customer by his or her first name. Do it a lot. "I'm sorry, I didn't catch your name."

"Jim."

"Jim! We have over two dozen FamleeVans in the back lot, Jim. Just delivered yesterday, Jim."

For spice, some salesmen use overfamiliar permutations: Jimmy, Jimbo, Jimster, Jim-My-Man. And you're supposed to say something like: "Jim. That's a great name. My dad's name is Jim. Heck, my boyfriend's name is Jim, too. When I have a kid, I'm going to name him Jim. I even go to a gym. That's how crazy I am about your name. I like you, Jim. And because I like you, I'm going to give you a *great* deal."

We always tell our ups that the car they want is in the back lot, a quarter-mile walk from the showroom. During the walk I'm supposed to "qualify" my up—that is, find out if he's a deadbeat. We walked between two rows of cars, a gauntlet of glass and chrome. Sunlight bounced off a bumper and into my face. My eyes watered.

Jim was an accountant from Manhattan Beach. "I'm surprised that you're a woman," he said.

"Really. Would it be less surprising if I was a man in drag?"

"I mean, such an *attractive* woman, working *here*," he added, as if I had taken his comment the wrong way. As if I need him to reassure me that he finds me physically acceptable. As if I derive all of my self-worth from the way I wear my hair.

I have problems with guys like this, and they seem to gravitate toward me—I'm not sure what it is about them that bothers me. They look at me, a tall, athletic young woman with lots of blonde hair, and instantly I'm not *me* anymore. I'm someone who needs to be harassed or protected or fucked or ignored. Or condescended to.

Once I upped a guy who insisted that he recognized me from a Swedish porn film. I spent two hours with him, demoed a few trucks, and finally he announced, "I'd like to talk to a *salesman* now. I'm ready to buy."

I don't get it. I don't understand why people see me the way they do, and behave toward me the way they do. I'd like to figure it out.

Anyway, with a lot of excruciating smarminess on my part, I landed Jim on a fully-loaded FamleeVan Grande XL. I said things like, "Jim, you're a successful professional—the kind of guy who'll settle for nothing less than the best...." pumping him. He drove the FamleeVan around the block a couple of times and wanted to take it on the freeway.

All demos are risky, but freeway demos are the most dangerous. There's always a chance you'll get taken for a ride. That means your up kills and/or rapes you and/or dumps you by the side of the road and steals the car. But if I refused to go on demos with potentially frightening customers, I wouldn't make many sales.

Joy was right—L.A. isn't a place for losers, it's *the* place.

But the drive went well. When we got back to the lot I put Jim in the box. I gave him a cup of coffee from the vending machine. He sipped and stared at the DynoCoat Truckbed Protection poster on the wall. It featured three women clad in plastic wrap: Babes in Truckland, it read.

I went to the desk to run Jim's credit. Squatty smacked his mouth as if he was tasting something peculiar, puckering and unpuckering his lips like a mud sucking carp. He raised his eyebrows when he pulled the stock number.

"This is a biggie, Suzanne," he said. "Think you can handle it?" Squatty knew that price negotiation was my weakest suit. I was good at doing demos and getting customers to like me, but when it came down to price, I had no edge. I felt silly and petty dickering about money.

"No problem, Squatty." I tried to convince myself as well as him. "This guy adores me. If he doesn't sign today, he'll be back. He has to talk to his wife."

"Be-back is weaksuck greenpea talk. I'll write the deal."

"But he's mine. I can do it. I need a whole deal."

"Half a deal is better than none. Get back on the line."

I hesitated. Squatty was right. I'd probably blow it. Half a deal *is* better than no deal. But a whole deal would mean a bigger commission....

"Go!"

I slouched out of the showroom, out to breathe the hot, fetid streets, feeling road grime on my teeth from smiling so hard, waiting for another up. My hosiery felt sticky. I squinted as the sun carved deep lines into my face. We're not allowed to wear sunglasses. Squatty says that sunglasses make us seem insincere. "Customers want sincerity," he says. "Even if you gotta fake it. Fake it 'til ya make it, that's what I say. Act like a good salesman and boom! you'll be a good salesman."

You go to the Department of Motor Vehicles; you pay fifty bucks; they take mug shots, fingerprints, chromosome samples; you get your sales license and boom! you're a buttwipe.

Car salesmen are desperate people; we'll do whatever it takes to get a deal. From intimidation to fabrication to begging, anything goes. Except skating — that's when you steal someone else's deal and refuse to split the commission money. If you skate, as Squatty says, "You might as well be a shark gushin' your own blood, cuz all your buddies will eat you alive."

After a few minutes of watching the traffic roar past me, I turned around to face the showroom. Reynolds stormed through the glass double doors and stood at the end of the outdoor display platform.

"Heyya, Suzanne."

He hopped down and walked toward me. Heat rose off the asphalt in watery, wavy sheets. The breeze from the boulevard traffic animated a few stray tufts of Reynolds's red hair, making it look as if his head was on fire. The reddish brown stubble on his chin made him look less boyish than usual.

"Gil sold another one, didja see that?" he said, disgusted. "Some rich laydown paid full pop. How can such a jerk close so many deals? Really fries my ass, I can tell you that." Reynolds ran his palms over his rumpled suit—it needed to be cleaned and pressed.

According to Squatty, Gil is the best salesman on the lot. He knows how to pack his deals and stroke his ups. He's never made less than five hundred bucks on a sale—*so they say*. Naturally, Reynolds and I hate Gil's guts. He's blond, clean-cut, marinated in cologne.

"Which one did he sell?" I asked.

"The brown Skyward 600 with all the bells and whistles. Squatty'll spiff him double cash for unloading that ugly heap of crap. That car's been here longer than I have. Look at that. Breaks my goddamn heart," Reynolds said, wrinkling his freckled nose.

We watched as an elderly couple shuffled out of the showroom to admire their new Skyward. The old man pumped Gil's hand for five minutes saying, "Fine young fella." The old man broke away from Gil and helped his wife into the car. She smiled and waved. The man got in the car, too, and smiled and waved. The car crept out of the lot and inched down the street. Reynolds and I smiled and waved as they drove past us.

"Just like Ron and Nancy fuckin' Reagan!" Gil shouted as he jogged toward us. "Hey, hey, I'm hot. What do you say, Suzanne? Wanna have dinner with a winner tonight?" He straightened his tie. His milky teeth glistened. His hair was bulletproof.

"No thanks, Gil." At first when Gil would ask me out it was kind of flattering, despite my being a lesbian. But now it was annoying.

"Hey, come on. After that deal, I can afford you. Squatty spiffed me double cash. I'll take you someplace nice. Wine and . . ."

"For crissake, you moron!" Reynolds howled. "She said no. Every day you ask her and every day she says no. Take a clue, Gil, wouldja, pal? This is getting embarrassing."

Reynolds sometimes assumed the role of my protective older brother. Again, flattering at first, annoying now.

Gil's eyes narrowed. "The sale starts when the customer says *no*. If you were a decent salesman, you'd know that, Reynolds."

"If you were a decent human being, you'd know that she doesn't buy the shit you're shoveling," Reynolds said. "You can't make people do things they don't want to do, Gil."

"Oh yeah, Reynolds? Oh yeah? Well let me tell you. The only difference between rape and seduction is technique. Obviously, that's an area in which you're lacking."

"Fuck you, Gil," I said, shoving him.

"I've had better offers, Suzanne." He mischievously grabbed my ass.

"Aw, don't you worry about ol' Gil, Suzanne." Reynolds gave Gil a sharp jab in the arm. "He has the smallest cock I ever saw in my life. The size of a Vienna sausage. A little cocktail wiener. You could snip it off with a pair of manicure scissors."

Gil and Reynolds stood like two rabid dogs, muzzle to muzzle.

I half laughed, amazed and insulted by both of them.

We heard a volley of shouts. Jim, my up, stormed out of the showroom. Squatty hounded him.

"No!" Jim yelled.

"Don't be a fool, Jimmy pal," Squatty persisted. "You'll never find a better deal."

"How many times do I have to say it? No!"

"C'mon, Jimbo buddyboo. What'll it take to sell you this car today? I can knock off another hundred, but that's as low as I can go, rock bottom. I'll even throw in free floor mats," Squatty wheedled, scuttling alongside Jim like a barnacled crab.

Jim got in his Volvo and peeled away from the lot.

Unbelievable. *Squatty* had choked on the numbers. I felt a pang of pity. He is getting older, after all. Then I remembered how he'd dismissed me from the deal in the first place. "There goes my rent, Squatty," I said. "Thanks a lot."

"If you'd done your job, we would've had a deal," Squatty snarled. "We had flat nothin'. And why? Cuz you're a weaksuck greenpea who doesn't know how to build value. You can't sell worth shit."

"That guy was ready to lay down, Squatty," Reynolds leapt to my defense.

"Squatty, the guy was an accountant," I said. "You can't pack the numbers and expect a guy like that to lay down. You blew him out of the box, not me."

"If it were up to you," Squatty said, "you'd *give* the damn things away." He lumbered back to the showroom.

"She's *already* giving it away—" Gil shouted. "To Reynolds!"

Before I could think of a response, Gil said, "Incoming Mustang. He's mine." He scrambled toward the curb.

Reynolds shouted, "Incoming family. Walking. Mine." He positioned himself on the display platform and greeted a young couple and their two kids.

In a heartbeat I had lost a deal, two ups, and some dignity. I clenched my fists, squeezing all my frustration into firm, manageable handfuls, like icy snowballs. *Losers!* A city *full* of losers.

Does that make me a loser, too?

I watched Reynolds for a while. He was developing a rapport with his up—the family—addressing some of his patter to the little kids who were pretending to drive one of the cars. I hoped he would write a deal on this up. Nestor, the lot boy who preps the cars, told me that Reynolds sleeps in one of the custom vans in the back lot. He keeps all his clothes in the backseat of his car.

Reynolds was nice to me right from the start. During my first week, other salesmen would say, "Hey, greenpea. Check out a few stock numbers for me, willya?" or "Greenpea, go find out about the new trucks." I was happy to oblige, rushing all over the lot. I thought I was being helpful until Reynolds pulled me aside and said, "Kid, don't let them throw you under the bus like that." Using a ruse to keep other salespeople off the line—reducing competition for ups—is known as "throwing them under the bus."

After an hour or so, Reynolds was still doing well with his up. He'd demoed two FamleeVans so far. He could make a killing on this deal. Other than that action, the lot was dead. Gil's up had walked before he'd even demoed a car. I leaned against a blisteringly shiny sedan and yawned. Squatty must've seen this. He swaggered toward me. When traffic is slow he comes out on the line to harangue us.

"You wanna be a good salesman, Suzanne? You gotta watch Gil. He's hungry. He's gotta big ol' tapeworm in his belly."

"I'm sure he has," I said.

"You don't like Gil, do you? A little professional jealousy, that's what I say. But you could be just like him."

I nodded. But Squatty, my dream is to be like *you* and have flecks of tobacco stuck in the foamy corners of my mouth.

He put his pungent lips to my ear and whispered, "You can wait for your ship to come in or you can swim out to it. We're sharks,

Suzanne. Gotta keep swimming or we drown." He looked at me hard, watching this ominous news sink in.

I gave him a serious looking frown as if I had just gained deep insight. He seemed satisfied.

We both turned to see Gil walking toward us. "Squatty, phone call. Sounds important."

Squatty hurried away. Gil had a nasty smirk on his face.

"What's so funny?" I asked.

"You'll see," Gil said. "Bad news for Reynolds."

I ignored him.

"Looks like Reynolds has a sure deal." Gil whistled tunelessly for a few moments. "Too bad. Toooo bad..."

"Okay, Gil. What?" I hated to capitulate—but I wanted to know.

"Reynolds is going to put his up in the box, write a gravy deal, and not make a dime for himself. That jerkoff let his sales license expire last week. You can't sell a car without a license. If he writes a deal, it'll be a house deal. His name won't be on it. He won't make a dime."

"Why didn't someone tell him this last week?" I demanded.

"Reynolds is a big boy. He oughta know when his license needs to be renewed."

I walked to the back lot and Gil followed. I caught Reynolds's attention and explained the situation in an urgent whisper.

"No way," Reynolds hissed. "I renewed it last year."

"You have to renew it every year, jerkoff," Gil said. "But I'm willing to close your deal for you while you go to the DMV."

"Forget it, Gil. I need a whole deal. Besides, I don't trust you."

"C'mon, Reynolds. Half a deal is better than no deal. I can get *gravy*. I want this deal as much as you do," Gil said.

Of course I was suspicious. But Gil was hungry; he might get twice as much as Reynolds could. That way, half a deal would be just as good as a whole one.

That's probably what Reynolds was thinking when he turned and glanced at his up. The entire family was beaming, sitting in the van as if they already owned it. "Okay," Reynolds conceded. "But no funny stuff."

"Agreed."

Reynolds was gone just long enough for Gil to push the deal through the desk and out the door. Reynolds returned in time to smile and wave as the family sped away from the dealership in their new van.

"He threw me under the bus!" Reynolds yelled. "I didn't have to renew it."

Bastard. "Did he skate you?" I asked.

"Nah, he'll have to split the money. Just makes me look stupid. No harm done."

"Congratulations, Reynolds," Squatty said as Reynolds and I stormed through the big glass doors of the showroom. "You got half a deal."

"Damn funny, Gil...got half my deal...slithering asswipe," Reynolds growled.

"It was fun, pal, but it wasn't worth it," Gil said. "Don't spend your twenty-five bucks all in one place."

Gil had lowballed the customer and had written a pathetic deal just to screw Reynolds.

"Gil must be losing his touch," Squatty said.

Gil shrugged. "I'll make up the difference on my next deal." He grinned, waiting for something other than shock to register on Reynolds's face.

"Twenty-five dollars?" Reynolds said. "Twenty-five crummy bucks?"

"Suzanne, babe," Gil gave me a wink. "Thanks for all your help."

Reynolds's eyes widened, hurt and sad, as if I'd stabbed him in the heart. He shuffled outside and sat on the edge of the display platform, his head in his hands.

What can you do? What can you say? "Buck up, Reynolds. Take it like a capitalist. Things will turn around." Give him a rosy-cheeked, all-American pep talk? Mickey Rooney and Judy Garland never worked on a car lot.

Bitey
Boy

MARTHA TORMEY

My mother's fleshy underarm is dripping warm blood onto my new Levi's. She's in more shock than pain and my lack of compassion is no doubt adding to this shock. "He's a biter, Mom," I say. "Do you get it, huh, do you finally get it?" I want to slap her. I want to shove my mother into the stove. I want to scream. Instead, I order her to "stay there," and head for the bathroom to search for some gauze. She whimpers something and shrinks in her chair.

For years my brother and I had come home with similar wounds. "Bitey Boy did it," we'd shriek, tearing through the screen door, checking for (always hoping for) blood. But Bitey Boy didn't always draw blood; frequently, the mark he'd leave wouldn't last the twenty or thirty seconds it took us to race the distance from the attack into the refuge of our home. Matthew Charles Roland was, and apparently still is, Bitey Boy. He has been O.O.C. (out of control), as my older brother Jerome refers to him, for at least the ten years he and his parents, Dr.'s Beatrice and Martin Roland, have been our neighbors. I was about nine the summer they moved in, Jerome was eleven—Dad was out of town and Mom was always hot. Matthew Charles was only seven but he was big, and he had a scooter, and he had a bike. Jerome was the first to be bitten that summer, and though I can remember the exact day that it happened because I got three cavities drilled that afternoon, I can't remember the actual bite occurring, although Jerome swears I was standing right there and even took a swipe at Matthew Charles's head before he lunged his mouth toward me and Jerome and I raced each other home.

Over the years my brother and I have had dozens, maybe even hundreds of friends in our yard—birthday parties and barbecues—and it just became an accepted thing between us all: "Stay away from Bitey Boy. Keep your limbs to yourself when Bitey Boy is out." I came up with his title at the end of that first summer. We had been calling him the usual until then—mental, sicko, retard. But Bitey Boy stuck like a perfect nickname does. We made up stories about the many possible demises of Bitey Boy, burning sun through magnifying glass being my favorite.

My friend Stevie, who lived a couple of blocks over, had some twins on his street named Nickey and Mikey. They had snakes and knives, but they lived way down Stevie's street and didn't come out much. We, on the other hand, had a vicious sicko regularly terrorizing us, right next door. The thing about Bitey Boy that made him so scary is how normal he could be most of the time. Even after we knew, after every kid knew, he could still coax you into having a simple game of Frisbee with him. First you'd say no a million times, and if anybody else was around they'd be saying, "Don't do it, man," but finally you'd think to yourself, "Hey, there's no way he'd try anything with all these kids around," and you'd give in and say, "OK, just a short game," and half an hour later Bitey Boy'd be sinking his teeth into your wrist, his body crushing the air out of your chest so hard you thought you'd never breathe again, the Frisbee somewhere safe under a bush.

I return to the kitchen with a giant Band-Aid, a white one with Mickey and Minnie dancing across it. "What!" my mother cries. "I need a bandage, Jules, a big bandage."

"Mom, it's not even bleeding anymore," I say. "This'll be fine."

"My God, that boy's a lunatic. I've never seen such a look on a child."

"He's eighteen, Mom." I force myself to calm down, breathe, and gently wash my mother's wound. Until five minutes ago I thought she understood what had been going on out there all those years. She'd hug us, touch our tears, and use these Band-

Aids even when there wasn't blood, so what was I to think? I stand
with my back to her now and attempt to sponge the blood off my
jeans. The longer I scrub the more I am astounded by her ig-
norance. "Who did you think was biting us all those times?" I ask,
my voice cracking. "Did you think I was making it up? Did you seriously think Jerome was making it up?"

"Well, I don't know, honey, I don't know. The boy's a nut—he
had a smile on his face, for God's sake. I was checking the mail,
just smelling the dogwood, and all of a sudden Matthew Charles
has got his teeth in my arm. My God, I've got to call your father."
My father lives in Colorado. We live in Maryland. I remind my
mother of this continually and now I can't help adding, "Sure,
Mom, call him. I'm sure he'll fly right out." Behind her back I
mouth, Don't you get it?

"What about a rabies shot, shouldn't I get a shot at least?"

"We never got shots, and we're fine," I say.

My mother turns around to face me and finally I think she lets it
start to sink in as she stares me down. Her gaze travels slowly down
my body and holding it on my forearms she whispers, "Did he
ever leave a scar?" Silently I hold my left arm out for her inspection. I stretch the skin tight across and it appears: a jagged half-
moon, without color, and as she runs her fingers across the width
of it I know what she is feeling, as I have felt it myself countless
times since the afternoon of that last bite. The afternoon I held
him facedown in the April mud so long Jerome and Stevie were
afraid I'd killed him. The afternoon I thought he'd finally stop.
My mother starts to cry and clings to me and although I am further from her than I ever thought I'd be, I also feel my anger
crack, just a bit, and confusion and sadness fill the crack, and we
stay like that for a while, she weeping and stroking my scar, me
staring out the window into our neighbor's yard, urgently willing
something, but not at all sure just what.

An hour later Mom's at the mall and I'm on a mission. From my
place at the kitchen table I watch the clock on the microwave
change numbers and it's just flashed "7" when the phone rings.
I'm about to answer it on the millionth ring when he appears on
his back porch and all at once I realize that this moment has been
eight years in the making. I'm finally ready and the phone contin-

ues to ring as I stalk him across his yard. I wonder if he even knows I'm back. I've been at school for two years and before that his parents took him to Europe, but those years apart do nothing to slow my adrenaline now—rushing like it did when I was twelve. When getting away was more important than getting back. The ringing stops as I hit our screen door. There is a short row of bushes separating the two yards but in several spots they've thinned, trampled by a collie the Rolands owned years ago. I choose my path and silently approach the back of Matthew Charles. He has something in his hands and as I get closer I make out an electric car—one of those ones you control with a remote. The car beeps as it circles the patio. Matthew Charles hears me before he sees me, but my hands are around his neck before he can drop the control box. I squeeze as hard as I can and look past his reddening cheeks as his Camaro rams the leg of the barbecue and stays there, furtively climbing and falling. He drops to his knees at some point, and I don't even consider not following him down, my fingers tiring but still clenched tight. From his knees he rolls onto his side, and I release my grip as his head cracks the pavement. The Camaro has ceased its grinding and beeping and it is truly just as an afterthought that I lean over Matthew Charles and fix his cheek between my teeth. I clench my jaw slowly, and only cease when the taste of his blood has entirely filled my mouth.

It's only when I'm back home and absently wipe the edge of my hand across my lips and feel the warmth that I look at my bloodied palm and wonder what I did with that mouthful of blood. I try to picture it on the pavement, the lawn, on Matthew Charles's shirt or shorts. There is a tiny red spot on the sleeve of my T-shirt. I scrub at it and walk over to the open doorway. I stand there and watch without cowering as my neighbor pulls himself up his back stairs. With one hand clutching his cheek, he uses the other to fumble with the latch on the door and noises I have never heard, noises I wouldn't know were human if I wasn't watching, come from his lips.

I'm showered and changed by the time Mom gets home. She stands at the bottom of the stairs and screams up for me. "Honey, did anyone call for me?"

"No." I am perched on the top step peering down at her. She

has left the front door open and behind her a shower of dust fills the light from the afternoon sun. I remember the ringing phone (was it less than an hour ago?) as my mother shuts the light and goes about her day. Lowering myself to the carpeted step, I hug my bare knees and listen. A kitchen cupboard is opened, a tune is hummed. I run my fingers around my lips and know that this is a taste I will remember.

Self-
Deliverance

ELISE D'HAENE

1. It is important to have food in the stomach. Make it something you like: toast, applesauce, cereal are recommended.

So far, so bad. Every light I approached turned red. I needed to get strawberry ice cream so I went to the Quality Dairy on my way from work but couldn't get a parking spot so I thought, what the hell, I'll go to Kroger's, and only one checker's working so it took me about a half hour. I went to call Ginnie on a pay phone to remind her to pick up some flowers and lost two quarters. I was so worked up when I got home I went to the fridge to drink milk, which usually calms me, and discovered, not with my nostrils but with my taste buds, that it was sour. This about did me in, upset my already knotted-up stomach so much I had to run to the toilet. I had no toilet paper.

With my jeans at my ankles, I wobbled toward the kitchen like an aging football player through a maze of old tires. The paper towel holder wasn't holding paper either, just brown cardboard. My last resort was newspaper. I've got plenty of it, piles of it, sky-scrapers of aging newsprint and magazines line the walls of my apartment. That's how I got my nickname, Alfie. It started at the restaurant. When I'm on break I bury my head in a book, a news-paper, a magazine, any kind of written material left behind by a customer. Victor, the owner, started teasing me. "What's it all about, Alfie?" It just stuck, that name, like gray gum on the bottom of your shoe. So anyway, I grabbed the thick classified section from some Sunday past, and wobbled back to the toilet. I tore a neat slice down the middle of the top page. After I wiped, I had this thought running through my head: '65 Mustang nu blk pnt/V8 $4,800. It's a good thing they don't print words on toilet paper since I'd have to read every square inch before I used it. You know how bugs are at night, how various kinds just swarm together under the porch light? That's how it is with me and words.

I smell like fish and tartar sauce because today is Friday and we had fish and chips on special for lunch and the Lady's Madonna Circle from St. Gerard's came in for their monthly luncheon. Of course Victor gives them to me, all twenty-seven of them, saying I was the only one he could trust to do it right. Which really isn't true. I'm the only one who'll put up with twenty-seven cackling Catholics who leave me a whopping twenty-five cents apiece. What's really annoying is this one woman, Dorothy O'Conner, actually counts the number of filets on everybody's plate to make sure they all get the same amount. I tried to explain that the cook weighs the portions and that some pieces are bigger than others. That didn't go over well and she complained and Victor said give them what they want. So every time they come in, she walks to each table and reads me her list of who's short. Ginnie says I should spit on her food, but I can't, it doesn't make me feel better. I do, however, throw a few of her french fries in the trash. She doesn't count the french fries.

I made lots of mistakes today. Mixed up my orders, forgot to get this guy an ashtray after he asked three times and I thought he was going to punch me. Spilled-milk kind of mistakes, so no use crying, but I did. Every chance I got I ran to the bathroom and just bawled my eyes out. My busboy, Tony, covered for me even though he doesn't get much either when those ladies come in. I think he was worried and said something to Victor because Victor let me go early without having me clean my area or fill up the salt, pepper, and sugar containers. Victor pulled me aside, asked how Teddy was, and I mumbled, you know, the same, and then I walked out fast. Victor is Catholic, and I mean *very* Catholic, and I've heard all his opinions about Dr. Kevorkian and I know he'd go ballistic if he knew what Ginnie and I are up to. The book I got said that we're supposed to act like nothing's unusual so that nobody gets suspicious. I almost blew it today, though, because when Dorothy O'Conner was saying, "Margaret Mary at table two, Kathleen next to her, and Doris, over there, all need one more fish filet, dear," I came real close to pulling a Ginnie and telling Dorothy to go fuck herself and enjoy it for once.

My apartment is a mess, especially my bathroom, which I hate cleaning because when I was eight years old, cleaning the bathroom became my assigned lifetime chore. My brothers got good chores: raking leaves, taking out garbage, mowing the lawn, shoveling snow, and helping my father clean the gutters along the roof. These were good in my mind because they were all outdoors, out of the house, out of mom's reach, or grip (depending on her mood), out of her line of vision. Back then, I gagged at the smell of boy-piss, the sight of splashed brown stuff underneath the toilet seat, the mixture of hair, toenails, dust, and foot powder on the floor. My brothers would stuff washcloths, stiff as cardboard, behind the toilet with gooey and crusty white globs of some alien substance sticking to the crumpled mess. I had to pick them up and put them in the clothes hamper and when I did, I'd put on my mom's yellow plastic gloves and hold those washcloths out as far as I could from my nose.

Ginnie and Teddy can't believe how nondomestic I am. Teddy wouldn't even use my bathroom, except the time he had an accident. Accident, meaning he was driving to the restaurant on his way to work and felt like he was going to have a bowel movement before his brain registered that he'd already had one. This was an early sign of his dementia. He was just down the street and called in a panic. I told him to come right up, I had some sweats he could wear, and boxer shorts. After I hung up the phone I ran for a sponge and scouring powder and scrubbed the tub. Teddy was crying by the time he got to my door and I just led him into the bathroom, rubbing the back of his neck, telling him it was okay, don't worry, get cleaned up, sweetie, you'll feel better. I called Victor and told him Teddy wasn't feeling well, then I called Ginnie and she went in and covered for Teddy. I feel tenderly toward Teddy, like a big sister, even though we're both twenty-seven.

I always wished I had been born years and years before my brothers so I could feel tenderly like that toward them, instead of being afraid of their unbelievably strong arms and legs that used to pin me down like a butterfly on paper. I was terrified that my limbs, like flimsy wings, would just crumple underneath them. There was a brutal hate coursing through their veins, a hate that laughed and drooled and poked and pounded, until they were bored or my mom snapped at them to go outside and play. I was left with handmarks, bruises, and sticky saliva on my face.

Long since my brothers got girlfriends and pinned them down instead of me, I've had this pressure on my chest, this weight in my body, and I'm always expecting to get slammed to the ground. Teddy's the first person I'd ever met that felt as pinned as I do, held down by some unseeable force that leaves us both gasping and struggling and trying to break loose. I wish I was more like Ginnie. She'll wrestle anyone to the ground who tries to get in her way. She's big, almost six feet tall, with strong arms and legs and a mane of dark hair. Sometimes, when wisps of her bangs hang down over her huge dark eyes, it's like she's got two bold exclamation points on her face. That's what Ginnie is to me, a big exclamation point.

At times, Ginnie and I sleep together. It started out that she would just show up at my door at any hour of the night, let herself in, and crawl into bed with me. She'll get real close, wrap her long legs and arms around me tight, and fall asleep. That's when I like to stay awake, feeling all six feet, all 163 pounds of Ginnie, like a sleeping stallion, exhaling and inhaling next to me. It's like nothing I've ever felt before. That weight in my chest dissolves and I can breathe, my wings are loose and I fly, fearless through the night. Since Teddy's been sick, Ginnie and I sleep together all the time. Sometimes, I guess you could say we make love. Ginnie will just bring her face close to mine and we'll start kissing and groping at each other like we're deep-sea diving, and one of us is out of oxygen. It's pretty frantic. We never talk about it, we don't call each other girlfriends, but I think it helps both of us, and I realize now that even Ginnie gets afraid.

She's coming over in an hour to help me pick out an outfit for tonight. I'd better clean out my closet, use those metal things called hangers instead of the floor for my clothes. She'll be disgusted if she gets a look at my wardrobe strewn everywhere like piles of donated clothes after a disaster. The only outfit I clean regularly is my waitressing uniform because Victor pulled me aside sometime last year and talked to me about appearance and pointed to the stain on the back of my dress, that may have once been brown gravy, by then edged in a green growth of some kind. I agreed it was disgusting, but how often do you get a good look at yourself from behind? Then he pointed to my once-white shoes that were splattered with coffee, chocolate milk, soda pop, and bacon grease. Okay, I said, I'm not only a slob, I'm a clumsy slob, a bit disheveled, but my tables are always filled, standing room only when I work the counter, and I tip out at night way ahead of the pack. Ask the busboys; I am exceedingly charitable with them, because without 'em, I'm nothing; they are the spine to my whole waitressing operation.

I get tipped better than Ginnie and even though she doesn't understand why, I do. The women who come in aren't threatened by me, my looks don't arouse envy then hate, so they don't need to scrimp. I'm a plain Jane, like them. The men don't peck and paw and pinch me like they do to Ginnie, so they don't feel bruised, their egos don't wiggle limply between their legs like they do when Ginnie snaps her glare and has them begging for mercy. Teddy made good tips before he had to leave. Even the big, burly truckers tipped him well because they didn't have to spit faggot behind his back. Teddy just handed them faggot on a plate. He was the sideshow freak at the circus. "Fruit juice from the fruit." "Dairy from the fairy." "Straight up, or over easy, big guy?" He'd put himself down, let them laugh "with" him as he swished his hips into the back kitchen, where his smile would drop as quickly as the cigarette butts he dumped into the trash. This was Teddy's way of protecting himself from dissolving into a heap of quivering Jell-O. If some unknown guy came in and even seemed the teeniest bit aggressive, Teddy would ask Ginnie to take him. He's gotten beat up before, more than once. Bruises may fade on the outside, but you can't erase that particular look in the eyes, that look somebody gets when they see that fist coming at 'em. It's in Teddy's eyes all the time now. I guess death must look like a fist.

2. After eating, take two antinausea tablets.

Alf called to remind me about the flowers for tonight. I don't know what we'll do after Teddy dies. I was supposed to be in California by now. That alleged Hollywood agent I met at the airport in Detroit said long-legged dark beauties like me are in demand. I had two responses to his saying this to me: One, I wanted to kick him in the nuts. Did he think I was a fucking asshole born yesterday? Two, this is my only way out. I hate Michigan. I hate Grand Ledge. If I had to stay for the rest of my life, I would look for a ledge, way up high somewhere, and take a grand fucking leap.

Yesterday, I was driving by the high school and the cheerleaders were revving up the football team as they packed on a bus headed for Petoskey. I remembered that moment of horror my senior year when Rich led me under the bleachers and was sticking his tongue down my throat and all I could hear were the cheerleaders screaming, "Eat a cowpie! E-A-T-A-C-O-W-P-I-E! Eat a cowpie!" The stomping students above Rich and me screamed in unison and I just vomited, lime vodka and a hot dog, partway into Rich's mouth which, I'm not sorry to say, was a peak experience. I swore at that moment that I would not live out my days in Grand Ledge, or anywhere near this godforsaken place. Even though I technically live in Lansing, the capital of the state, I can't tolerate the ordinariness of my days. I'm thirty now, not eighteen, and I'm still as stuck as a snowball on a wet mitten. I would have moved three years ago, I swear, with or without Alf and Teddy, but Teddy got sick and everything changed. We're his family. We take care of him. The four hundred dollars I had saved up for my plane ticket is gone. I sometimes feel like vomit is pooling up in my stomach and headed toward my mouth.

After I saw the cheerleaders I stopped at my mother's to pick up a flashlight and a casserole dish to make macaroni and cheese for tonight. She hardly looked at me, didn't ask how Teddy was, and told me to be sure I didn't break or crack her cookware. "Don't let Alf take it home with her." My mother hates Alfie because she's from a "low-rent" family. All that means is we own our piece of shit shoebox and they don't. I sometimes want to give my mother a heart attack and tell her I lick Alf's low-rent pussy every night. It's weird with Alf, but I love her, and I know she loves me. It's weird with my mother, but love doesn't enter the equation. She doesn't mention Teddy because it's widely known in the Grand Ledge area that Teddy Shepard is a homosexual and when my mother says "homosexual" she makes it sound like a kind of yellow pus oozing from a scab.

I ran into Teddy's mother at Kmart about three weeks ago. My shopping cart was filled with cotton swabs, adult diapers, plastic sheets, bottles of juice, and soft foods, all for Teddy. I spotted her in the women's clothing area going through a sale rack of sweaters designed by that famous TV star from "Charlie's Angels." She had a greedy, shit-eating grin on her face as she edged her fat elbow into the woman next to her. I couldn't help myself, I rolled my cart right over to her, nudged her with it, and announced loudly, "Mrs. Shepard, remember me, I'm Ginnie, I'm a friend of your son, Teddy, remember you have a son, a homosexual son who is dying from AIDS! What the hell's wrong with you people!" I just couldn't hold my tongue. First she just glared at me, her jaw dropped along with the sweaters cradled in her arms, and then her eyes were like faucets and water gushed down her cheeks and landed on the sweaters pooled at her feet. I backed up slowly, wanting to apologize, but not wanting to at the same time. She started to say something, but it sounded garbled, like talking under water. My lower lip started to tremble and I noticed that a crowd of people stood stock still, staring at the space between Mrs. Shepard and me, too frightened to make eye contact with either of us. Then I just screamed at them, "What the fuck are you looking at, fucking assholes!" I turned and got out of there fast, leaving my cart behind.

I went to the restaurant and pulled Alf off the floor. Victor gave me the evil eye, but didn't say anything, cuz he knows we're taking care of Teddy. We sat out back and I confessed what happened. Alf just shook her head, saying, "Oh, Ginn, oh, Ginn." She has a way of dipping her voice when she says my name like that, in response to whatever trouble I've gotten myself into. It usually makes me feel like crying, but I just bite the inside of my mouth and fix my eyes on the ground. Then she handed me a copy of the *Hollywood Reporter* to cheer me up. She started subscribing to it for me, underlining auditions and circling casting calls with a bright red marker. When I left and went over to Teddy's apartment there were two grocery bags from Kmart on the stoop. On top were two of those sweaters, with a note from Mrs. Shepard. "For you and Alf. Thank you for taking care of him." I shoved the sweaters behind a bush and walked inside with the bags. Teddy was asleep on the couch, and I looked at his face, a thin version of his mother, and I whispered, "I'm sorry." Which I am, but I'm still disgusted. She added a big tin of peanut brittle to the groceries, it used to be Teddy's favorite, and I wanted to scream again and slam my fist so hard into the folds of flesh around her stomach that she'd lose her fucking breath.

I've got to get out of here.

3. Combine the medications with the right dose of alcohol. This will multiply the toxicity of the drugs by about fifty percent.

I watched a documentary with Alf about that oil spill in Alaska, and thousands of dead birds and fish covered in black were scattered on the beach. And this oil slick was spreading everywhere. That's what it's like, inside my body, creeping real slow, like it's taking you over. Mostly, I stare at the ceiling or the TV cuz I won't look at myself anymore. Sometimes when Alf or Ginn get real close, hooking up a needle to the tube in my chest, or putting medicine in my mouth for thrush, I can see myself, my face, in their eyes. I ask them to stare at me, because it's like you're looking into a shiny, round marble and your cheeks puff out and your whole face is wide and round as if the flesh that has vanished has come back.

It reminds me of these mirrors that lined the walls of the now famous rest stop off the freeway between Lansing and Brighton. It's where I used to go before the police sting operation about four years ago. They set up hidden cameras inside the men's bathroom because it was known to be a gathering place for sex. Then they arrested almost fifty men for lewd conduct and printed their names in the *Lansing State Journal*, or "State Urinal," as Alf calls it. Important businessmen, doctors, politicians, and two priests were listed. I wasn't there that night, even though it'd be no big scandal if my name was in the newspaper under a headline naming local perverts. Alf was so mad that she wrote all week on her customers' checks, "You who are without sin cast the first stone. Alf." We're supposed to write, "Come again," or, "Have a nice day," but Alf's always writing down quotations from the stuff she's reading.

The funniest thing about the rest stop were those mirrors. They puckered out so that everybody was distorted, big and bulgy, like those trick mirrors at circuses. I liked it cuz it's not like you want a good look at who you're with anyway; that's the point, it's ruined if you really see each other face to face. So the mirrors kind of worked, because you couldn't really get a look at yourself, I mean what you really looked like. I used to go on Saturday nights, to pass time when I was horny, or when I was lonely, or when Ginn and Alf were working, and there was nothing to watch on TV.

If I were to stand in front of one of those mirrors now, it would look like I have four heads. I've got three tumors the size of golf balls. One is at the top of my head, one above my right ear, and one at the base of my neck. We joke about it, Ginn and me. Ginn will swing an invisible club in the air, like Johnny Carson, and yell, "Fore!" They are only going to get bigger, like lemons, oranges, then grapefruits. The doctor said that all the problems I'm having, like the seizures, memory loss, hallucinations, temporary blindness, result from the tumors pressing on my brain, squeezing different parts. Alf described all of the brain functions to me and how it was happening. Knowledge is power, is what she said, like I'd be less afraid if I knew the facts. She reads to me all the time. I like the sound of Alf's voice. It's low and gentle and with my eyes closed, I imagine curling up on top of her, like a cat, with my face pressed against her chest. I don't tell Alf that most of the time now I can't make out a word of what she's saying. I'm afraid she'd stop reading to me then.

My sister Doreen used to read to me when I was little; she's two years older, and we were really close. She knew about me too; when I started high school and Mom kept asking why I didn't have a girlfriend, Dor would tell Mom to shut up and leave me alone. Then Dor's best friend, Candy, started going to this church where they speak in tongues, so Dor goes too, and then we weren't close anymore. You know that feeling when something's over, like a movie, the screen goes dark and you leave and pretty soon it's like you'd never gone to that movie at all. You were laughing or crying and forgetting your troubles and then, there you are, right inside those troubles all over again. That feeling reminds me of Dor now.

I've been having these dreams a lot lately, except I'm awake when it happens, and it's like you're a car and you're speeding toward a brick wall and nobody's driving, cuz you're the car. Usually I scream and the sound of it splits my head in two, and a nurse or Ginn or Alf will be staring down holding my face between their hands. I told Ginn that when this happens, I'm always disappointed that I scream because I really want to hit the wall. Then Ginn got real close to my ear, cuz the visiting nurse was in the room, and whispered:

"Y'know, Teddy, I feel like a car too sometimes. Not my Mustang, more like a Ford Pinto, you know the ones that can explode. My heartbeat just thumps like a tire over speed bumps on some endless freeway. My eyes are headlights, and all I can see ahead of me is a straight yellow fucking line broken up into pieces, and deep inside I'm just waiting for a nail to puncture the air out of me, send me flying off the road in some other goddamned direction."

I knew then that someone finally understood about my dream, and what it meant. Even if she made it up about wanting to explode. She was grinding her teeth, I could hear it, and she pressed her lips against my ear and a couple of tears ran inside my eardrum, which tickled, and I started laughing and told her to be careful, she was watering my tumor.

4. During the process that follows, the patient's breathing should be monitored. Breathing will become slow and shallow. Put a mirror in front of the nose or mouth to detect breath.

It was weeks ago when I drove to this little bookstore across from Michigan State. It's dark inside and crowded with stacks of books. I went up and down the crammed aisles scanning the slips of paper taped to the shelves. I found a section called Death and Grieving, but the book wasn't there. I kept replaying Ginnie's voice in my head saying, "Don't be afraid, Alf, we have to do it." I finally mustered up the courage to ask the clerk who was behind the counter typing into his computer. I tried to sound light and cheerful when I asked: "Do you have the book *Final Exit* by Humphrey?"

He didn't even look up from the screen and said, "The practicalities of self-deliverance and assisted suicide for the dying. Yes. In the self-help section toward the back."

After I paid for it, he smiled and said, "Have a good day." When I left the store, I accidently knocked into a group of five chanting teenagers on the sidewalk, clad in oversized T-shirts and huge, baggy jeans that seemed to spill onto the pavement. They were unfazed by me and my quivering apologies, and just kept walking, clapping, and rhythmically rapping, "If you don't give a shit, like I don't give a shit, then wave your motherfuckin' hands in the air." I watched them for a while as they parted the sea of oncoming pedestrians like a boat. I crossed the street and decided to walk onto the campus and find a bench under a tree, maybe near the river where the ducks are.

After I graduated high school, I used to come on campus all the time to read. I'd drive all the way here from Grand Ledge just to sit among the old brick buildings while students walked with books tucked under their arms, and professors strolled together absorbed in serious conversations. I used to think people at colleges were deeper thinkers, more thoughtful than the people in Grand Ledge who came into Victor's.

After I met Teddy, I stopped coming to read on campus. He dropped out of hotel/motel management as MSU and came to work at the restaurant, and I found out that he was tied up by some guys in his dorm who gagged him and put him underneath the library in these underground tunnels that run like a maze from building to building. And they urinated on him and did all sorts of terrible things and left him there. The guys who did it weren't even disciplined or anything because they were on the football team. Teddy was moved to another dorm.

The day I got the book, though, I sat on a bench, I thought about those tunnels that have now been boarded up because two students died there mysteriously while playing Dungeons and Dragons, and I thought about Teddy being down there, gagging on the smell of boy-piss, terrified like I was with my brothers. I opened the book and the first thing I read was, "Be sure you are in a hopeless position." I was wishing I had brought Ginnie with me because she would have suggested we go for a beer or shoot some pool, play pinball or something. She would have probably walked out of the bookstore with me and joined those teenagers who didn't give a shit. For the first time in my life, I didn't want to keep reading. I closed the book, put it back in the sack, and left.

I drove straight to Victor's and sat at the counter through the rest of Ginnie's dinner shift. She kept coming up to me, taking drags off my cigarette, leaving the stain of her lipstick for me to taste. She brought me a piece of pecan pie with vanilla ice cream. Victor said, "Who's gonna pay for that?" Ginnie told him to put a lid on it. Then Victor said, "I oughtta fire both of you," then winked at me.

At one point Ginnie came up from behind and brushed herself

against my back, real lightly, like a cat, then leaned into me. When she did that, she was telling me that we'd go back to my place and go right to bed. That's exactly what I wanted, but I'd never ask.

5. The extremities will cool, but this is a sign of reduced blood pressure, not necessarily evidence of death.

I don't care if they pump Teddy's stomach and find my god-damned fingerprints on each pill. That's what I told Alf when she read the part about only the dying person should mix the sleeping pills with the ice cream. Then it said don't unplug the phone or answering machine because if someone tries to call and no one answers it could alert them that something is wrong. I say, something is fucking wrong because nobody calls Teddy. His family lives three miles from his apartment and not one of them is the least bit interested that he is dying. Why should it be different, why should it change now? That's what Alf kept saying. They weren't interested in his living, why would they be interested in his dying?

Teddy's sister, Mrs. Doreen Born-Again, had the balls to come into Victor's. She must have heard that Teddy wasn't working anymore. She dragged in her four snot-nosed brats last Wednesday night and Victor tried to put them on a four-top with a child seat, but she insisted on sitting in a booth. I've got booths on Wednesdays, and she ordered four fried chicken baskets for the runts and a dinner salad for herself. She knows who I am but acted like the Queen of fucking Sheba. After I bring them all of their food, I say, "Can I get you anything else?" I said it three times. But she doesn't answer because they're all holding hands with their heads bowed, praying. I slam their ticket down and say, "If you want anything, ask Jesus for it," and walk away. Then she starts banging her glass with a knife, getting everybody's attention, and she says, "Oh, miss, miss, this spoon is dirty, this glass is chipped, you didn't bring enough honey for the biscuits." Shit like that. Clarise at the counter saved my ass from being fired. She swooped up behind me and said, "You're on break, sweetie." Clarise belongs to the same church Doreen does, but at least Clarise asks how Teddy is and says she's praying for him.

I was driving over to Teddy's to relieve Alf and I caught a glimpse of my face in the rearview mirror and my eyes were all pinched and my mouth was twisted and tight and I've got Bruce

Springsteen blaring "it's a death trap, it's a suicide rap," and I purposely slide the car to the left, right over the speed bumps, and I want it to be over, I want Teddy to die, I can't stand it anymore.

I watch Alf with him, you know, all soft and cleaning out the shit in his nose and combing back his hair the way Teddy likes, like the picture of George Michael on Teddy's wall. I just can't be that way; I joke around all the time, keep Teddy laughing, act out these stupid scenes with him from his favorite movies, like *The Way We Were* and *Out of Africa,* and I have to be Robert Redford. Teddy says I'm a cross between Cher and Geena Davis and Alf is a mousier version of Meryl Streep. I play along, it used to be funny, but it's not anymore. Sometimes I want to scream at Teddy, wake up goddammit, your fucking life is over, it's gone. I want to slice off this part of me because it swells up and makes my face twisted and my eyes throb and then it feels like nails are being pounded into my forehead. It only stops when I'm with Alf, when I lie down and I'm breathing hard and it's like hot steam is shooting from my mouth, bouncing off her back, and she draws it in as if her skin is a sponge.

Alf and I tried to explain to Teddy what was going to happen, and after hours, I just couldn't talk. It's impossible to know what goes on inside Teddy's head. He kept saying he didn't want to be here anymore. Then, when we asked if he understood what we were going to do, he said, "Yes, when I wake up, I'll be dead, right?" He has to completely understand. Finally, he says, "Just like you're the end of a movie." Alf said, "That's exactly it, Teddy."

He fell asleep then and Alf and I sat in his kitchen and drank beers. Sometimes Alf gets real quiet, and we're sitting at the table and our legs are touching, and she's staring at her beer can, reading the ingredients, and I know she's upset and probably wondering why I'm so angry. I'm on my third beer; she's still sipping the first, and we're passing a cigarette back and forth and I hotbox it cuz I take in a huge drag and hand it back to Alf and the burning ash falls into her lap and we both jump up and I pour beer onto the chair but it's already melted a hole in the green plastic cover. She's still not saying anything. She dries her chair off and sits back down. So I barely say sorry, and she slips her leg in between mine. We're just staring at each other and I'm waiting for her to say something and instead she lit another cigarette and out of her mouth she blew a whole bunch of tiny, per-

fect smoke rings, like balloons they rose to the ceiling and we followed them with our eyes. Then we both started laughing and I
did the strangest thing, I plunged my whole body into her lap
and I push my head down between her legs and my mouth opens
and I just chew and chew and the skin on my face is on fire, like
burning your knees on carpet, until I can smell her and the
crotch of her jeans is wet and we forget completely that Teddy's
in the next room sleeping.

6. Be absolutely sure that death has occurred. Test pupil contraction by shining a bright flashlight in the eye.

The name of the game was where does it hurt the most. Alf's
brothers would get on top of her and hold her down and then
pinch her all over to see where it hurt the most. She told me
about it after I told her about what happened to me on campus.
We were behind Victor's smoking a joint waiting for Ginn to finish
cleaning her area. Allen, the night cook, came back and took a
few hits and said, "Where are you sweethearts going tonight?"
He's such an asshole.

When Ginn finished, we drove out to the Ledges and climbed
up to this spot above the river where all these caves are that the
Indians used to live in. Ginn is using a red marker and changing
the names written on the rocks. Like if it says, Paul and Tammy
Forever, she adds an "ette" onto Paul, or maybe she put an "o" in
Tammy. I can't remember. Alf and I were pretty high and Ginn is
drinking a beer and Alf starts saying that they have the remains of
an Indian girl who was buried up here in one of the museums at
Michigan State. They have clothes on her and put these things
that look like marbles in her eye sockets. It says she died of unknown causes although there were indications that she had a
concussion or something, like an indent in her skull. Alf said it
was really sad and that they'd never unbury someone at a ceme-
tery and put them on display like that. She complained to the
person in charge and wrote a letter to the "State Urinal," but they
never published it.

We were all quiet after that story and I kept thinking about Alf
getting pinched and then I said, "So, where did it hurt the most?"
Alf looked at me and smiled but didn't answer. I felt kind of bad,
like I shouldn't have asked. Then Ginn stands up on a rock and

screams, "Fuck this place!" Her voice kept echoing for a while and then I stood up like Robert De Niro in *The Deer Hunter* and yelled, "Okay!" over and over, just like him. Ginn did it too, but not Alf. I've never heard Alf yell. She was laughing, though, but at one point I looked down and I think she was remembering that Indian girl because she looked so sad.

That was so long ago, way before I knew I was sick. These things keep coming back to me, stuff I thought I'd forgotten because when I remember it's like suddenly having someone else's memories. It's hard to explain but they don't seem like mine anymore, like old photos of yourself and you don't recall looking like that at all. The one picture I have next to my bed is me, Mom, and Dor. Mom and Dor look like themselves but I don't. We're up at Mackinaw Island and I'm probably ten and I have these shorts on and my legs look like stiff pencils. I'm not wearing a shirt so I'm sunburned and I remember standing there with them and I'm shivering cuz I just got out of the lake. My dad keeps yelling at me to stand still cuz I'm shaking and the louder he yells the more I shake. And Dor's saying, "Stop yelling at him," and then he takes the picture. The only one smiling is Mom.

The worst part is going home and I'm sitting behind my dad who's driving and his neck is red from the sun and we have to say quiet the whole way because he can't stand noise when he drives. Dor and I are faking, like we are talking to each other using our lips and faces and mouthing the words. My dad looks back at me through the mirror and he's staring at me like he has something rotten in his mouth. I know it's because I am acting silly and maybe he can see I'm pretending to be a girl.

I keep that picture, though, because it reminds me of swimming in the lake and I made two friends up there, Todd and Brad, they were twins my age. We're swimming together and dunking and splashing and watching each other piss in the water. They're both taller than me so I get up on their shoulders and they hold my legs and I squeeze my thighs around their heads and it's the most fun I've had with guys my age. When we shower in the public bathroom we stare at each other's peckers and our eyes swell up as they get bigger and then Todd keeps watch while Brad plays with mine. We take turns. When my family's leaving I almost start crying saying bye to them and we swear to come back the same time next summer. All year I bug my dad about where we are going for summer vacation and then my dad got laid off from Olds and we never had another vacation after that.

All these things keep coming back to me and it's like opening a door and there you are. I like it too, because I forget my body then, the burning and this needle I think someone stuck in my back and left there.

You know, it's like you forget you're here and where it hurts the most.

7. After death has been confirmed, make sure all medications are put away. Be sure to wash the dishes. Wait at least an hour, then call the police. Tell them the patient had a terminal illness.

I read in *Science* magazine about Albert Einstein being on his deathbed, and his doctor told him that there was an operation they could try that might save him, but it was very risky. Einstein said no, for everyone there is a time to die; it is my time. There was a moment tonight when Teddy said almost the exact same thing and I wondered what happens in the brain or maybe the spirit that leads somebody to know this so clearly. I didn't see that terrified look in Teddy's eyes at all, like somehow death wasn't a fist anymore, it was more like a cup of warm milk, at least that's what I'd want it to be like, a warmth that eases into your pores and lulls you to sleep.

It didn't take long for Teddy to stop breathing, just a few hours. Ginnie and I sat next to him and just talked to him, then when he was asleep Ginnie kept talking, going scene by scene through *The Way We Were*. When she got to the end where Robert Redford and Barbra Streisand part for the last time, both of us were crying. Then we were quiet for a while and just watched Teddy's chest going up and down and up and down and I fell asleep for a minute because I started breathing like Teddy. I was jolted awake when my book slipped out of my hand and hit the floor with a loud thump. It's a huge, thick book of great poems that Ginnie gave me years ago. She said she found it, but I could see that the paper pocket for the library card had been ripped out. I've been reading to Teddy from this book for the last few months. Mostly because I knew he couldn't follow a story or an article anymore, and I thought that at least with the poems he could listen to the words, he didn't have to know what they meant, all he had to do was listen. When I reached down for the book, Ginnie stroked my back and said, "He's gone, Alf."

After Teddy died, Ginnie carried the dinner dishes into the kitchen. There was a small amount of melted strawberry ice cream left in Teddy's bowl and she scooped it up with her tongue. The police came first and then the coroner. I was surprised how routine everything was. The worst part for me was when they put Teddy in the black plastic body bag. I was sitting next to Ginnie on the couch clutching my book when they zipped it up. The sound was so loud and jarring, and as if she read my mind, Ginnie pressed her palms over my ears. It shouldn't be that way at all. It should be real quiet like sealing an envelope or closing a book.

I'm driving us back to my place because by the time everyone left, Ginnie was feeling real drowsy from Teddy's ice cream. In the car she starts talking about giving Victor our notice, selling her Mustang, and how we would use the money to get to California. Then she asks me to slow down and just drive over the speed bumps on the road. She closes her eyes, leans her head back, puts her hand on my leg, and falls fast asleep. Every so often her muscles twitch as if she's got an electric current running through her and when she twitches some of that current is released.

It seems like it's only Ginnie and me driving under the moon tonight. When I glance at her sleeping, she reminds me of a night flower, the ones I read about in the California desert that bloom when the sun sets. She opens outward and whatever's clamped down inside just unfolds. Most people think Ginnie's a harsh person, but she's not, really; Teddy and I know that. Right now, in the car, I can feel that stiffness in her body drop off and she's soft and yielding like an old pillow, just like a pillow you can burrow into and you feel sort of sad when it's time to wake up and lift your face to the day.

I wrap my hand around her wrist and feel the rhythm of her pulse as it navigates us toward home. When we get there, I'm going to press my body real close to her as she sleeps. Then I'm going to talk to Teddy, tell him about flowers that bloom in the night desert, until my words start running into each other, just like those bugs that swarm under a lighted porch before it goes dark.

ALEIDA RODRÍGUEZ

The pharmacist came running from his tiny white office and tried
to stop her. She screamed and sobbed and beat herself as though
her own arms and hands had turned against her. While he held
on to one arm, the other one came around, hitting her on the
side of the head. She hit her face, her chest; she pounded on her
hips and thighs with her fists. All the while raving, wailing. He
tried to talk to her, but she only shook her head more violently, as
though his words were bugs trying to enter her ears. When he
couldn't get her to calm down, or even to recognize him, he sent
for the paramedics.

But she had worn herself out by the time they got there. She
had collapsed, sobbing softly on the floor, though still dazed, in-
credulous, like someone waking from a dream. The paramedics
probed her and took her blood pressure, but found that she only
suffered from a severe case of disbelief. The customers drifted
back to buy their Dr. Scholl's footpads and Vicks VapoRub, which
in her country had been called "*veevaporoo.*" The pharmacist
helped her up as though moving a sleeping child from the backseat of a car and called her husband.

Roberto wasn't the typical husband from her country. He was
dully good-natured. He never got drunk at parties like the other
men who huddled on the stairs outside their friends' apartments,
smoking and making jokes about women. He drank his beer
slowly and grinned at them with his big teeth and protruding lips.

And he had never beaten Tomasa. The money they earned at their factory jobs they kept in an account with both of their names on it. He trusted the finality of her decisions.

Tomasa was practical and regarded as something of a skinflint by their friends. She didn't demand a new dress with every paycheck and was usually seen wearing the same pair of black low-heeled shoes with the little silver buckles. That is, unless she was going to work; then she wore the white nurse-type shoes that gave her support on the assembly line. She was short and stocky, and no frilly, impractical dress would look good on her anyway. She had resigned herself to looking *decente*.

That's how she and Roberto had managed to start a little savings. Unlike the other Cubans who worked the same kinds of jobs, they had bought a tiny house in a lower-middle-class Mexican and white neighborhood on the west side. It was white and had a manageable, trimmed strip of yard in the front, surrounded by a chain-link fence. The house hadn't cost much, and because of the tax break it gave them, they were able to save, over several years, the sum of ten thousand dollars.

Maybe Tomasa was inordinately proud of that accomplishment. She told the woman who lived alone in the apartments next door. They had become friendly, talking over the fence, then having *café* together in Tomasa's spotless blue-and-white kitchen. When they went grocery shopping, the neighbor often commented on the amount of time Tomasa spent doing price comparisons. Maybe it was during one of these times that Tomasa had snapped, irritated, and told her that pinching pennies had helped her amass ten thousand dollars in the bank.

The neighbor, Lourdes, said she was married and that her husband, still in Guadalajara, would soon rejoin her. Tomasa had known Lourdes for nearly three years, but the husband hadn't managed to make it over in all that time.

One day Tomasa was waiting for the bus on Venice Boulevard. She clutched her change purse in one hand, wedged between her legs, as she stared straight ahead on the green bench. A bus came. It wasn't hers, but she had started walking toward it to check the number. It read "Out of Service," and when it passed without stopping she began marching back to her seat like an obedient child.

A man, a Latin-looking man, suddenly appeared from around the corner and walked right up to her. She started at his direct-ness and stepped back; she didn't like him getting so close. He asked her, in Spanish, if she might possibly help him. She thought he was going to ask for directions or have her translate some-thing, but he held no torn piece of paper creased and unfolded in his outstretched hand.

Instead, he began to tell her about his infirm mother, *la pobre*. How he had had to put her in a nursing home because of her fail-ing health and his inability to take care of her. However, that had left him with the problem of what to do with her house. He wasn't from here, he said, otherwise he'd know whom to turn to about this. But, as she saw, he'd had to petition a complete stranger for help. And he thought she looked like an honest, sensible woman. Did she understand that there was nothing else he could do? Yes, she could see that, and right beside it, an image of her recently married son living in a cramped bachelor's apartment.

While Tomasa leaned into the stranger's face (now the face of a charming man in a bad predicament) listening, a woman joined them on the bench and soon she too was caught up in the poor man's dilemma. Tomasa was surprised to feel so immediately at ease with this man, whose gently receding hairline reminded her of the bays of her island back home.

He didn't expect her help for nothing; no, if she would con-sent to help him there would be rewards for her beyond the ones God would surely heap on her, such a good woman, so con-cerned and willing to help a stranger who shared only her lan-guage. The three of them agreed to meet again, to work out the details.

The teller at Tomasa's bank is unduly curious, she thinks. Why doesn't she just mind her own business? Isn't it her *own* money, money she had slaved to save while other Cubans with similar jobs have nothing to show for their miserable lives here? But only one signature is required, so the teller lets Tomasa withdraw the full sum.

For the previous two weeks Tomasa hadn't been telling Roberto about the meetings and her deal with the nice Spanish-speaking man. She wanted to surprise him and besides, she didn't want to hear his stupid reservations, his doubts. If she had listened to him, they never would've bought their house—and look at how investing some money had brought them the biggest savings they'd ever had in their lives! No, she wasn't going to tell him until it was all over.

Tomasa and the man and woman met again in the little park by her house. She pressed her black handbag under her arm as she watched them cross the street toward her. They smiled and she beamed back. The sun made dappled patterns on their clothes as they approached under the trees.

Then suddenly the man felt ill, a headache, some slight dizziness. Did she know of a place nearby where he could get some medication? Of course she did—he was lucky. Right on the corner was the Rexall where the pharmacist was Cuban. He knew her; he provided her with tetracycline without a prescription whenever she needed it.

So they strolled together to the corner and crossed the street, not making much small talk. How comfortable one can feel with certain people in such a short time, Tomasa thought. How pleasant this man was. How gentlemanly. And he treated her with such respect.

When they entered the Rexall, Tomasa led them to the corner where Ignacio had his prescription counter. She leaned over the countertop, calling his name, craning her neck to see if he was asleep in his office. To hoist her belly up onto the counter so she could peer down the hall, she handed her purse to the woman. But she couldn't see him. She turned back to her friends, to explain that sometimes he took little naps in the storage area where no one could disturb him, but they had disappeared. She looked down a couple of aisles in both directions but didn't find them, as she had expected, loitering in front of a display.

All at once, as if bolting awake from one of her recurrent dreams about plummeting from the top of a skyscraper, she felt drenched by the cold realization of what had happened. How could she have been so *stupid*? Of all people, *her*, Tomasa? Ay, and all that *money!* Clearly, she deserved to die.

She ran out of the store and threw herself in front of traffic, but brakes squealed, cars swerved, and someone dragged her back onto the sidewalk. He was asking her something, but she couldn't hear him above the screams of someone nearby. She watched as her own hands came up and yanked at her hair. How could she face Roberto? The man pushed her into the drugstore, yelling for help, and that's when Ignacio appeared from behind his counter.

Roberto was silent as he brought her cups of chamomile tea and stroked her head. Never had he seen her that way. At least they hadn't murdered her, he responded, when she demanded to know why he wasn't yelling at her. At least they both still had their health. No, he shook his head, of course that didn't mean he was happy, but they were both still strong. They had lost everything before—remember?—their country, everything. And they had been able to start again then. They could start again.

When the police arrived to take the report, they asked her if she'd ever drunk anything with the two strangers. She growled that she didn't drink and insisted that Roberto verify it, which he did, calmly. The cops shifted their weight slightly and asked again: no soda? coffee, maybe? But no. They'd never been together long enough. Their meetings had always been short, she now remarked, and always in parks or on street corners.

Hadn't she suspected anything? But then Tomasa started to whimper again like she'd done when he had picked her up at the drugstore, so Roberto had to intervene. He extended his arm and gently ushered them toward the door. The police left, saying it was a clear case of bunco, and that things like this happened every day. The people are usually never found, and in this case, considering how much money those two had gotten, they were probably long gone past the border.

After they left, Tomasa asked Roberto what they had meant about the *banco*. Had these people also robbed a bank? But Roberto hadn't understood either; he shrugged. Standing over her as she lay on the flowered sofa covered in plastic, he looked as lean and tall as when they'd first met, strolling the Saturday night promenade in their hometown. Timidly, she started to reach for one of his hands, but he turned away without noticing. She saw the folds on the back of his green work shirt expand and fall back into place. Sliding his fists into empty pockets, he squinted out the window in the direction of something at a great distance.

Defiance

CAROLE MASO

It's a memory so she can change it—warp it along the lines of infinity if she likes, stretch it into submission so that the hand ab-
stracts across the sky in veins of light and the pain is only thunder.
Turn the ring into a star, the star into a code pulsing in a lost language. What does it say? *Harbinger of love. Safe.* Something senseless. It's a memory so she can prolong the moment before rain,
turn down the thunder, change the emphasis, rearrange. Perfect
the scene, straighten the crooked man, and the little girl—
straighten her splayed walk home. It's a memory so she could allow it to collapse, implode, or she could close it down altogether.
Crush the hero seed in her palm.

She could count. Count every vein in every leaf, count every
leaf on every tree out the window of the tree house now. Is that
thunder? She might divide the vast night into quadrants. Or paint
the world by number. All the threes will be indigo blue—and the
twos that sort of blowsy green of summer. Is that lightning? Paint
it white, fluorescent white. Not to forget purple tinged with rust in
the bruised morning. . . . Pink.

Look to the sky. Straighten, no matter how painful, the bow-
legged Cassiopeia in the star-filled night. It's gorgeous up there,
you've got to admit. Objectify your fear. Put all that longing and
sadness and trust into an oblong box—no wait, that's not a box—
that's a tree house; and they are just about to climb into it again.
There. There now.

The hiss of the trees in the strange sky. In the distance—why does this story linger there—after a lifetime? A lifetime of calling it up. You can try to make it come closer. Make it surrender its heavy-handed revelations. Who's that on the glib horizon? Almost within sight now—*Janie, is that you?* Harbinger of love.

She can be reckless if she likes. She can call the black volts right up to this house in the trees—it's only a memory, for God's sake. She'll be okay, safe; their meager positive, negative, positive, flickering in the night, is nothing to her. She might shout to the lightning, call it boldly to her side. Cassiopeia weeping in the night without gods. Take out your small box of paints. She can color this shape, the one that has lingered for a lifetime on the periphery, like some wretched sadness or crimson—illegible banner from the static inner life—useless, stupid equation.

Is that lightning? Don't worry. *I'll keep you sheltered from the storm.*

Paint it red and up close and hard and blunt inside. It's like she's drawing and dreaming and remembering and wishing all at the same time. He'll keep you sheltered, not to worry. And safe. It's a memory so she'll make it all right in the end. It's a memory and she'd like the last words to be certainly, or of course, or without doubt, or doubtless.

He gives her a hand up and into the tree house. *I'll keep you sheltered.*

So much blood, don't worry, it's only a dream. And the fields and fields of rice and soy he'll run through. Cotton, can that be cotton, yes, in a drenched fist. It's only a dream. Paint it—six will be gray. Gray of the factory floor and father and son. Pale droning of factory and trash fish. Paint the little girl in the corner pink.

It's memory so there aren't the same rules. She could choose to alter the central fact—that he is going to die—but she doesn't choose.

In the distance now, thunder.

Three will equal red. Six will be magenta. Two will be purple. And seven will equal darkness, tinged with blood.

On the sharp edges of the frame, where the boundaries are clear, neat, razored away, stands—who's there?

Couldn't there be a nice, a reassuring voice of some kind coming from offstage right somewhere—at the scalloped border, some comforting, gorgeous, lilting song drifting across the field from the trees; or rescue—bleeding into the scene? Warm. Tinted rose. Flowing. A curtain of soft blood.

It's a memory, so she might make it pretty. The world will be glowing and lit. The trees will caress. Will bow down and protect them. Anyone, even you, is entitled to wish.

Cruel, insoluble equation of rich and poor, splintered dilemma of day and night, peace and war. The black man in the broad-rimmed hat whispers, *run.* See, there's help if you concentrate hard enough. *Run,* he says, getting smaller and smaller as he runs toward the impossible night-scalloped border—

Where there are always guards and guard dogs, waiting of course.

In the interval between dark and light and dark again in the light-ninged night—she might change from child to adult—in a light-ning flash back to child again in the dream—ridden, eternal night.

She can turn down the sound so that no thunder is heard. No barking or darkness or dogs. For a while. So that the girl and the darkness tinged with blood... Paint it five if you like.

In the interval he changes from brother to man, then to soldier boy, bye-bye. The child cries. The mother tinted sepia like a real memory waves a pretty scalloped handkerchief as if this were another war. It's the old movie version of herself, and in it she waves the perfect square of grief and cries.

Don't go.

Is that thunder?

Don't cry.

If she could have protected someone, she'd have picked him in the night-tinted sepia like a memory, so safe. But not here, not here, and no one suddenly we know or recognize.

It's a memory so when the child cries out in the dark in the trees with the dogs, someone certainly will be within the reach of her voice.

The university students change out of their polo clothes, shower and prepare for the evening meal. Put down their racquets. Powdered. Cologned.

Shouldn't we go now?

Behold: a child in a flowered dress touched by light. The brother already defeated, nearby. He takes her hand. The bitter choreography of their lives. The darkness of poverty and dogs.

The sky with its dumb green glare. And eight will equal ...

Surely someone will be well within the reach of her voice. The brother? He's already left. He's been gone for some time now. She barely recognizes him anymore. Can't anyone —

Help.

Surely someone...

In the multiplication dream she triples herself. Becomes four-fold, then five, then God—

In the elaboration, she's ten feet tall. It's so lovely up here hovering above the rest of the world. You can touch the tops of trees, imagine infinity.

You've never seen such beautiful shapes. She bisects the night, places the stars into their quadrants. Dispels from the earth the anvils and weevils and fish and the weeping floor of the world. The dogs—banished. Divide right, bisect, left, forward march, so they are only barking heads. Nothing to fear. Remote, elongated parallelograms. The world, the known world, predicted, color-keyed: friendly maps, smiling guides, nothing to fear now.

She looks at them tiny from the edge of the scalloped, sepia-tinted frame. Integers on an infinite plane. As if by design. How lonely she is out here, where she's always stood.

They're whispering. Whispering. All right—she can turn it up, but not without risk. Let's listen for a minute.

Don't go.

And her mother reciting, as if in her sleep, the terrible numbers of the phone company.

They are there in the trees in the early evening turning dark and the brother is saying good-bye to his friends. He is about to leave, about to go at the height of the action, to the stupid, unpopular war. A volunteer of all things, in perverse, reverse fashion. As if to spite them. But how can she stop him? What can she do to make him stay? *Stay. Don't go.* She's only eight years old and it's already far too late. *Don't*—the only one she ever loved...

Beloved... *go, don't go, don't.* But no sound comes out.

Isn't that thunder? Shouldn't we go now? She loves him so much. It's only a memory locked in the prison of a woman's head.

He's standing with his friends, this pathetic fraternity. In the riotous, raw night. The boys slapping each other on the back, passing out beers, *what the fuck—hey, where's Jane?*

In the bannered, meaningless, jingo-jargon of the poor, who always go. Why must it always come to this? The hungry, defeated Irish, and the solution that is always alcohol and the war.

In the star-spangled night. O voluptuous dark. Seedy on black velvet. Doomed, flaring horses carefully painted by number, above the couch and the Virgin, and Elvis.

All this is played out in a woman's head who has time on her hands. Time to burn, time to kill.

In her pretty cerebellum. She's pretty on the inside.

It's a memory so she can keep it as something in a locket if she likes: little and perfect and finished and carry it around, glittery fetish, press it up to her fiendish and bitter breast.

You could count your heartbeats. Turn the body into the calibrated, exquisite machinery it is. It is, isn't it? You could dissect the heart. Admire it. Finger its perfect valves. God, it's warm and bloody in there.

Is that lightning? *Nothing to be afraid of,* he whispers to the little girl. *I'm right here.* You can bring him up that close—but no—

Your heart would break—not again.

So that the dogs and the darkness and the increasingly drunk, senseless friends recede. And the trees—God, the trees are beautiful aren't they, this way, backlit? She could count every leaf.

And he fingers the hem of her dress in this version—like a prayer shawl, and weeps.

Hail Mary Full of Grace, lightning bayonets the night. In her body she swears she can feel its jagged life. Crazy Janie, darling of the hallowed night, where are you?

We enter this story at a point where there is little left for them—or for us—but to let them march on the tracks already laid down to their preappointed destinies—he to the fields of resignation and rice and she to the shiny

Lightning chair at the end of the too long hallway.

Oh, the perversity of it! There's no reason to go, save for what glints in him. He feels the hero seed inside. Death head. Dog star. Brute—blunt—she swears she can feel—

That's lightning. Lust to be a hero—the chance—the one chance in a million. Take it, take it—it's yours. Once and only once in a lifetime.

Take it, take it, it's yours now. So that the filthy, the factory, the no hope, recedes now, the no chance lets up for a minute—the mother's suffering, the father's stupid, penniless pride. Is that what he's thinking? Or maybe he didn't think anything; not one to fix emotion with words. Bleak, inchoate—

Just get me outta here. And when I come back I'll marry Jane.

The pounding relentlessness of Jane, Jane, Jane in her brother's—

Rain now.

Rain.

Gutted and gutless.

Rage.

Oh, for a muse of fire!

In the foreground, lightning. Count. The thunder still some fifteen or so away. Not to be afraid.

He sings, *In a gadda da vida*, something senseless, made more so by repetition and his slurred—

In a gadda da vida, baby—don't you know that I love you?

Behold a child suffused with light—the small genius of her being.

If she could make Janie appear. It's a memory after all, and she'd like to, she's a magician after all, but she can't and he's getting drunker and drunker and it looks like she's not going to come and I shout, *Janie* across the decades. *Crazy Janie.* He's waiting for his sweetheart to come and say good-bye. And she'll come, sure. Doubtless. No Doubt.

To bid him adieu. If she could only change the tone. Throw in some French so as to escape the dismal and wretched and small— transform the scene for a while. It is, as you know, a memory. The thunder can't hurt you anymore.

Janie, where are you? The war's on and he hears the dark hero music. Isn't that just night breaking apart again, or the mother crying? Nope. It's music of friend and brotherhood and doomed music of country. Attention. Then, forward, march. Discipline of the ages. *Attention!*

A woman weeping. Yeah—that's their mother, all right.

Veins of light illuminate the sky, there's an enormous hand in the sky, palm side up—lighting up one, then another line. Life line. Heart line. This will happen. And this. All this. A sky of fearful possibility. You'll be—

Lucky in love. He's waiting for his Jane, his true love now. He's got the ring in his heart pocket. He'll marry her when he returns; it's a promise. And he's waiting in the night, in the trees with the little girl, after his friends have gone, for Janie to come.

In the memory, this small locket, anchor, the woman wears around her neck—this small killing bottle she dangles like a charm and looks into occasionally—in the memory in the bottle —place of dog hair and tooth and velvet, lightning, cries—he opens another beer and waits: in the cruel, stupid, baffled punishment of his life.

No more factory at five A.M. No more dirt and darkness and dogs. There's a war.

He fingers the hem of her dress like a wound or a code.

Was that thunder, and closer now? Nothing to be afraid of. But she is afraid. She's just a little girl, seven, maybe eight, yes, on the verge of her eighth birthday. *Take my hand.* And she does because she loves him and they climb up, up into the tree house in the sky in the thunder, in the lightning into the trees, and she knows better, but she does not care if she dies—*she would give up her life*—silly, melodramatic, inappropriate late, last overtures in the sky in the night. Give up your little life, Bernadette—soldier, pilgrim, stone. And *hurry*, he says and, *careful, take my hand, little saint*—before the rain.

If there were a goddess—if there were someone up there—just for her—who might understand.

That's lightning—now count—1,2,3,4—then thunder.

The sky with its dumb green glare. Take my hand. Paralyzed like an animal in the headlights of a truck.

Bewildered. And his friends. Fists at his back. A kind of pummeling. *Nuggies*, they say. Neck vices, and other displays of affection. *You dumb fuck.* A term of endearment apparently, holding him tightly. Tears. Yes, perhaps tears, marijuana and bloodshot eyes. *What's up with Jane?*

Rain now. I'll keep you sheltered.

Ridiculous, black comedy, and I the crippled, nostalgic vaudevillian—thumping, thumping out a useless code. If there had been even one shred along the way, of hope.

One-legged tap dancer, mute singer of the great arias, blind landscape painter. Bloodied, knocking—

In the clubhouse in the trees up high. Psychedelic posters on the wall. Jimi Hendrix and his swirling sunglasses—the purple and orange and acid-green sky, paint it nine. And the music. *Are you experienced?* the hero-brother asking—rhetorical, drugged, numb rage.

In the lightning flash—look: a bitter young man, a joint in his mouth on his way to the war.

Don't go.

He licks the hem of her dress like a wound.

I'll keep you sheltered, he sings, sweetly. But now he is crying, standing by the beaded curtain. *Please don't cry, Kennedy.* And the little girl. The little girl trembling holds his hand and the dogs howl. She's afraid. And he combats the black forces of his psyche and the lightning night for her. She's just a child. The sky cracking open. The lit gagged grass.

Fingering, like a hollow rosary, the child

Clinging to his jacket, behold, shouting something—love or don't but no sound coming out.

Thumping with one foot on the rim of the bloodied door: a telegram.

How can they find the right address with everything covered over like someone's already died. The draped path home.

It's a memory. She ties herself to him. Sets fire to the tree they are perched in. Feels them both go up in flames. Watch them burn. Before the telegram and the terrible purple bunting. Flames —because she doesn't want to live without him. Dead together in the electric night. Because she knows he will never come back alive.

Eenie, meenie, minie, moe.

Electrocuted, drowned in light, bound.

It's a memory so she can warp it, open it along the lines of oblivion. Now coming into the foreground, licking the edge of the frame: fire. The disintegrating frame.

Behold: a child suffused with light. The small genius of her being.

The short-circuited sky alive. Cruel and violent. Indifferent executioner. *Maybe we'll be struck,* he says, laughing. And somewhere someone is already weeping.

It's the black man, deserted, in a field of cotton. In the distance, dogs.

It's their mother being passed the telegram from the government.

All this held in the prison of a woman's head. Still. If she could only stop the dogs or the sobbing or the gagging for a minute.

And she repeats, *Boys will be boys will be boys,* something senseless, made more so by repetition. To calm herself she counts the blades of black grass, beads in the beaded curtain, leaves, graves. Blessed rage.

This passion play. Look:

He helps her up the tree house ladder. Takes her hand. Come on; it's okay.

Pink. It's okay. He'll even sing.

Through the skylight, the heavens framed. *If you lie on your back you can see all the stars.*

You can paint the heavens black and red and blue, lit up. You can divide the night into fractions, divisible light, manageable, while he weeps and sings.

Defeated, handsome, still handsome—he was always her hero —defender.

The stars are howling tonight, the stars are baying, the stars, the stars, count them—fix them. Blessed rage for order. Fix your place.

Where's Providence tonight? How did we end here? So far. Where's God?

Pink.

No one is listening, he says, pointing to the heavens and running. It's the nigger. And the dogs.

The world is lit for a moment and she sees him, running to the border, and her brother marching and marching—what can they be thinking?

She wants to be brave. She wants to be lionhearted. She wants him to be proud of her. Admire her. *If you lie on your back...*

Don't go. Stay.

A small, stunned creature as if paralyzed, caught in the head-lights of a truck, don't move—

If you lie on your back you can see all the stars. There's the Archer, bowled Dipper, the bow-legged Cassiopeia.

The gagging Virgo: strange, double-jointed freak. Sirius—the Dog Star. Fierce Leo. She wants to be brave.

Fuck.

The nigger with fists of cotton and rage, with dog tags runs to where the war is.

One-legged, thumping, injured—

There's a little girl with a ring in her fist. There's a little girl with a ring.

I love you. She always loved him. They went to the river. Caught fish. Glittering. Small trajectories of hope.

The world is lit by fish for a moment and she sees:

I'll keep you sheltered.

The lit grass gagged.

And she sees: a crooked life. Beetles and weevils in the choked grass devouring

Weeping fields of—

Potato eaters. The parents of the parents of the parents, singing an Irish song of potatoes and beer and crooked jigs. And she sees:

A man bends down, singing a song soft and low and rises holding—if you can, *run.* Fields of cotton, then rice, dry your eyes, don't go—then dark.

And she sees: Janie. Janie will come, sure and doubtless, and no doubt.

Lie on your back. The broken-veined sky at night. Is that lightning?

And she sees: He takes off his jean jacket and wraps her in it. And she's gray-faced, poor urchin in her red flowered tangled dress and she begins to cry—as if she's grieving already. Of course she is.

Then light. The scene is lit again. *Hey you, how about a pony beer?*

What does she see? What does she want from this warped passion play as they escort each other through the last stages of his suffering?

And she sees:

He looks in the distance, clear-eyed, intent on his death. He feels the hero seed, strange grenade inside him

About to ignite, about to explode. Lie on your back. Count the stars. Fix your place.

He prays the edge of her dress like a rosary.

Bow-legged Cassiopeia. Poor Virgo. And Sirius

The Dog Star dangling around his neck. The dog tags. She'd follow him, if he'd let her.

And the dogs, whom she fears, might protect after all, bark— but now no sound comes out. And she tries to hear the numbers her mother speaks in sleep, but no sound comes out anymore—

And the awful mute dogs and the night. Lift up the mute button. Let them howl, fuck, hold indigo night in their jaws, life in their leaded black balls. Fuck and howl, but no sound comes out. *Help.*

It's a dream so the rumblings and hurt and the ache in her body and fear is only thunder. The tremblings are thunder. Look, you can quiet them.

The awful mute pleas coming out of her mouth. Who will hear her?

You'll die. If she could only stop this. Console him. Stop this. *You'll die,* she says, but no sound comes out. If she could let him know what she knows—but she can't stop it—she can't do anything to stop it—and she knows that it is—it must be—it's her fault. She can't make him stay. He is going to die. Because there is nothing she can do.

But *Boys will be boys will be boys will be boys will be boys will be boys.*
No one is listening.

Paint the planes of his face green and gray and brown and beige. Camouflage him. Keep him safe.

Because she can't keep him. Help him now out of his gray factory dressing gown. And she in tangled flowered dress. Then Catholic school uniform. Take it off.

Arrange then rearrange them. Ram. Archer. Bull. Sea monster. Medusa. There's a little girl with a ring in her fist.

I swing this cruel killing bottle where they are trapped, dying, back and forth, ruinous and continuous. Under glass. I watch the bruised morning come. And they make their crooked way toward home.

What flares from the corners of the frame now is hurt. Burn it, burn it if you can. What makes us blind is grief.

Poor wretches, who shall save them at five A.M.? Walking toward the defeated, squat town where the mother—a litany, a small rapture of numbers might help, no? It's OK, isn't it, to hope? God, the trees are beautiful at this hour, even now as they turn into a paint-by-number backdrop on cheap but durable cardboard and the girl. It's pretty nice here in the sore morning awkward—

Bow-legged child, gagging on her own sadness and dress and he is already there in a thicket of—a dense tangle of jungle and disgust. The ring is her fist—

Never say. Never. Never say a word to anyone. Never say a word. As they walk home. In this memory, this terrible sepulcher, he was her hero—this terrible sore light of day—*never say a word.*

And the mute sound comes out barking and crooked, help me please. Never say—Never...

How about a glass of milk, Stringbean? he says, later in the dingy kitchen.

Behold: they stand emblematic of all that's been lost, in the failing light of morning where there are numbers. Everything charted. She'd like to paint all the threes purple, she thinks in this injured light. The fives black, all the sevens pink, pink like a girl, pink like a little girl. *Never say a word.* About the pink or the ring or the man you saw with the cotton who whispered, *run for your life, run through this or die—*

Father and son on the banks of a muddy river long time ago, here catching trash fish. Back in Africa, long long time ago catching—

Miraculous fish. What went wrong? Long time ago.

I'll keep you sheltered from the storm.

Glass of milk.

She'd just like to keep this, she'd just like it to be something in a locket now: little and perfect and over.

Glass of—

Flowers on stilts and black, red, white and blue ribbons at the funeral and the mother hissing at every mention of country, God. Who is that puppet-child crying, without a mouth?

Color the sky violet.

And many times before this they had come to this spot. He sang her songs: "In-a-Gadda-da-Vida" and "Purple Haze." "I'll Keep You Sheltered from the Storm." Number the purple haze now. Put the voice away in a locket.

And many times they had to come to this place. Higher and higher in the trees. Sky and clouds and the surrender of green. No one can hurt us here. *No one can get us here, little one.* Posters, a mattress, a record player, beer. Let me take you higher. Let me take you higher to this—

Terrible Sepulcher up in the trees. Pity them, these quaint costumed players: she in her childish sundress, he in his shirt and muscles and jeans. He puts his arm around her. She can see every hair on his hand. He'll keep her sheltered....

The tumored fish thrown back. Nothing ever works out.

Is that rain—or just Bernadette weeping now?

Who will help them? Doomed. Roaming toward home.

Back to the bleak house. *Where was Jane? And why didn't Jane, anyway?* Incoherencies of night and day. And the little girl with quiet doll mouth, doll arms, doll legs, and the little girl, he loves her so much—she holds the ring.

Cruel puppeteer with no face. Shriek without a mouth and pulled back hair now, exaggerated: the little girl holds the ring.

She'll bury it in the yard like a bone. So no one will know. No one will ever know. Garden of ring and roses. Garden of sharp diamonds and pointed thorns.

It's yours, it's yours, it's yours now, he whispers in the trees; it's yours now, take it. Terrible microscopic bride. Engagement without end.

Never let her know, if you see her, that there was a ring or a dream.

Everything is wrong angles and vertigo. She in her cotton tangled dress of pain, he in his jeans and jean jacket—poor children, and the dogs—rusty, roaming through an immense, a vast landscape of bright light.

So that you think you see something; you think you finally understand something—but then dark—again.

Behold: this bitter choreography.

Who will protect them on their crooked path without numbers? The draped path home.

In the memory now I paint almost everything black or red. I worry.

It's a memory and I thought I could stop it if I wanted. Erase the ring and the grass, escape the killing bottle, break it, even. Round off, scallop the sharded edges. There's something so hard and sharp. In bleak recurrences—sad, repetitive, persistent, without warning or permission—in the middle of the night—and in daylight. The little girl grown now with only months herself left to live. An unseemly sentence leveled on her head.

I call it back—for her sake, poor child, in the thunder, in the dark, with the only one she ever trusted or loved about to be taken—

Killed by friendly fire. *You dumb fuck.*

Home of the panicked, indentured, home of the poor.

Jane, I am writing across the abyss of the years. Surely you have a good explanation for that night. . . .

Is that thunder? Yes.

They haul their dumb love and rage across the ruined terrain.

Rest on the way home in the flowers if you like for a while.
Flowers don't speak or cry. You can animate them though if you
like. Paint them. You can try. Sure you can try. You can dream.

You can dream about catching fish—and not only trash fish, but all
kinds.

It is thunder. They haul their dumb love that weighs a ton
across the bleak terrain and rage—hobbling home as if injured.
But grief can do that, we've seen it many times before—in the defeated dark of their father's house. He'll never be able to pay the
bill. The lights shut off again.

Look: she stands huddled in the dark at the small stove, boiling
and boiling the gray potatoes. She's had to plead again, make
promises she just can't keep, with the phone company and the
other demons. And the father gone out again—

In a rage. Eenie, meanie, miney moe. Why?

Why have you left us here alone another night?

It is lightning. There is rain. Her brother's hand across the sky.
The doomed, illuminated veins emblazoned to the pink of the
little girl. A universe of pain; all over her body—she'll never get
away.

There was a crooked man who walked a crooked mile.

She's so pink.

The moon watches resigned in the electrocuted night; she
wants nothing more to do with this.

And the stars—

There aren't enough stars for these kinds of wishes.

Where's Ireland tonight? Where's Africa? Where's Providence,
even? Where's that obliterating yielding equation that might elu-
cidate, might clarify, that defiance of light?

Crooked wife. Crooked cat. Crooked mouse. They all lived
together—

The tree house down, the indentations in the grass where you
lay gone, grown over—the mark of how far one's come—away
from that night, away from the beaded curtain, bleak rosary, the
thunder, the pointed trees, the fistfuls of cotton and rage and rice
and the droning, enormous, unending gray floor of the world,
that is everywhere.

They'll never get away.

The banners hung. Strange music of country and God and the
bunting blackened. Fear for them.

I bolt upright at five A.M. I fear for them. Where they will go. What they will mistake for shelter—in this prison within a prison within a prison; I baffled now, as he was always, back then, I guess. And the terrible pink. And the little girl.

$$E=mc^2$$

WENDI FRISCH

I spied her sitting at the bar of the Palms, drinking a cappuccino, her long legs wrapped around the barstool. It was August, and she wore wool kneesocks with clogs, a black dirndl skirt with draw-string waist, and a tea-green beaded sweater buttoned to her neck, where a Peter Pan collar shyly peeked out. I judged her to be about my height, five six, and sensed that beneath her demure clothing a curvaceous figure lurked. Although I lift weights to keep in trim, I like women built like women.

Her hair was red, obviously dyed, pulled back into a coarse knot secured with crisscrossing chopsticks. She seemed to vibrate in an energy field all her own. She sipped her cappuccino with a dedication matched only by the concentrated gaze with which she appraised her reflection in the mirror above the bar.

The question of where she'd gotten a cappuccino in the Palms, a West Hollywood watering hole for lesbians, had barely formulated in my mind when I found myself slipping into the seat next to her.

"Where'd you get the cappuccino?" I asked.

She tore her eyes away from the mirror long enough to look me over from head to toe. "Across the street. I get it to go. I save on sales tax that way."

I wondered if my bleached-blond flattop, horn rims, "Top Dog" T-shirt, black jeans, and military shoes passed muster. I could see she was staring at the shoes, so I volunteered, "I got them from my cousin. He's in the navy."

"Cool," she said and went back to her own reflection. One of her crimson curls pulled loose from the chopsticks and swung across her right eye. Languidly, she reached across the bar for a swizzle stick, which she used to spear the deviant strand.

I felt her slipping away, so I leaned forward and asked, "What do you do for fun?" I inwardly cringed at the predictability of the question.

For a moment I thought I saw her eyes light up. Then, with a dramatic flourish, she produced a copy of *The Stranger* from her leather knapsack. "I'm studying the connection between the French existentialists and the street people in Los Angeles. Are our homeless a reflection of a deeper societal problem or is existentialism on the upswing? I'm a graduate student at USC. I'm also active in a guerrilla theater group." Brains *and* an artistic streak? I was beginning to feel as frothy as her cappuccino.

I watched as she scraped some of the foam from her cup with her index finger. She sucked her finger for what seemed like a long time then said, "I only come here about once a month. It's nice to meet someone interesting for a change." She was staring in the mirror again, so I wasn't sure if she meant me or her reflection.

We sat compatibly for a few minutes, neither of us speaking. Sipping my mineral water, I pondered her neckline, what I could see of it above the Peter Pan collar, and my good fortune in having met her. Her? I realized with a start that I didn't even know her name.

I cleared my throat. "My name's Sparky," I ventured. I'd gained the nickname because of my ability to fix anything electrical. When I wasn't playing backup, I could usually be found fixing music equipment for the local bands.

"Nice to meet you, Sparky," she said, not looking away from the mirror. She began stroking *The Stranger* absentmindedly with her left hand. Her fingers were long and sensitive looking. I wondered if she ever played guitar.

Suddenly she pounded her fist on the bar. Staring deeply into my eyes she said, "I am Adara. I haven't been in a relationship in six years." All this and single too? "It's been pleasant chatting with you Sparky, but I really must be going now," she said, shoving off of the barstool.

Tossing back the remains of my Crystal Geyser, I said gallantly, "Let me walk you to your car."

Adara didn't look back as she strode purposefully to the exit.
Taking her silence as assent, I stalked into the steamy night after
her and overtook her just as she reached a beat-up looking VW
parked about a block from the bar on Santa Monica Boulevard.
Seeing me glancing at the front bumper, which was secured with a
Bungee cord and what appeared to be a racoon's tail, she said, "I
haven't had time to get it fixed. Too busy saving the world."

I couldn't restrain myself any longer. Grabbing her shoulders,
I pressed myself against her, her against the car, my lips against
her lips. Her ripe breasts teased me from beneath her sweater. I
nuzzled her neck, left teethmarks on the Peter Pan collar. She
smelled of patchouli, baby powder, and Ben Gay. I wondered
whether she wore underwear and if so, what kind.

"Let's stay together tonight," I said.

To my surprise, she reached into her knapsack, retrieved her
keys, and unlocked the passenger door. Needing no further invi-
tation, I slid in and leaned over to unlock her door.

"Your place or mine?" she purred, suddenly coy. My nuzzling
had caused the top button of her collar to come undone. A pulse
throbbed there, visible in the light from a street lamp.

I usually took women to my apartment for the first time, but it
was Friday night and I was feeling daring. "Your place."

We drove silently across town, pulling into the driveway of what
appeared to be a mansion or a haunted house in the middle of
Koreatown.

"Welcome to my domicile," Adara said. Slamming the car door
behind her, she said over her shoulder, "Come in."

The first floor of the house appeared to be completely empty
except for a glow-in-the-dark skull that sat inside the fireplace in
the living room.

"Would you like some tea?" Adara drifted toward what I assumed was the kitchen. It wasn't what I'd had in mind when I'd
asked to come home with her but, not wanting to appear rude, I
answered, "Sure."

I stood nervously in the entryway while Adara made the tea.
When she returned with the teapot and cups on a tray, she was
wearing nothing but a black merry widow, her kneesocks and
clogs, and the Peter Pan collar, which turned out to be a dickey.
Her lightly freckled breasts were well-formed under the flimsy

cloth of the lingerie. Her waist was small and swelled into voluptuous hips and long, shapely legs.

"Let's go," she murmured, turning to climb the stairs.

I no longer felt as confident as I had kissing her on Santa
Monica Boulevard. Adara had quite suddenly gained the upper
hand.

Staring at the tantalizing bit of ass that peeked out of her lingerie as she maneuvered the steps, I followed her into a bedroom
that contained little more than a bed with black satin sheets.
Adara placed the tea tray on the far side of the bed with a crash of
china. It wasn't until she pushed me down on the bed that I noticed the mirror on the ceiling. Adara pulled my T-shirt up with
her teeth and began vigorously massaging my breasts with a bottle
of oil she'd grabbed from a nightstand.

"What was Einstein's most famous equation?" she spat at me as
she rubbed the oil against my now-hard nipples. She was simultaneously squeezing my hips between her thighs and grinding
against me, making it hard to concentrate.

"Could you repeat the question, please?" I gasped, stalling for
time.

"What was Einstein's most famous equation?" she almost
screamed. Her palms were making small circles over my nipples.

"$E=mc^2$?" I asked doubtfully.

"Yes," she said encouragingly, sliding one finger under the
waistband of my jeans.

"Who was the greatest writer of the twentieth century?" she
challenged, beginning to unbutton my jeans with one hand while
stroking herself with the other.

"I...I don't know," I blundered. I reached for her but she
slapped my hands away.

"Think! Think!" she ordered, tugging my jeans down as far as
my ankles.

"Who did you read as a child?" she pressed. One hand teased
me by stroking my cotton underwear. The other hand pinched my
nipples alternately.

"Lewis Carroll! Beatrix Potter! A. A. Milne!"

She turned me over and pulled my underwear to my knees. She
spanked me twice, hard, and said, "You can do better than that."

"E. B. White. Carolyn Keene." I bit the sheets in frustration.

"No." Slap. "No." Slap.

Digging into a deep reservoir of my past, I tried again. "Beverly Cleary. Hans Christian Andersen." Was he even twentieth century? "Zilpha Keatley Snyder. Robert Louis Stevenson." Silence. "What do you want? Help Me!" I begged. I thrust back against her, feeling the wetness of her through the silk lingerie.

Four more slaps in answer.

I twisted back to see my reflection in the mirror above the bed. The spanking had left red prints on the curve of my ass.

In desperation, "Dr. Seuss!"

"Yes! Oh God, yes!" Adara shrieked, moving spasmodically against me. "Dr. Seuss was, is, the greatest writer of the twentieth century! God, this is good!"

I flung her dickey, kneesocks, and clogs into a heap with my T-shirt and jeans. This time she didn't resist. We united in a perfect fusion, and there were no more words until Adara came again screaming, "Venus! Take me, Venus!"

HOLLY HUGHES

Performance Art. What causes it. Where it comes from. And what can be done about it. Three case studies.

NUMBER ONE. "Performance Art as a Tool of Social Change."

I launched my careers as a lesbian and as a waitress simultaneously. For a while they kind of fed off each other, there was a certain symbiosis. (Someone has suggested this had something to do with me working in seafood restaurants, but I would never say such a thing.)

Initially, I admit I wasn't very adept at being either a waitress or a lesbian, although I was fast and mean and this was somewhat of a plus in both departments. I remember standing over the naked form of the woman I lived with. The woman who everyone in town thought was my girlfriend. Everyone, that is, but her. I wanted desperately to have my way with her. But I had no idea what my way might be.

Meanwhile, back at the Red Lobster, I was working very hard to present myself as a lesbian separatist waitress. It's not so easy to combine those particular sets of identities. If you want tips.

It was hard to persuade anyone I was even the most benign form of feminist since most of the women would run when they saw me coming. They knew I was apt to start quoting *Ms.* magazine at the slightest provocation and that I loved to chase people around the salad bar trying to persuade them how oppressed they were.

But I was respected, if not actually liked, for the principled stances I would assume at our staff meetings, which were held every Tuesday at eight A.M. The rest of the waitresses would just be trying to wake up. They'd be all hunched over a cup of our famous burnt coffee that we'd whiten with a little liquid paper we'd try to masquerade as cream. Eight A.M., and your feet are already rebelling against the vinyl prisons they've been sentenced to. And the manager, he's introducing the "Bermuda Triangle Platter," or talking about the latest all-you-can-eat deep-fried sea monkey special. Or the drink du jour. The Moon Rocket. It was always our drink du jour no matter what jour it was because it was blue and frozen and on fire. All at the same time.

And I'd say: "WAIT JUST A MINUTE! While we're sitting here trying to come up with a few more ways to push shrimp cocktail, women in Africa are having their clitorises cut off! And I want to know: WHEN IS THE RED LOBSTER GOING TO DO SOMETHING ABOUT THAT!"

As a lesbian separatist, I was more successful in the latter category than the former. I pretty much separated myself from just about everyone.

It's something you never read about in radical political theory. The loneliness of the pure.

And I wanted so desperately to experience some of that sisterhood I had read so much about. Finally an opportunity presented itself in the form of a five-state employee talent contest. I decided to inflict my talent on all the waitresses because I had read: "None of us are free unless ALL of us are free!" So I called all the waitresses together and I put pillowcases over their heads. Then I proceeded to interpret, choreographically, the wit and wisdom of my then-heroine, Andrea Dworkin, as set to the music of Randy Newman's "Short People Got No Reason to Live."

This was my big chance! This was my opportunity to strike a blow against the capitalist patriarchy! But do I look like someone who's got all the answers? So I danced a joke instead.

And we won.

NUMBER TWO. "Breaking the Fourth Wall."

Like most children, I had various chores I was expected to do around the house. The most odious of which was, in my opinion, kissing my parents good night. I realized, however, it was an important job. One that apparently they could not do for themselves. And I would be paid.

One night, sitting next to my mother on the couch, I had a sudden epiphany. Fortunately, the fabric was Scotchgarded, so I didn't cause any permanent damage. But all of a sudden I realized that my mother wasn't just my mother. She was a *woman*.

I knew what that meant.

I'd already figured out that being female was a chronic medical condition. You couldn't cure it, but you might be able to learn to live with it. If you got the right treatment in time. And I had an idea for a new treatment for women.

I noticed I had an audience. This made me very happy because I'd heard in science class that a tree falling in the wilderness made no sound. I wanted the world to know about my new treatment for women. So I stood up and looked at my audience. It consisted of two people. My father and the other person, who I will alternately refer to as my sister and my father's girlfriend.

It's important to know who your audience is.

I went over to my mother and when I got to her I straddled her. Kind of like I imagined I would straddle that pony I knew by then my father was never going to buy me. And as I mounted Mom, I turned and I looked at my audience, as if to say: "I bet you wish you'd just bought that pony for me, now don't you? Maybe all this ugliness could have been avoided."

Then I proceeded to kiss my mother good night in the following fashion: I applied my mouth to hers with all the suction power I could muster in my prepubescent frame, and I began to rotate my mouth against hers in a precise, almost scientific manner.

When my mother was, at least in my opinion, good and kissed, and would stay that way for quite some time, I turned and I looked at my audience, as if to say: "You could be next."

All that kept me from breaking the fourth wall at that moment was my mother, who said: "Where did you learn to kiss like that?"

"On TV," I answered.

"Well, you're doing it all wrong, hon. You got to open your mouth. Like this."

I opened my mouth. I leaned forward. And yes, I did kiss my mother good night in the way she so obviously wanted me to. As I did, a small voice in the back of my head warned: "What do you think you're doing? Now you've gone and fucked your life up but good."

And I was happy.

This was the first time I realized *I had a life*. Something of my own to fuck up. And I felt powerful. Like the most powerful thing I could imagine, which at that time was a waitress at Howard Johnson's on a Sunday morning, seeing that room full of the interminably ravenous and thinking: "I know what to do."

As I made out with Mom, I heard a small sound. Like a door closing and locking behind me. I knew I would never get back to that place where I imagined I was safe. And yes, I knew what I was doing was wrong. But I was surrounded by people who were suffocating under the burden of A Normal Life. I knew I'd rather be wrong than safe. I guess I was at that age when most

girls start looking for shelter from the storm. But I started looking for the storm.

NUMBER THREE. "I Was Forced to Participate in Performance Art
as a Condition of My Parole."

I wasn't actually in jail, though I desperately wanted to be. Anywhere my family wasn't.

So when my mother asked me if I realized what I had done to
Lynne Colbert in the back of our garage was a crime, I said: "Yes."
Then she asked me if I realized that people in this country went
to jail every day for what I had done to this young girl and I said:
"So what."

Every day my mother would confront me with a list of my crimes
and misdemeanors. I had, for example, told my little sister that
she was adopted, that her real name was Gertrude and that no
one was going to buy her a Christmas present. I had broken a
branch off the ornamental cherry tree and gone over to the
neighbor's freshly poured cement driveway where I created a little
bas-relief depicting, if I recall correctly, the history of bullfighting.
In Michigan.

I believe it was my first triptych.

Every day my mother would try to get me to admit how bad I was.
I would always plead innocent. But after I had Lynne in the
garage, I cracked. I surrendered to my essentially criminal nature.
I knew I never could be good enough to please my mother so
maybe I could be good at being bad.

I resolved I would go from bad to worse as soon as it could be
arranged.

But my eager confession didn't seem to please my mother. I guess
I had robbed her of the joy of interrogation and those long,
lonely hours until she would start to burn dinner just stretched
out empty before her. She asked me to consider the particularly

heinous nature of my crime. I knew she was just stalling. But I thought about it because I liked thinking about it.

What I had done is I had taken Lynne Colbert (my sometimes best friend and often worst enemy) out behind the Buick, and I had persuaded her to let me give her a little haircut.

Lynne Colbert was widely believed to be the most beautiful girl in my elementary school. But that was *before*. Before I got out my father's toenail clippers and started hacking away at those long blonde curls. As I hacked, I persuaded her that (A) she didn't look hideous; and (B) her mother would not beat the shit out of her when I was finished.

She believed me.

I couldn't believe she believed me! Any more than I'm sure Jim Jones couldn't believe it when people started drinking that Kool-Aid! As I ravaged Lynne's locks, I channeled the spirit of my first lesbian role model—Paul Lynde. Particularly Paul Lynde as he was manifest in that seminal piece of queer cinema, *Bye Bye Birdie*. His spirit sneered through me that day in the garage. I said: "Kids."

I did not consider myself a kid. I walked among them but was not of them.

When confronted by my mother I liked to imagine a big prison devoted to people whose crimes are merely aesthetic. In particular, I liked to envision a big holding tank filled with bad hair stylists.

Of course, I was too middle-everything to be sent to anything as lively as prison. But I was expected to participate in the nearest equivalent for someone of my milieu.

Community theater.

I was under psychiatric orders to work on a production of *The Sound of Music*. This wasn't just any production, oh no. This was a production under the direction of one of the most renowned thespians in the entire "Thumb" region of Michigan. (She'd won kudos for her previous season's one-woman *Man of La Mancha*.)

I wasn't allowed to act. Instead, I was expected to work on the set crew. I was entirely responsible for the Alps. The Alps are of supreme importance in *The Sound of Music*. You got no Alps, you got no music, you know what I'm saying? I was also expected, during the run of the show, to lower a microphone during "Edelweiss" so the Von Trapp children could be plainly heard making that touching homage to those little fascist flowers.

Opening night. By some fluke I've managed to get the Alps up on their hind legs. I lower the microphone on cue. But one of the Von Trapp children has another idea. Instead of belting out "Edelweiss," he pivots and farts. Into the microphone.

I have no idea how many of you, if any, have experienced first-hand the sheer destructive power of amplified flatulence. But let me assure you, it's nothing to sneeze at. The one thing we had in Saginaw was a damn good sound system.

Pandemonium broke out, praise the Lord. The first thing to go were the Alps. You'd think I'd be upset because they were *my* Alps, after all. But I was delighted. Because all of a sudden you could look backstage and see—*the nuns and the Nazis were the same people!* It was just a question of costumes and phony accents.

Finally the play made sense.

I thought: "This is what I want to do with the rest of my life!"

Joshua

ROBIN PODOLSKY

Sacred soil. Reeking of history, nourished with new blood. Land of grapes, olives, oranges; juicy, heavy-flavored fruit. A colonized, a chained land.

This land demands vehemence. It lives in deep color, immense gesture, gigantic significance. This haunted holy land, this womb, slaughterhouse, this potent field.

Little Joshua caught between his father's rages: "Lay the boards straight, you little bastard"—the callused mallet of a hand across his head like the hammer of God—and his mother's fantasies: "I wouldn't let Yusef give me any babies, I stole seven hairs off his balls and knotted them in linen soiled with chickenshit, I buried it all in the garden, he can't put a kid in me, you're my miracle, I made you in the moonlight when the angel fucked me, you're my magic boy...."

When she was a girl there was true quiet power. Towers and webs of thought, a deep irresistible flood of ideas. And visions. And dreams that came true. Her family was afraid of her. All but the brother who had taught her to read, whispering Torah under her father's nose. They tried to beat the dybbuk from her body. They married her to Yusef, the quiet carpenter who could not stop staring when she passed.

Barabbas: "I got to talk to him in prison a little bit. Hell of a sweet guy when he was lucid. He did have something. It was beyond charm. He was—compelling. He made you like him so much, you wanted to believe whatever he said. And that got pretty scary. Because he knew what was coming and he wanted it. He didn't want to live for the cause. He wanted to die for it. He had something going on inside him, bad dreams, visions, whatever you want to call things like that. By the time it was over, I think he really believed that he was the Messiah himself. What a pointless, pathetic waste. And what a strange idea of God he had. What kind of father would torture his only son?"

"I'm gone for three weeks building a mikvah in Galilee to put a roof over your fuckin' head and you get your silly ass knocked up? Crazy slut has the nerve to smile up into my face and tell me an angel did it? You always make fun of me. You probably think I'm stupid enough to believe that shit, you whore, you PIG!"

She lies on the ground, smiling her hatred up at him, a new bruise blooming on her cheek. As always, his lips quiver and thicken before he cries, just like those of a child.

"Goddammit Mara, I used to love you so much, you were so pretty, you were so smart, why couldn't you give me a chance, you always hated me, it wasn't my fault you didn't want to get married, every woman gets married, who do you think you are, couldn't you just try to be happy, what did you want from me, you always looked at me like I was a dirty animal and that's just what I feel like whenever I'm around you, it isn't my fault, I really loved you, goddamn you fucking bitch, you fucking whore, goddamn you, goddamn everything. I don't care about anything anymore. You happy now? I don't care. I don't give a shit anymore, I really don't. Okay, Mara? I don't care anymore. Are you happy now? Mara? I don't care. Okay?"

Prayers rise from the lips of davening old men and circle the air like lazy bees. His lessons done, Joshua lies curled at the feet of his favorite teacher, baking in the hot, damp air. He loves the old synagogue.

Here he finds order, peace and quiet. In this dim, still place, elders find time for questions that were ages old when they were boys. Here the prayers for sunrise, for washing up, for blessing the books are always pronounced with care, exactly when they're supposed to be, in the same beloved rhythms all the time.

It is a special indulgence for a boy to be allowed after school with the scholars. Joshua is a special boy. He asks so many questions. Grimacing with embarrassment, he must give voice to just a few of the riddles that throng his brain.

Little Joshua, curled in a flaccid ball, lets the prayers wash over him. The old men mumble and sway.

In a confusion of harsh sound, the door flies open. Framed in the white afternoon sun is a bulky bearded man, roaring. The Roman soldiers have gotten drunk and decided to visit the synagogue.

Joshua does not move. His trance becomes an aching watchfulness, as he takes in every gesture of the massive Roman's arms and legs. He sees the tremor of muscle, the web of saliva that connects the bawling lips, the uneven stubble that crawls over the bull neck.

Joshua sees the pain trapped in the soldier's eyes, the baffled hurt that drives the man's stubborn aggression. Joshua sees the eyes of a child who, knowing that he will be hit, continues to yell, demanding that everybody stop what they're doing and look at him.

This man is the leader. The rest hang behind him, leaning on their spears and giggling or staring at their feet. They will wait for their captain's permission to burn the books, make the old men dance and cut off Joshua's hair.

Joshua discovers that this Roman, outlandish and bestial in his bowl-shaped helmet crested with a filthy spray of plumes, reminds him of no one but his father, even though his father looks nothing like the soldier at all. Yusef wears his hair and beard long, as tradition demands. His spadelike hands, crusted with years of callus, have never held a weapon of war.

But Yusef, a patriarch with no authority to defend his family, a craftsman begging work from people taxed to the limit of survival, Joshua's father has eyes like the Roman soldier's eyes. More and more he smells, like the Roman does, of wine and stale sweat. More and more often he enters his own home as the soldier had entered the synagogue, a miserable invader, demanding a welcome that, long ago, he lost all hope of receiving.

So Joshua knows what will happen when the soldier runs out of curses. He holds very still, aware that he can never be small enough to escape the blows when they come.

"Maybe my father *was* an angel."

"Maybe your father was a ghost, you're so pale, you look like you're sick, maybe your father was a *Roman!*"

"Maybe he was. Maybe my father was a soldier."

"Yeah, Joshua's father is a Roman and his mother is a soldier's whore."

"His mother is crazy."

"Here's Joshua's father—'Hi, lady, I'm an angel, you want to fuck?'"

And then Joshua's hatred grew claws and a voice and his tormentors fell to the ground, vomiting black stuff while trying to scream.

They were all too afraid to tell. But one of the old men knew.

"Joshua, you think your power is so very special. You think you're the only one. A lot of people have it, really.

"You need to discipline yourself. You need some control over this gift you have. And let God control the rest. You could heal people some day. You could learn to see things that will help people understand the world. You could do a lot of harm, also.

"Joshua, you still have a choice. Stop thinking you're so special. Try to understand—wanting to be so special is making you *less* than you are." The old man stared at something that Joshua could not see. "And something horrible will happen. To all of us, Joshua, because of you. Something really horrible, more than you could ever imagine. But, now, you still have a choice."

Pilate: "Dirty bastards, huddling together all the time, mumbling that filthy language in their ratty beards. I never know what they're thinking. I suppose they hate us all. Their absurd dignity—why can't they learn to walk like slaves? Herod knows how to handle them, only he doesn't go far enough."

Joshua had to go to market by himself. His mother sits at home, rocking on the floor. She has been like that for two days. Her belly swells, she drools. Her hair drags against her mouth. Joshua can't look at that, it makes his own face itch.

Someone should stand up for him. He's only ten, he shouldn't have to go through this by himself. None of the other boys he knows have to suffer like he does. His teachers tell him that there is a reason for everything. Sometimes he hates them for saying that. He wants them to be on his side, to get him out of that house. He can't stand to hate his teachers, they're all he has. He resolves to take their word for it and study harder.

Joshua likes to read about the great martyrs. He pores over the details of their excruciations, exults in the purity of their triumphs. At night, they visit his dreams.

Joshua arrives home to silence. He cannot dare to believe his luck. His father, an empty wineskin cradled against his stomach, lies motionless outside the door. Quivering with relief, Joshua puts the groceries where they belong.

His mother is no longer where she was. Joshua wants to find her, to throw himself in her lap. He will forgive her for everything if she'll just hold and rock him while he cries. She does that sometimes. Mara is not in the house or the yard or the outhouse.

Unable to hold back his tears, Joshua runs to the stable, his favorite place. He can curl up in the hay, with the gentle mule for company. Afraid that his retching sobs will tear him apart, he stumbles inside his refuge.

He almost trips over them. His mother and a stranger are fucking in the hay at his feet.

Joshua runs off to a field. Surrounded by barley, he drops to the ground and rocks himself. His open mouth pulses around the shape of remembered sobs, his shoulders hunch in rhythm, but he is silent, dry-eyed. He will not cry again for years.

Joshua the preacher has been called to judge the adulterous woman. Through a curtain of bodies, he glimpses her, whirling in terror, long brown hair spiraling around her. Joshua can barely breathe. He wants to see them smash her, to have them tear the clothes from her body and mutilate it in front of him. He wants to throw himself over her, to shield and cradle.

Someone in the crowd sees him, calls his name. Others take up the cry and, grabbing the woman, throw her to the ground at his feet. His heart batters his ribs. He feels his muscles drain from his bones like running water, he is dissolving in the wind. Only his member, a striking animal imprisoned in the folds of his robe, has life, appetite. Self-disgust settles him. Weight and sensation return to his stolid flesh.

She stands in front of him, holding herself, gulping little sobs. It shocks him that he has to look down, not upward, to meet her large brown eyes and that he can find nothing there but the most ordinary calculation and fear. He lets her go. "And daughter—sin no more." The enormous eyes widen further. He will be her god forever. Dizzy, he watches her run away. He shivers for a long time.

Judas: "What difference does it make how it started? You can't fight Rome. They had me, three months after I came to Jerusalem, for stealing a centurion's coins. They were going to sell me out to sea. Or that's what they said they would do. They can do what they want, they could have let me go or they could have locked me up or nailed me up anytime they wanted before I stole anything, even; they never need a reason. I think they saw something in me. I think they arrested me just to save my pride, so I could pretend they made me a snitch to save my life. They know what they're doing.

"I knew this would be the last time. Too many people had heard things. They were always warning Joshua not to trust me. But he thought he knew everything. I'll never work again, but this time, I got serious money.

"Now I'll be a rich man when I die.

"I never planned that part. I don't know why I can't stand myself anymore. Just one job too many, maybe. Not that I ever believed I'd die old. I thought if the Jews didn't catch up with me, the Romans would get around to it themselves. No. Really, I always knew. Someday I'd wind up alone with time to think, knowing there's not a living soul I could turn to who would tell me not to go through with it. It feels funny. Like all of a sudden I'm getting dramatic or something.

"But, then too, why not? It's quick and clean, and I've already lived longer than most people I know. Maybe that's more than I deserve. Story of my life, grabbing more than I deserve and getting away with it. You can call me a traitor if you want, but I didn't make the world the way it is. You can't fight Rome. If you're smart, you can use Rome for a little while and then you can die rich, like me."

Barabbas: "You know the trouble with wild-card populists? They're charismatic and they're diligent, really driven, but a bitch to work with. They stink of ego. No belief in the people, no cooperation. That render unto Caesar business. Why didn't he talk to us before he made a conciliationist speech like that? But it's alright to attack the money-changers in the Temple and fuck up our united front.

You notice how he saves the really nasty venom for his own people? But he's full of compassion for the oppressor. Like we really need this shit right now, there weren't enough factions to keep life interesting."

The evening stumbles forward. Joshua is conducting a Seder. Everyone else is nervous because he has been petulant for days. He put a curse on a tree that didn't have fruit when he wanted it. Even John was embarrassed.

There were confrontations in the city. With the priests who have heard of Joshua's claims to prophecy, his increasingly broad hints that he is the son of David himself. They are incensed at the blasphemy, querulous at the thought of reprisals that some new challenge to Rome might bring.

Confrontations with the Zealots. They are impatient with Joshua's unpredictable mysticism, his wild swings between pacifism and unfocused ravings about blood, and they have truly had enough of his arrogance. They don't want to work with him anymore. They agitate for his flock to disperse and join them in the hills where they prepare to fight.

Staring fitfully at his apostles, sensing their distance, Joshua begins, visibly, to seethe. "One of you is going to betray me tonight." Matthew rolls his eyes at Mark. He is thinking that they ought to leave together. First thing in the morning, while the rest are sleeping it off.

Mark smiles and rolls his eyes back, indicating Peter with a cocked brow. Peter, who will believe anything, is staring at Joshua openmouthed. Like a child who has been told that a favorite pet is never coming back.

Joshua gazes back into the wide, soft face. While despising his own nastiness, he shudders with contempt. And a cold, private fear. Often, he really does know things. His prophecy reverberates in his ears and throat. Was it a prediction or a command? He feels certain that by naming his fear, he has made it inevitable. In a whisper of an image, as insubstantial as odor, a memory of Mara takes form. Joshua bats it away.

Enraged at the apprehension that crouches like a hungry dog inside him, Joshua digs spitefully into Peter, his shadow. "You. You're going to betray me tomorrow. Three times. You'll say that you never knew me." He really is scaring himself. Why can't he stop this?

Peter's eyes fill, visibly. Rigid with mortification, knowing that everyone is hating him for being mean, Joshua wraps himself in indifference. Like an old man donning a tallith, becoming holy and unapproachable.

Joshua shakes his head. His ears are buzzing now, his pulse an angry tide. He is eager and furious, at what and at whom, he doesn't know. He doesn't want to go to prison. He doesn't want to die.

"I *don't* want to die." He says this inside, over and over. With each repetition, the denial tastes more and more blatantly false. For a moment he is certain that he has said it out loud. The faces around him won't reveal if this is true; they've been furtively appalled all night.

It is time to bless the wine. The brothers are calmed by the familiar ritual. They sip pensively as Joshua pronounces the words, "Blessed are you, oh Lord, our God, who has made the fruit of the vine." Relieved, they raise their eyes from their cups to see Joshua trembling with agitation.

"This wine you're guzzling—it's my blood." The voice is flat and shallow. "Well, don't stop. Drink it. Drink my blood."

Something dreadful here. The reek of dissolution. None of them can say it now, but they will take it to their beds. They will consider how it would be to break away. None of them wants to be the first to leave the group—none of them wants to be the last.

Pilate: "Alright, we'll give them a choice, Joshua or Barabbas. Whoever they pick, they'll be condemning one of their own and the survivor will get blamed for it. Barabbas's people will probably carry the crowd. But I want it done right. Our agents yelling for the death of Joshua and the release of Barabbas. The religious will blame the terrorists. The terrorists will blame the priests who will run screaming into our arms. And Joshua's cult won't last without a leader."

Mara: "I saw angels before all the bad things happened, before he started beating me, my visions were different and they were so beautiful, I swear it wasn't supposed to be like this, nothing I do ever comes out right, nothing."

Barabbas: "How could this happen? Why didn't people smash the crosses where they stood? I feel dirty to be alive. And ready to sob with gratitude not to be nailed up. What am I supposed to do with this?

"Well, maybe this will be the atrocity that finally brings Jews together. When the Empire slaughters mystics who preach an accommodation with Caesar, everybody has to see they might as well fight back before we all get wiped out. All Judean people will form a solid wall against the West. It's historically inevitable. It can't go any other way."

Joshua on the cross: "It hurts, it hurts, it hurts, help me, Pop, Dad, I'm bleeding, I'm really bleeding, you insatiable bastard, is this what you wanted, Mama, help me, help me, it hurts, oh god, I don't want this, it hurts. It hurts, I want my FATHER...."

Joshua goes off into the desert alone. For days he eats nothing. He scours his body with hot sand and thrashes himself with thongs until he is a mud man, caked with blood and grit.

He prays that the Father see and accept his sacrifice. Sometimes the Father will not answer and Joshua's rage bubbles like restive magma in his belly. He knows that he has done something wrong. So he flays his scabby wounds again, and the white heat in his belly erupts; he feels its flame cut rivers into his flesh. He falls to the sand and squirms there.

Then the hard blue dome of the sky opens for him, clanging like a great brass gong, and he sees the angel, its wings of white flame spread before him. And behind the angel, shimmering in the heat of those immense wings, he sees his Father's face.

God talks to Joshua as Joshua has always wished that his Father would. God tells Joshua that everything will be all right. His suffering has pleased the Lord. He is almost ready. He will get to live with his Father in heaven. His mother will be named holy. All the people will cry for him. Everyone will love him forever.

Joshua is satisfied. He can return to his followers. He will tell the trusted ones everything. They will be his witnesses when the time comes.

Yusef: "I knew the little bastard would die on a cross one day. He never was good for a fucking thing except getting in trouble."

Rat
Bohemia

SARAH SCHULMAN

Last summer the mayor of New York decided to cut back on rat extermination. He also cut back on streetlights. As a result, night increasingly meant these dark outlines of buildings surrounded by the scampering of eighteen-inch varmints. Ten million of them at least. My best friend, Killer, and I spent a lot of nights that summer just walking around because we didn't have any money. I was saving up to move out of New York, and Killer hadn't had a job in two years. She came over every night to eat and then we'd take a walk. She'd forgotten how to even look for a job. She'd forgotten how to sound employable on the telephone. One day I glanced over her shoulder at the Help Wanted pages of the *New York Times*, only it wasn't what you'd call *pages*. It was more like half a column. One Saturday we saw a kid get shot in front of the Unique Clothing Store Going Out of Business Sale and the next day we watched a guy go crazy and throw glass bottles at people for twenty minutes. I've always wanted to shoot rats.

Killer and I are hard-core New Yorkers. But when we were kids the only homeless person you'd ever see would be a wino on the Bowery or an occasional bag lady. You never saw anyone sleeping on a subway car unless they were coming home from the night shift. The streets were not covered with urine then. That was considered impolite. There have always been rats, though. I remember as a teenager watching them run around on the subway tracks waiting for the Seven train to get me out of Jackson Heights. But mostly, when I was a kid, rats were something that bit babies in a mythical, faraway ghetto. You never saw them hanging out in the middle-class sections of Queens.

An average rat litter is twenty-two little ones, and they can reproduce at the rate of six litters a year. Some time in the 1980s I started to see them scampering regularly in the playgrounds of Central Park. Reagan had just become president and I held him directly responsible. Rat infestation felt like something the U.S. government should really have been able to handle. That's when I started thinking about getting a gun and shooting each one of them on sight. Picking them off the way hillbillies shoot squirrels.

That guy, last Sunday, who was throwing glass bottles? All he cared about was himself. His personal expression was more important to him than other people's eyes. That's the kind of attitude that makes this town a dangerous place to live. You never know when it can hit. The shooting in front of the Unique was more reasonable. It was just a bunch of friends killing each other. Don't have friends like that and it will never happen to you.

Every morning I go over to the old Veteran's Administration building on West Twenty-fifth Street and wait on line to go through the metal detectors. The lobby walls are covered with these old World War Two murals of soldiers getting fitted for artificial legs by nurses in starched caps. The women lift up the veterans' new legs and demonstrate how to use them. Once I make it through, I have to ride up in the elevators with all the wacked-out veterans scratching and getting into fights. Then I get off at the seventeenth floor, where there is the Food and Hunger Hotline office and walk past them to my office. Then I sign in at Pest Control and waste about half the day unless I get sent out on a job.

When I'm sitting in Pest Control, hanging out, waiting, I pay close attention to the goings-on at Food and Hunger. I want to see everything I can. Everything. I want to be a witness to my own time because I have a sneaking suspicion that I'm gonna live a lot longer than most of the people I meet. If I'm gonna be the only one still around to say what happened, I'd better pay close attention now.

Killer usually stops by the office at ten for coffee and peanut butter sandwiches. Then she checks in at a couple of restaurants to see if they need any prep cooks. I know for a fact that they're only hiring Mexicans and Israelis. Everybody knows Americans aren't good for restaurant work. They want to talk on the phone in between high salaries and free meals. In the meantime, she's living on forty dollars a week from watering plants for a couple of offices and boutiques. The rest gets paid by the bed-and-breakfast guests she hustles at those four-dollar cappuccino places. Mostly Swiss people or Germans. They think it's quaint. She gives them a bed and then tells them to make their own breakfast. Then she comes to the office to eat some of mine. We've been living on this schedule for a long time already. It is one big fat habit. You know one thing I don't like about homeless people? They ask you for a light and then hold on to your lighter for forty-five minutes blabbing on and on about some misfortune. The whole thing is designed to make it seem that they don't realize that they've got your lighter. But the fact is, they know they've got it.

Killer was brought up to be a racist. One night I went over to her place to watch TV and her parents brought over some food. Next thing you know the news came on and it was all "nigger" this and "nigger" that. Her parents had these sharp teeth whenever they said that word. They scrunched up the skin around their eyes. It wasn't said calmly. Killer knows better but when she gets emotional, that's what she falls back on. Like one time some Puerto Rican guy was beating up his kid in the hallway and Killer said, "Look at that low-rent over there."

"Shut up," I said. "You haven't had a job in two years. If you had enough patience to stand in line you'd be on welfare yourself."

"I'd be on welfare if it wasn't for the strength of the Euro-dollar," she said as some blond couple rolled over in the bed. That was the way she looked at things.

God, that summer was hot. There's that way Puerto Rican girls sit close together on the stoops. They have skinny arms and those ten-dollar pink dresses. They smile and wear their hair long with a headband.

Every day homeless people come into Food and Hunger looking for food but they only get Contact Cards. I gave Killer one of those cards but she said the food they advertised wasn't nutritious.

One time, before breakfast, Killer walked me to work but she wanted to stop off at the Xerox store on Tenth Street that was run by some Moonies. They were clean-cut peculiar and wore polyester pants up to their necks.

"They give away free bread and free Chinese buns," she said.

When we walked in it was kind of slow and real hot. It stunk of Xerox fluid. The polyesters had a few day-olds sitting on the counter and a bag of day-old buns.

"Don't eat it," I said. "It's old pork."

"Hi, Killer," they said, handing her two loaves. Then they turned to me. "What about you?"

"I don't need free food," I said.

"Look," Killer whispered. "Take it. I need it. I'll give you a fresh one later for your birthday."

"OK. No, wait. I don't want bread for my birthday. I want a colander."

"Do you think I need a professional portfolio?" she asked.

Killer was still thinking about jobs.

"How is everything going?" Killer asked the Moonies, remembering to be gracious.

"We're having problems with rats," they said.

That woke me up.

"Do you have big ones?" I asked. "One-pounders?"

"Yep," they said.

"Did you put out poison?" Killer asked.

"Poison doesn't work," they said. "They're too strong. Besides, if you kill one that way it's just gonna stink up your place and bring maggots."

"Did you try traps?" Killer asked, trying to cut me off because she knew what I was about to recommend.

"Traps don't work," I said, ignoring her. "The rats are too smart. They spring the traps and get the bait."

"What about walk-in traps?" one of the Moonies asked.

"Too expensive," I said. "Doesn't work on a massive scale."

"Well, what do you suggest?" he asked.

"You gotta shoot 'em," I said. "You gotta get 'em one by one."

The reason that all of this background information had been on my mind was because I spent most of last summer thinking about the fact that, frankly, I have not made as much of my life as I would have liked. I have never learned how to achieve. That's why I've been saving up to move out of New York. Florida might be nice. Learn how to drive. Go swimming.

Working this job is a real downer except when we go out for the kill. That's the best. But in the meantime, I have to sit here with the crew from Food and Hunger and listen to them make small talk. Especially that Mrs. Sabrina Santiago. She almost always has a city worker attitude and therefore kicks my butt psychologically and regularly. Everything is about her territory and her ability to lord it over me. But she has nothing to brag about since she moves real slow and wouldn't say, "How are you?" if it was worth a million dollars in food stamps. These types of relationships and social encounters are what have made me question my life.

Killer and I talk about this all of the time, about how we are going to better ourselves. The problem with Killer is that she's a pretender. She pretends that something is going to happen when nothing is ever going to happen. Then, when it's over, she pretends that something did happen when actually it was nothing. I love Killer. I don't mean to judge her but I have to.

Mrs. Santiago called me from across the hall and asked if I would messenger something over to the computer store on Forty-third Street. Now, I knew that she was supposed to bring that over herself because Food and Hunger doesn't have the kind of money to buy a messenger service. I also know that Mrs. Santiago lives in Bushwick, Brooklyn, which is in the opposite direction from Forty-third Street. So, out of the kindness of my heart I said *yes*. Then she made me stand there, freezing my butt off in that central air conditioning, while she chats away on the phone for forty-five minutes. City worker.

Of course I'm eavesdropping because I've got nothing else to do, and the whole conversation seems to be about these store-rooms filled with flour that the City got ahold of. But all of this flour doesn't do hungry people any good because most of them don't know how to bake bread. Or, if they do know, they've got no place to make it. Especially if you are a person with a substance abuse problem. You will never find the time to make bread. Therefore, all this potential food was sitting there going to waste. Mrs. Santiago was suggesting on the phone that they could get all the new prisoners in all the new jails to learn how to bake bread and they could bake up all this flour and distribute it already made. She was suggesting that, in the future, when they build prisons, they could include bread baking facilities and kill two birds with one stone.

By the time she actually handed me the package and I got

downstairs, I found out that Killer had been waiting around in the lobby because both detectors broke down and everyone was being searched by hand.

"Fuck that," I said and we both set off for the computer store.

Unfortunately, we decided to take the subway, which promptly got stopped between stations.

"Fuck that," I said.

After about ten minutes the conductor's voice came on over the PA system.

"Attention, passengers. Due to a police shooting at the next station we have been temporarily delayed. But we will now proceed with caution."

"Proceed with caution?" Killer said. "What is this, *Stagecoach?*"

"What are we going to do?" I asked.

"Look," she said. "When we pull into the next station, duck behind the seats. You gotta get lower than the bench in case the bullets come through the window."

So, when the train eased into the next stop we ducked. But we both kept sticking our heads up to peek because we wanted to see what was going on. Sure enough the place was swarming with cops and a bunch of medical personnel, all looking very tired and overworked. Then the guy across the aisle from us started to have a psychotic episode. He started meowing. At the next stop, Killer and I got off the train.

"Killer," I said as we walked uptown. "Tell me something. What the fuck are we doing? What are we doing with our lives? I think about this all the time now and I can't figure out what category I'm in."

"Category?"

"Yeah, I mean, I don't have any money but I'm not *poor*. I have aspirations but they're spiritual ones, not careers. I look around at how people are really living and I can't identify. But when I turn on the TV I don't understand that either. What the hell is going on, Killer?" I asked. "Who the hell do we think we are?"

"We're bohemians," she said.

"What?"

"We're bohemians. We don't have those dominant culture values."

"We're bohemians?" I meekly asked.

"Yeah," she answered. "Ever heard of it?"

"Of course," I answered indignantly. "It's people who go to foreign movies."

I was identifying already.

"Look, in the past there were decade-specific names," Killer said. "Like hippies, beatniks, New Age, punks or Communists."

"What do we call them now?"

"That's the whole thing," Killer said, her black hair flapping carelessly against her green skin. "Nowadays it's not generational. Bohemians aren't grouped by clothes or sex or age. Nowadays, it's just a state of mind. Anyone with a different idea is in."

We were standing by the front door of the computer store and Killer obviously wasn't planning to enter. So we stayed out on the sidewalk and discussed existence like any New Yorker would do in our place. We were outside in that inside kind of way. There's weather and a sky at the top of the corridor. The walls were made of buildings and streets ran on like cracks in the plaster.

"But what about turn on, tune in, drop out, Socialism and other social outcast stuff?"

"Listen," Killer said. "In the fifties, the Beats, those guys were so all-American. They could sit around and ponder aesthetic questions but a cup of coffee cost a nickel. Nowadays, with the economy the way it is, you can't drop out or you'll be homeless. You gotta function to be a boho. You have to meet the system head-on at least once in a while and that meeting, Rita, is very brutal. Nowadays you have to pay a very high price to become a bohemian."

SANDRA GOLVIN

When the sickness takes hold of my body like now it always looks the same: head stuffed, throat swollen shut, skin that hurts to touch. I'd say it's the flu but the truth is there's a pain that's deeper than this ache in my bones and the swelling in my glands. I don't want to talk about it, though, not even to myself. Searching for clues in my journal of these past six months I find I have recorded only the happy moments, the small successes that have come my way. I do not mention the missed connections, the not belonging, the constant search for myself in others that is wearing me down.

I do not describe how I wake up and reach for the phone. How that time between dreams and morning is the time of confrontation. Though I hunger for solitude like mother's milk, I find it unbearable. I fall in love over and over, sometimes it's a person, sometimes an organization, but always an idea I have that this person, this group, has the answer I seek. At last, this time, I will feel at home, I will belong somewhere, I will no longer be alone. There have been so many I can't name them all and besides I'm too ashamed.

Everywhere I go on the hot L.A. streets I am looking. In my fever I see everyone else where they belong except me. Everyone else has the right job, the right home, a satisfaction with their lives. In this sickness I envy even the street people because they seem to hang out together, to belong somewhere. Because I imagine that their lives have been stripped of the illusion of security, that they know better than to try to wrestle certainty to the ground. I hate

myself for this disgusting romanticism. And for still trying to pin security to the inside of my pocketbook like my ninety-seven-year-old
grandmother used to do with her keys before she got moved to the
Beverly Hills Retirement Hotel and didn't need them anymore.

The people who have more, the people who have less, all are
to be envied. I can see my way into their lives, into their satisfac-
tions with their lot, into the things they have that I don't: their
backyard picnics and barbeques, their street-corner powwows,
their block parties, PTA meetings, neighborhood watches, community gardens, cultural centers, camp-outs, churches, Al-Anon
meetings, and family reunions. I am queer, I am Jewish, I was
born in L.A. I know everything there is to know about not belonging, about wiping out history, about having everything stolen
from you including the words to explain how it happened, but I
only know it in my bones. In my family there were no fond remi-
niscences, no stories told by the fire. Don't look back, they might
have said, had the instructions come in so many words; it's
maudlin, stupid, useless. There's no one there after all, and only
pain.

Chinatown sits just across Sunset Boulevard from City Hall where
Sunset ends at Olvera Street, the tourist attraction that was once
the center of the newly founded El Pueblo de Nuestra Señora La
Reina de Los Angeles. Due east across the concrete-bound Los
Angeles River is Boyle Heights where, in the first decades of the
twentieth century, my parents' parents settled with thousands of
other Jewish immigrants, the next-to-the-last stop on their west-
ward trek from Poland and the infant Union of Soviet Socialist
Republics. The very last exit is where I grew up, the suburbs of
West L.A. at the end of Interstate 10: as far as the immigrants'
children could get from the memories, as close as they could get
to the sea.

Chinatown is a strange kind of coming home. I recognize something of myself in the small, sturdy, unadorned women with blunt
haircuts who wear ankle-length man-tailored pants and carry plaid
mesh shopping bags in both hands. When I was growing up,
Chinatown was one of the only places in L.A. where life took place
on the sidewalks. Today it is one of the only places in L.A. that, to
me, still looks mostly like it did in my childhood. The smell of gar-
lic, grease and ginger floats on the thick downtown air and carries

me back. In an old brick courtyard I see again the gift shop whose door bears the signs "happiness," "good luck" and "long life" in gold letters on red lacquer, one of the many stores selling treasures from across the Pacific—delicate gold wind chimes and buddhas of porcelain, large paper umbrellas in bright colors with bamboo handles, white bowls with special spoons perfect for soup. Old men sit in each doorway on aged wooden folding chairs, next to hand-lettered signs announcing, I imagine, the special of the day.

In search of herbs I go up New High Street past Yee Mee Loo, the site of my introduction to Chinatown. From the clean, well-organized and mostly empty streets of Cheviot Hills my parents would sneak east, back toward their chaotic roots, Chinatown and a good Chinese meal as close as they allowed themselves to come to the old neighborhood, now populated by a new generation of immigrants, from the south this time. Through windows steamy from cooking I could see chickens and ducks strung up like Christmas ornaments. Under the high yellow-stained ceiling my family would sit in the back corner at a round table with a lazy Susan that spun around loaded with plates of egg rolls, ribs, sweet and sour chicken, white rice and tea in a porcelain pot with a picture of a dragon on it. "A great neighborhood bar," my father would say.

Continuing my quest, up on Broadway I spot a large sign bearing a picture of a giant white ginseng root looking very much like an earthbound relative of the squid I see early Saturday mornings at the harbor by my house. Slightly feverish, I head into the first store I find, a small and somewhat antiseptic place. The woman at the cash register speaks no English. I pantomime a sore throat and she gives me bottled cough syrup, loquat flavored, and a package labeled "American Ginseng Tea." I buy it and a hunk of fresh ginger and wander out with the sense that I have not yet found what I am looking for.

I discover that all the stores along this block have herbs in them. The one I choose this time seems large and particularly well populated. I see glass counters stocked with plastic trays of dried things. Gold wooden boxes stacked behind them look like large library card files. Abundant baskets of roots, shells and herbs have been piled on top of one another to fill the center of the room. People hang out on tall stools talking in a Chinese dialect, which one I cannot tell.

I approach a young girl I hope will speak English. I am in luck. I tell her I am sick and would like some herbs. She says they cannot dispense herbs without a prescription. But, she adds, there is a doctor on the premises with whom I could consult. She waves toward the back where cartons are stacked ceiling high along a narrow hallway. It will cost ten dollars, she tells me, and I decide: I'll do it.

She points again to the rear of the store, this time directing my attention to a bright yellow sign with red Chinese characters hanging over a doorway in the rear hall. I go back through the saloon-style swinging doors where a man sits at a battered metal desk in a small closet-sized room. He has a broad face, thick lips and a receding hairline. He wears a beige short-sleeved shirt with faded vertical orange stripes. His pants are also striped, but wider and on a darker fabric. He smiles at me and folds up his Chinese newspaper. Gesturing for me to wait, he leaves, and I understand he has gone to retrieve the young woman to assist with the translation of my ailments.

He returns. While we wait, he hands me his card, all in characters except the address and telephone. He turns the card over so I can see the back. I hope for a translation but I get more Chinese. We laugh. The granddaughter arrives (I have decided this is who she is), and I tell her my problems. She speaks to the doctor in their Chinese dialect. He asks a question and she asks me if I have fever. I explain that I have chills and that I crave orange juice. The translation is short and I suspect she has left out the part about orange juice. She leaves, telling me he will take my pulse.

He places a red-and-white striped pillow the size of a small rye bread on the desk in front of me. It is quite worn, stained yellowish from long use. I lay my left hand, wrist up, on the pillow. He gently places his fingers on my wrist, concentrating on the messages from my body. Then he does the same to my right wrist.

As he works, head bent down over my open palm, I am struck by the noninvasive nature of the diagnostic process. Simple human touch, with attention to detail. I try to imagine his life, where he came from, what brought him here from his country of birth to this back room on a street in L.A. Where did he get his knowledge? Was he venerated for his healing wisdom, or simply another member of the community, no greater in stature than the person who picked the herbs, or dried them, or dispensed them with a delicate handheld bamboo scale?

I am hungry for a life rooted in community, as I perceive the good doctor's to be. I think of my grandmother's liquor store in L.A., her deli in Long Beach, her health food restaurant in New York, peopled by the immigrant Jews from Russia and Poland and Germany. Other languages, whether Yiddish or Mandarin, seem to rise from the very center of these elders' beings as they gesture and engage and laugh.

English isn't like that for me. It's a language of limits, hard edges, one in which I am always reaching for the right word or phrase sitting just beyond my grasp. I want to speak gibberish, guttural sounds that rise from the belly and open the throat when joined with air. I want to pound the cobblestones with the language of the streets of my ancestry where only ghosts now live. I want to accentuate that inflection in the sentence, a song rising at the end, each sentence a question, each ending a beginning.

So nu?

I want to stand among the hawkers and the fish sellers, the pushcarts of old books and the bolts of cloth, streets filled with Jews speaking the *mamaloschen*, the language of the women of my homeland. I want to pour my crunchy steel English into the heavy cast-iron meat grinder my mother used to make chopped liver, attach it to her cutting board and crank the hard edges into a bloody pulp of syntax and breathing flesh, into a language I can smear on my breasts and bellow from the open window of my mouth. I will crank and grind the bits, make them scrape like nails on a blackboard, and let the smell of spilled oil, expensive cigars and welded steel girders attack my nasal passages.

As I crank and grind, crank and grind I will force alchemical transformation to earth, blood and bone that will plop steaming into that yellow porcelain bowl, the largest of that matched set my mother kept in the cupboard under the cutting board along with a lifetime supply of empty jars and large brown paper bags. Here in my mother's small kitchen among the old pickle jars, iron pots and mismatched glasses will I resurrect the language of my people from the ground bits of history I can retrieve from the refrigerator, the cupboards and the three drawers of bagels and rye bread, of onions and potatoes, of dishcloths fringed and frayed. I will find those sounds lost to me in the America of John Paul Jones. I will find them in the grinding in my mother's kitchen.

In Eastern Europe the *bubemiesehs* appropriated the Hebrew forbidden them by their scholar husbands and the choice German tidbits gleaned from their Aryan landlords. To this they added the spicy flavors of the fish market, of a good negotiation, of *chrane*—horseradish—strong enough to make you cry, to cook up a Yiddish language totally satisfying in its specificity, its ability to describe the guts, the insides of life in the human community. Likewise the old mothers of my Sephardic friend Michele, the Jewish women in the hot deserts of Spain and Turkey, mixed the useful portions of those languages with the ancient Hebrew, to make a word stew as pungent as kalamata olives, feta cheese and baba ganoush with cracked bread and cold beer on a Mediterranean summer afternoon.

From these women I learn that I need not be content to use words that do not vibrate with the truth of my life. I want to speak without fear in the voice of my ancestors, guttural sounds and all, to release that assimilated speech my parents taught me to protect me so I could pass and not be too Jewish. I want words for my uniquely queer experience, an as yet unheard lexicon that embodies my queer life as surely as Yiddish and Ladino did for my old Jewish grandmothers.

I want a word for who my Cuban girlfriend is to me that isn't girlfriend, partner, lover or roommate and that encompasses how we come together hard sometimes like two fiery worlds colliding and so easy sometimes like slipping into the Caribbean sea on a steamy day.

I want a word for when your first girl lover becomes your best friend but not before years of navigating to make sure you don't end up at the same events on Saturday nights, moving to other cities and breaking up with the lover you broke up over in the first place.

I want a word for who Michele is to me when we've been negotiating our queer connection ever since we demonstrated together in Berkeley against the Vietnam War and almost had sex together one time but not really and instead she slept with my brother.

I want a word for who Doug and Luis are to me when I think they're smart and sexy and get excited when we're going to get together but they're faggots and I'm a dyke and what the hell does that mean?

I want a word for "queer family" that's about *meschpuchah*, which roughly translated from Yiddish means "the whole fucking extended family," and that's also about invention and vision.

I want a word for the guy at the AB 101 demonstration with the shaved head, earrings that looked like buttons off my grand-mother's good coat, floral print skirt and combat boots, for the dykes who did such a good imitation of the Village People I didn't know they were women, and for all the genders in between and beyond.

I want a word that says we queers are the unifiers because we live and love in every culture, race, religion, class, age, sex, tribe, village, town, city, country in the world, and we do it passionately across every single one of these constructed human boundaries.

I want words as extravagant, edgy and stylish as the interna-tional visual language we've constructed with our finery, pierc-ings, tattoos and drag.

I want a word for the kind of a world we're trying to make where fun, hot, sexy and profoundly moral all mean the same thing.

Because I can't envision a new way of being without the words to describe it.

With his two square hands the doctor selects a thin white sheet of onionskin paper. He takes a white ballpoint pen, the kind they used to give away at the bank, then very deliberately begins to write out my prescription. In addition to a red picture of the earth in the upper left-hand corner and writing across the top that is probably the store's logo, the paper already bears red Chinese characters on the other three sides of the page. The doctor con-centrates intently as he weaves his blue marks up and down and across the paper according to some mystical order that I cannot decipher. His focused attention is like a meditation for me, and I feel well loved.

He accompanies me back out to the store and we search out granddaughter. Holding his hands together he tells her how to instruct me on the preparation of my medicine. "You will cover the herbs with water and then cook for a long time until you have a thick, dark tea. Maybe it will take a long time, maybe more than an hour. We will give you three packs, use one pack per day. After three days you will be healthy." The doctor says more. "It's very important that you cook the tea long enough for it to be like a syrup, very thick." The doctor nods and smiles at me. I thank him and nod back to let him know I understand.

"Do you have a medicine herb pot for cooking?" granddaughter asks.

"I don't think so. Is it a special pot?"

"Yes, I will show you."

Among the dried seahorses and other riches I present my prescription to the gray-haired woman behind the counter on the other side of the store. She lays out three bright pink squares of butcher paper and begins to open the drawers behind her. After consulting the prescription, she pulls a handful of the appropriate herb and deposits it on the bamboo scale, which she holds up for inspection with a critical eye. Then she divides the herb into three parts and puts one on each paper square. She repeats this process until each square holds an aromatic pile of herbs, roots, grasses and unidentifiable dried things. She folds the papers into three solid blintze-shaped bundles and hands them to me. I take my packets and a box with the medicine pot, confident this time that I have what I came for.

At home I open the box and find a rough ceramic pot the same shape as, but slightly smaller than, my grandmother's yellow Bauer cookie jar. Two short hornlike cylinders protrude from the upper edge of the round pot so it looks like a cross between a witch's cauldron and the flask of a mad scientist. Nevertheless, it looks happy simmering away on my stove, filling the air with a kind of sweet chicory smell that only a sick person could find pleasing. An hour and a half later I strain a thick brown syrup into my special turquoise mug and sip my medicine very, very slowly. As the potion suffuses my aching body, I dream about roots and bits from Eastern Europe and far-flung corners of the queer community, of young boys in pastel dresses, smart old kerchiefed women, the smell of horseradish, the bite of kalamata olives, girls in black leather, the light of Grandma Rosie's candles on Friday nights and celebrations of the moon, ancient and new, cranked to a pulp in my mother's kitchen and sealed up in pink blintze-shaped packets of my own.

snap!

girlfriend

MESCHPUCHAH

¡Marimacha!

...So nu?

Notes
on the
Contributors

Lisa Asagi

Lisa Asagi was born and assembled in Honolulu. She likes to think of "Portraits of Desire" as an ongoing saga, occasionally a full-time hobby. It has exposed itself in public at various times as collaborative installations, spoken word performance, and, as soon as Lisa can get a good deal on a super-8 camera, perhaps someday a little film. At the moment she is in San Francisco helping to curate Queer Pacific Islander and/or Asian spoken word performance events and working on a novel obsessed with hatcheries, science, and the psychometry of growing up on an island.

Rebecca Brown

Rebecca Brown's most recent novel is *The Gifts of the Body* (Harper-Collins, 1994). She is also the author of two other novels, *The Haunted House* (Viking and Seal) and *The Children's Crusade* (Seal), the latter a finalist for Britain's prestigious Guardian Fiction Prize. Her novel-in-stories, *The Terrible Girls* (City Lights) was a finalist for the Lambda Literary Award. Her collection of short stories *Annie Oakley's Girl* (City Lights) was a featured title of the Quality Paperback Book Club and a nominee for the QPB New Voices writing award. Her work has been adapted for theater in the United States and Britain and translated into German and Dutch. Her stories have appeared in numerous anthologies including *Mondo Barbie, High Risk II, The Penguin Book of Lesbian Short Stories,* and *Good to Go.* She lives in Seattle, where she teaches part-time at the University of Washington, Extension, and volunteers at a soup kitchen.

Michelle T. Clinton

i have done most of my work as a poet & performance artist—feminist in promise & scope—though i consider myself a teacher &, now, prose writer as well. (books include *Good Sense & the Faithless,* West End Press, 1994, and *black sage,* Pennywhistle Press, 1995.) writing is a mystical act: conjuring language for self & community is immediate, indescribable connection w/ the unknown, w/ the divine. & essential aspects of the divine include issues of justice, of collective struggle, of small acts aimed toward our political evolution. lesbian culture & ethics (though technically, i would call myself bisexual) remain at the core of the impulse toward the shift into matriarchal rule. though much of my early work was aimed at illuminating the wounds inflicted by patriarchy & rage & recovery, now i am trying to find language for love of earth, love of the elements of natural lights & its miraculous relation to shadow. i study the martial arts: karate and tai chi.

Elise D'Haene

I placed the story "Self-Deliverance" in Michigan where I grew up. I have often wondered how my queer self would have emerged had I not moved far, far away. I may have been the character Alfie, finding solace in the pages of a book. Or Ginnie, edgy and hissing with a desire to escape. Their love for Teddy, who is dying of AIDS, leads them to perform the act of assisted suicide, or "self-deliverance." I love the sound of those two words. I find the hoopla around Dr. Kevorkian's methods almost comical. The queer community is filled with stories of helping our friends die—it's an ordinary act of love. I am completing my first novel, *Licking Our Wounds.* An excerpt from that novel was published in the anthology *Blood Whispers: L.A. Writers on AIDS, Volume 2.* A short fiction piece, "Married," was a winner in the 1994 Hemingway Short Story Competition.

Jacqueline De Angelis

"Joshuas in the City with a Future" is the middle story of a trilogy. The Charlene and Marge characters made it easy for me to look at contemporary relationships humorously and I had more fun writ-

ing these stories than I'd ever had before. I often go to the
Mojave, so taking them on a desert camping trip gave me the opportunity to use some of the journal notes and observations from
my own trips. Although I am a western writer by choice and tem-
perament, I was born and raised in Ohio's steel valley. Both my
poetry and short stories have been published in various anthologies and magazines. The last story in the trilogy, "Baby," was published in the Plume anthology *Indivisible*. My first book, *The Main
Gate*, was published by Paradise Press in 1984.

Kleya Forté-Escamilla

Kleya Forté-Escamilla is the author of two novels, *Daughter of the
Mountain* and *Mada*, and a collection of short stories, *The Storyteller with Nike Airs & Other Barrio Stories*, and of various short stories published in anthologies and journals. "As a writer who is a
lesbian, I'm interested in detailing the history of our evolving con-
sciousness in specific ways: through lesbian characters with lesbian issues. No less important is my concern with describing
Latina culture; however, both these things are the exterior of writing: The interior is the expression of the knowledge I've gleaned
from life, which can take as many forms as required."

Wendi Frisch

When I wrote "E=mc^2" I wanted to put a spin on the predictable
"Girl Meets Girl and Falls in Love" story. I chose two self-absorbed
poseurs as the main characters for a number of reasons: Because I
wouldn't have to worry about them falling in love; because I
thought they'd be fun to follow around; because it was easy to find
prototypes to observe. Although Sparky and Adara annoyed me
almost as much as they amused me, I enjoyed poking fun at a few
lesbian stereotypes with their help and exploring narcissism and
power shifts in relationships through their eyes. Los Angeles provided an ideal setting. My work has appeared in *Indivisible* (Plume,
1991) and *Snakeskin* (Anaconda Press, 1991).

Sandra Golvin

I was a corporate lawyer until the Whittier earthquake rattled me
loose from my office on the thirty-third floor of a high-rise in
downtown L.A. I've been flying, making it up as I go along, ever
since. I still don't have words for my heart's work but I try to do it

anyway. Living queer means I own my body and teaches me magic of the most powerful kind resides there. Living magic means how I live every minute is the art. Queer magic means smash, twist, burn, lick, sweet-talk, or otherwise reconstruct existing forms to suit my own purposes. Usually I feel I don't know what the hell I'm creating, "Chinese Medicine" being no exception—what is it? Essay, fiction, quasi-autobiography? I have the same experience with the visual art I do. In the end I can't let the category get in the way because, as difficult as not-knowing may be, that unknowing place holds the magic, the truth, the imagination, and is where I must go.

Eloise Klein Healy

Usually I write poetry and nonfiction, but this story literally forced itself on me. What I needed to engage with was the range of feelings brought about when my lover was diagnosed with breast cancer—particularly going through the ordeal as a lesbian couple. I wanted the narrative to be fairly straightforward but not chronological, to set forth experiences and imaginatively document the complicated process by which we were confronted with the impact of cancer. In the process of writing this story, I discovered a new area of my writer's brain, not at all the one I wrote poetry from, though it did borrow some melodic elements of language from the poetry brain—sound and rhythm were as important in this piece as in a poem. The sound of words has always been of great interest to me. My last book from Firebrand Press was also released as a CD/audio tape by New Alliance Records under the title *Artemis in Echo Park/The Women's Studies Chronicles*.

Holly Hughes

Holly Hughes is a member of the WOW Cafe, New York's "home for wayward girls" and sometime performance space. She is a failed pornographer who turned to writing and performance art only in desperation after her first opus, *The Well of Horniness* was rejected by Poontang Productions. In 1990, then chair of the National Endowment for the Arts John Frohnmayer vetoed funding recommended for Hughes, saying her work was "heavily of the lesbian genre." With Tim Miller, she cofounded the National Fund for Lesbian and Gay Performance in 1991. She received an Obie award for *Clit Notes* in 1994.

Sarah Jacobus

I am a Los Angeles writer, radio producer, and teacher of English as a Second Language. My essays and short stories have appeared in *Bridges, Sojourner, Common Lives/Lesbian Lives* and in varied anthologies. I am a longtime activist in the movement for a just peace between Israel and the Palestinians and am currently working on a collection of stories drawn from my journeys to the Middle East over a period of twelve years. In "Welcome to Gaza" I am interested in using political context and a vivid sense of place to explore how lesbian sensibility informs perception and experience. This is an issue I am constantly looking at in my own Middle East activism, and I've found the portrayal through fiction illuminating—and fun!

Lisa Jones

"Los Angeles, City of My Dreams" is the first chapter of my first and as yet unpublished novel, *Another Articulation of Love*. I feel as if I'm a sapling of a writer, and with every word I write, I'm growing. I want my life and my vision to expand, like branches, to embrace everyone. My roots are in the people and places that I love. My love of women especially—that tense, sensuous heaven—nourishes me. Sometimes I think that the love of a woman is like a deep underground stream, a mysterious fluid vein of revelation and discovery. To tap this source, to draw this richness into myself, to bloom beautifully: This, I believe, is what it means to be a lesbian. I majored in European Intellectual History at the University of Colorado in Boulder and went through the technical writing program at Cal State Long Beach. I've worked as a copywriter in the health care field, the defense industry, and in mortgage lending. Currently, I'm a media development director for a cable television/interactive/entertainment corporation based in Englewood, Colorado.

Hildie V. Kraus

"Mrs. Yakamoto Comes to Stay" had its seed partly in a real-life incident, and its flowering in my fascination with the arrangements people live with and the secrets they keep. I don't see lesbianism as the main perspective that informs my writing, but one of many. P.S. I wrote this story before the film *The Wedding Banquet* was released.

Carole Maso

Carole Maso is the author of four novels: *Ghost Dance, The Art Lover, AVA,* and *The American Woman in the Chinese Hat. Defiance,* a novel-in-progress, is forthcoming from Dutton in 1996. Of her work she has said, "Almost everything is yet to be written by women. Let us bloom then, unreservedly."

Robin Podolsky

Robin Podolsky is a writer of fiction, essays, and poetry. Among the anthologies that include her work are *Blood Whispers: L.A. Writers on AIDS, Indivisible,* and *Discontents.* In 1991 she received a Special Citation from the PEN Center in New York City for her book-in-progress, *Roughing It Out.* She received, in 1991, a Media Image Award from the Gay and Lesbian Association Against Defamation and, in 1993, an Outstanding Journalism Award from the National Lesbian and Gay Journalists Association. "I wanted to take this story back for the Jews who were colonized and degraded under the Roman Empire. This brilliant grievance-ridden bastard boy whose mother saw visions was too good a character to pass up. Is this a lesbian story? A lesbian wrote it and it's about the terrible consequences of internalized oppression combined with a genuine desire to do good—a mixture that queers especially need to be wary of."

Aleida Rodríguez

Aleida Rodríguez is a Cuban-born poet who occasionally steps over the line into prose. This story was inspired by a phone call from her mother, who, though conveying what she knew in her usual dramatic style, was missing enough parts of the story to intrigue Aleida into trying to fill in the blanks. Aleida's poetry and prose have appeared in magazines and anthologies nationwide for more than twenty years, among them *Prairie Schooner, The Kenyon Review, Indivisible* (Plume), *An Ear to the Ground: Contemporary American Poetry* (University of Georgia Press), and *Cuentos: Stories by Latinas* (Kitchen Table Press). She is the recipient of an NEA fellowship in poetry and multiple grants from the California Arts Council. One of her poems was selected by Bill Knott to receive the inaugural Greg Grummer Award in Poetry from George Mason University in 1993, the same year her manuscript was a finalist in the National Poetry Series competition.

Sarah Schulman

I've published six novels and one nonfiction book over the last eleven years. At this stage in my development I feel an enormous frustration over the marginalization of openly lesbian work. Although generously supported and represented within gay and lesbian publishing, I am still virtually excluded from the mosaic of American writing. The prejudice of the reading public and of nonhomosexual artists and intellectuals seems to obstruct their ability to universalize an openly lesbian subject. Increasingly I see my most talented peers reverting to demurely closeted subject matter or to the old pattern of establishing themselves from a closeted base and then coming out. This seems to reflect the growing gap between gay people's rapidly evolving sense of self and the static mentality of the dominant group.

Christina Sunley

I was born in 1961 and moved to New York City in 1983. When my roommate sheared my hair to crewcut length, I quickly learned that humans of all ages, classes, and colors have an obsessive urge to assign gender—they will stare and stare until they figure you out. Lindy offered me a way to have more fun with gender fluidity than I ever had in real life. She's my superhero/alter ego. Beyond gender and sexuality, "Bizarro" also arose from my fascination with shape-shifting, power (super and otherwise), and difference. My short fiction has appeared in a variety of anthologies and literary journals, including *Conditions, Common Lives/Lesbian Lives, Nimrod,* and *The Cream City Review.* I have been employed as a teacher, legal proofreader, house cleaner, assembler of exercise kits, TV news monitor, and hot tub attendant. I now live in San Francisco and work as education coordinator for the NAMES Project Foundation, sponsor of the AIDS Quilt Memorial.

Jane Thurmond

So many of the rituals from my Southern Baptist girlhood strike me today as odd, befuddling, and sometimes downright silly. Even when I don't set out to include the events of my religious upbringing in a story, they creep in on their own. In the case of "The Great Baptism," I wanted to explore my own baptism. I remember dangling my legs quietly over the edge of the baptismal tank, and my desire to cannonball in and swim. My fictional characters did what

I never had the nerve to do. This is what I enjoy most about writing. One grain of truth can lead me almost anywhere. In real life, I write short stories and work as a graphic designer in Austin, Texas.

Martha Tormey

I started writing stories a few years ago. My first was one paragraph long and about a lady sitting in her car watching a snowstorm blow up. In the middle of writing this story ("Bitey Boy") I met several people at a party who had recently been bitten by adults. Different adults, in different circumstances. One guy showed me the teeth marks on his biceps. This is the kind of amazing stuff that keeps me writing. My first published story ("Safety") appeared in the *Santa Monica Review*. I currently live in Vermont.

Cody Yeager

I am a Northeasterner transplanted in the Pacific Northwest, where I share my life with my dogs and my partner. When I wrote "Against All Enemies," I was sure of two things: that Clinton would become president and that he would lift the ban on gays in the military. When only one of those two events took place, I realized my military career was a farce, a painful oxymoron. So, after ten years, I am a soldier no more and have returned to writing, reading, and struggling against the Oregon Citizens Alliance. Again.

About the Editors

Terry Wolverton

Terry Wolverton is the author of *Black Slip,* a Lambda Book Award-nominated collection of poetry from Clothespin Fever Press. Her poems, short fiction, essays, and dramatic texts have been published widely in journals and anthologies. She is the former executive director of the Woman's Building in Los Angeles, and the founder of the Perspectives Writing Program at the Los Angeles Gay and Lesbian Community Services Center.

She has also edited *Harbinger: poetry and fiction by Los Angeles writers* (with Benjamin Weissman, for the 1990 Los Angeles Festival), *Indivisible: new short fiction by west coast gay and lesbian writers* (with Robert Drake, Plume), and *Blood Whispers: L.A. Writers on AIDS,* volumes one and two (Silverton Books).

"In my own writing," she says, "I aim to demonstrate that truth is a complex entity. As a teacher and editor, I have two goals: to create opportunities for exceptional writers whose voices might otherwise not be heard, and to help raise the overall standards of craft and quality in the gay and lesbian literary community."

Robert Drake

Robert Drake is an educator, author, editor, and literary agent. His first novel, *The Man: A Hero For Our Time (Book One: Why?)* was published by Penguin USA/Plume in June 1995. With Terry Wolverton he co-edited the anthology *Indivisible: new short fiction by west coast gay and lesbian writers,* receiving two Lambda Literary

Award nominations. He is the book review editor for the *Baltimore Alternative*. He teaches writing at St. John's College and the American University, and resides in Annapolis, Maryland, with his dog, Pudsey Dawson—a white bull terrier with brindle ears, named for a "bully" the English poet Rupert Brooke went swimming with in Byron's pool at Granchester.

Acknowledgments

The editors would like to thank Robert Jones, Richard LaBonte, Christopher Schelling, and John Talbot for their support and interest in the development of *Hers* and *His*.

We are especially grateful to Betsy Uhrig, who made it possible. We also extend our hearfult appreciation to Susan Silton, and to Robert Flynt and Connie Imboden.

We are fortunate to have been able to work with the talented writers whose stories are collected in these books. To them, most of all, we offer our gratitude.

"Black Orchid" by Kleya Forté-Escamilla. Published in *The Storyteller with Nike Airs & Other Barrio Stories*. Copyright © 1994 by Kleya Forté-Escamilla, Aunt Lute. Reprinted by permission of the author and the publisher.

"The Great Baptism" by Jane Thurmond. First published in *The Iowa Review*, Volume 23, Number 1. Copyright © 1993 by Jane Thurmond. Reprinted by permission of the author.

Lines quoted in Lisa Asagi's "Portraits of Desire" are from "Poetry, Madness, and the Inner Ear" by Doug Thorpe, published in *Parabola, the magazine of myth and tradition*, Volume XVII, Number 2. Copyright © 1992 by Doug Thorpe. Used by permission.

All other stories reprinted by permission of the authors.